It Started With Tears

A PORTHGARRION STORY

by

Suzie Peters

GWL
PUBLISHING

First Published in 2023
by GWL Publishing
an imprint of Great War Literature Publishing LLP

Produced in United Kingdom

Cover designs and artwork by GWL Creative.
Watercolour illustrations by Tonia Tkach

ISBN 978-1-915109-23-1 Paperback Edition

GWL Publishing
Chichester, United Kingdom

www.gwlpublishing.co.uk

Dedication

For S.

Author's Note

This book contains medical advice, given by a fictional doctor, to fictional patients, about their fictional problems.
Readers should not follow the advice given, or treat it as sound, in any way, and if they find any similarities between the problems covered in this book, and anything from which they might be suffering, they should seek the advice of a real doctor.

Chapter One

Millie

I pull the front door closed, looking up at the clear blue sky. There isn't a cloud to be seen, and already I can feel the heat on my back, even though it's only eight o'clock in the morning.

I'm leaving fifteen minutes earlier than usual, because I need to pick up a few things on the way to work, but now I come to think about it, I'm not sure the florist's will be open yet. I should have checked when I walked past yesterday, on my way home. They have a sign on the door that displays their opening times, and I could kick myself for not paying more attention.

Still, I suppose I might as well go now. There's no point in going back up to my flat and sitting there for ten minutes, is there? If the florist's is closed, I'll just go to work early. Even if Robson isn't in his office yet, I've got a key. I can just let myself in, and carry on checking the files for people who need to come in this month to have their regular asthma, blood pressure and diabetes check-ups. It might only be ten weeks since I started work as the doctor's receptionist, but I've already discovered it's like this at the beginning of every month. I don't mind, though. It keeps me busy.

I double check that the door is locked, even though I know I've already turned the key, before putting them in my handbag, and then I start the walk down Chapel Mews. Most of the properties along here have been converted into flats. Some of them are permanently occupied, but I'd say roughly half are holiday lets, which means you never know who you're going to run into from one week to the next. Houses only occupy one side of the road, though. On the other side, there's a low wall, beyond which is the private parking area. There are two spaces for each house, which was probably enough when they were built. Now a lot of them have been converted, though, it tends to be a competition for who gets parked first. Fortunately, I rarely use my car, so it just sits in its space, and the couple below me on the first floor don't even own a vehicle. They cycle everywhere. The ground floor is a holiday let, which this week seems to be occupied by a young family, who've taken the other space allocated to this house… although, being on holiday, they're rarely here.

A lady comes out of her house. It's one of the ones that hasn't been converted, and she comes out backwards, pulling a pushchair, while her two young children mill around her feet. She seems flustered and scolds her son for wandering down the path by himself.

"What have I told you about going near the road?"

It's the quietest of roads, leading absolutely nowhere, but I can see her point. He needs to learn that roads are dangerous. He stops and looks back at her, then sidles towards the house again while she fishes around in her handbag. "What's wrong, Mummy?"

The little girl standing beside her looks up, her head tilted slightly.

"I can't find my keys."

As she says the word, I stop walking and quickly check that I've got my own. I know I have. I put them in my bag less than two minutes ago. They're safely tucked away in the zipped pocket, where I always keep them.

Why am I like this?

I know the answer to that, of course, but the fact remains… I never used to be such a worrier. I never used to be scared of my own shadow, either.

"Got them!" The woman pulls a bunch of keys from her bag triumphantly.

"Can we go and see Granny now?" the little boy asks.

"Yes, we can."

She sounds relieved, and I walk on before she notices me, then turn the corner onto Church Lane. Crossing over the entrance to St. Mary's Road, I glance up at the garage as I pass it, and then at the Italian restaurant opposite. I haven't been there, but I haven't been anywhere much since I moved here. I go to work; I come home. It's a safe, but dull life, and I need to do something about that before checking for my keys becomes the highlight of my day.

The door to the police station is open, but I ignore it, and turn out onto the harbour, grateful for the gentle sea breeze as I by-pass the estate agents, and the pharmacy, both of which are still closed. The bakery and café are open, and I'm familiar with both. I buy my lunch in the former, and occasionally grab a take-away coffee from the latter, although I don't have time today.

Next, I come to the florist's and I sigh out my relief when I see the door is wide open.

The young woman who works here is behind the counter, leafing through some paperwork.

"Is it okay to come in?" I ask, and she looks up with a smile.

"Of course."

"Sorry." I step over the threshold. "I wasn't sure if you'd be open this early."

"We're not usually. But we had a delivery, and it didn't seem worth coming in for that and not opening up."

"I see."

She comes around the counter. "You work for Doctor Carew, don't you?"

"Yes, I do."

"I'm Gemma Hughes. I can't think why we've never met before."

Probably because I don't go out very much. "I imagine because you haven't been to see the doctor for a while?" I say, and her smile widens.

"No, thank heavens." She chuckles. "That sounds rude, doesn't it? Robson's lovely, but it's always best not to have to see him in his professional capacity… not that he's not good at what he does…" She blushes and I smile.

"I understand what you mean. No-one wants to have to see the doctor. And you're right, he's very good at what he does." He's also lovely, but I'm not about to admit that out loud.

"Anyway… what can I get for you? Or did you just come in to cool off?"

"I didn't, but you're right, it is wonderfully cool in here."

"We need it that way for the flowers, and I'm not complaining."

"I don't think I would be either." I glance around. "There's a flamingo plant in the reception at work, and it's outgrown its pot. I wondered if you might have anything."

"All our pots are over here." She leads me to two cream-coloured dressers, the shelves of which are stacked with vases, and pots, and various ribbons. "Do you know what size you need?"

"Not exactly." I reach out for a white one. "That looks about right, though, and white seems like a good choice for a doctor's reception, don't you think?"

"It's neutral enough," she says, picking it up for me and putting it down on the counter.

"These are pretty." I point to the bud vases on the second shelf. They're made of brightly coloured glass, with a bulbous base and a silver ring around the neck of each one, and I can just picture them sitting on the windowsill at the surgery, catching the light.

"Are you open?"

Gemma and I both spin around at the sound of a voice coming from the door.

"Yes." I step back as she gives her reply, and the man comes in.

"Can you send some flowers for me?"

"I can, but I'm just dealing with this lady. I'll be right with you."

The man checks his watch, evidently in a hurry. "It's fine," I say. "I've got a few minutes to spare."

"Are you sure?"

The man walks forward, making it clear he intends to take advantage of my offer.

"Yes."

He smiles, nodding his head, and waits for Gemma to join him.

She pulls a large red book from underneath the counter and starts writing the details of the man's order, while I turn back to the vases. I think the windowsill at work will hold four of them, and I choose ones in green, turquoise, light blue, and purple, putting them to one side, while I wander over to the display of flowers. There's a lot to choose from, but my eyes are drawn to the gerberas, and I pick out four... one for each vase. The colours are bright and cheerful, and I select ones in pink, orange, yellow and red.

The man is just paying for his bouquet, so I hang back, waiting, and once he's gone, with a nod of his head in my direction, I approach the counter, carrying my gerberas.

"Can I have these, and the vases as well?"

"Certainly." She takes them from me, and I grab the vases, too, noting that she seems to be looking at my dress.

"Is something wrong?" I glance down, but can't see anything the matter.

"No. It's just that I saw you leaning over to get the gerberas, and I was worried you might have got some lily pollen on your dress. It's really hard to get off, and your dress is so pretty."

"Thank you."

"It looks very cool, too."

"It is… and thankfully, it's pollen-free."

She smiles and I watch her wrap the vases and the pot in tissue paper, feeling pleased with myself… not because I've completed my purchases, but because I felt brave enough today to wear a dress. I don't know what made me feel brave, and maybe that's the wrong word, because that's not how I feel at all. Maybe it had more to do with the weather than anything else. It's the first time I've stepped out of trousers in months, but with the temperature due to hit the high twenties today, I wasn't sure I'd survive. So I went through my wardrobe last night and found this dress. I've got several of them, all quite similar, but in different colours, and I know how comfortable they are. They're just sleeveless shift dresses, with a rounded neck, the hemline finishing just above my knee, so nothing to write home about, but I like them. This one is pale pink, and it's my favourite, although I couldn't tell you why.

Gemma finishes by wrapping the gerberas in brown paper, treating them gently, and I pay her with my card, tapping it against the machine, before I gather everything up and say goodbye.

Outside, it seems even hotter, and I complete my journey along the harbour, taking the turn into Bell Road, grateful that I'm nearly at work.

I only have to pass the little cottages on the left, and the art gallery and hotel on the right, and I come to the doctor's surgery. It's directly opposite Garden Close, and I push the gate open with my hip, my hands being otherwise occupied with holding onto the vases and pot, the gerberas balanced on top.

Before me is a grand, double-fronted house, built of Cornish stone, and I walk up the slabbed path, which is gravelled on either side, to the front door. It's painted in a pale blue, and beside it is a slate plaque, the word 'Surgery' etched in white lettering. The path forks around to the right and down the side of the house, where there's a separate entrance at the side of the house that has a similar plaque, only that one is marked 'Private'. It opens onto a hallway that divides the surgery, which occupies the front of the house, from the doctor's private residence, which is at the back. There's a doorway in the rear wall of the reception area that leads into the same hallway, so at least the doctor doesn't have to come outside to get into his own home.

I've never seen his home, but I've seen the hallway, when the door's been left open. The walls are a pale off-white, almost yellow, and the carpet is a rich, deep honey colour. On the wall, opposite the door, is a painting of a harbour. It's not Porthgarrion, but it's beautiful, nonetheless.

I have no idea what lies beyond.

I've never asked. It would seem nosy and intrusive. That's the doctor's personal space, after all, and as far as I'm concerned, if he wanted me to see it, he'd invite me in.

I have to put everything down to retrieve my key, and once I've opened the door, I pick up my purchases from the doorstep and cross the threshold.

It's stuffy and silent in here. Robson's door is closed, which may mean he's in there working, or that he hasn't surfaced from the back of the house yet. Either is possible, and I turn to the right, going straight into the reception and waiting area. It's a big room, which I imagine was once a living or dining room. The fireplace has been blocked off, and my desk sits just to this side of it, with two filing cabinets in the alcove close to the front window. The flamingo plant lives on top of the one nearest the fireplace, its scarlet, heart-shaped leaves brightening the otherwise dull room. My desk is grey, the linoleum flooring is grey, and the walls are white, as are the doors of the cupboards that fill the other alcove. Even the coffee machine that nestles beside the flamingo plant is black. Other than a few posters on the walls, which only serve to inform, not to delight, it's a monochrome space.

I put down my packages, taking care with the flowers, and leave my handbag on the desk, going to the front window and opening it outwards to let in some air, and then I go back and put the front door on the latch, so patients can come and go without having to knock, or ring the bell.

Returning to my desk, I switch on my computer and while it's powering up, I move around to the other side and set about unwrapping my parcels.

"Good morning."

Robson's voice makes me jump and I spin around to find him leaning against the door that leads to the front hallway, and ultimately his surgery, his arms folded across his chest. As usual, whenever I'm looking at him, my mouth dries, and my heart beats faster, butterflies flitting around my stomach.

"H—Hello."

He smiles, unfolding his arms as he steps into the room.

The butterflies go a little wild as the scent of his body wash assails my nostrils. The ends of his mid-brown hair are still damp, so he can't have been in his office for long, and although he's combed it, there's no denying it's far from tidy. It doesn't look as though he just got out of bed, but it's not what I'd call groomed, either... and it suits him that way. He's tall, without being imposing, and his dark grey trousers and white shirt fit his athletic build perfectly. He always wears a tie, and today it's a red one, although he hasn't done it up properly yet, and I don't blame him in this heat.

"What have you got there?" he asks, his grey eyes sparkling at me as he walks over.

"I bought a new pot for the flamingo plant." I nod towards it and he follows my gaze.

"Is that what it's called?"

"Yes."

"And this?" He picks up the turquoise vase.

"I got four of them in different colours. They're to go on the windowsill."

"What a good idea. Why didn't I think of that?"

"I don't know." He smiles, parting his generous lips and revealing perfect white teeth, and I wish, for the hundredth time, that he'd see me as more than his receptionist.

I've felt like this since the day I walked in here for my interview and he greeted me with that same smile and a warm handshake. Somehow, he broke down all my barriers in that first, brief, thirty-minute meeting. He didn't say anything special. He didn't do anything special, either. And yet, I felt safe with him... safe and comfortable. They were unfamiliar feelings, but I didn't fight them. I'd moved here to escape my past and start again, and I knew I wouldn't get very far if I railed against every instinct.

Because my instincts were telling me to trust him.

My heart was telling me to let him in.

When he called the following day to offer me the job as his receptionist, I was thrilled... not just because I needed the work, but because it meant I'd get to see him every day.

And I have… as his receptionist.

I might have felt something when we met, but it seems it was one-sided, because outside of these four walls, I may as well be invisible.

I'm not the most gregarious of people, and I'd never be able to throw myself at a man… or even to flirt with one. It wasn't easy for me to fall for him, but having done so, I wish he'd at least notice me… acknowledge my existence. There's no way I can make the first move, and it seems he doesn't want to. He never asks what I've done the night before, or if I've had a good weekend. I wouldn't have much to tell if he did. My evenings are spent alone, watching movies, or reading books. My weekends aren't that different, except I add in grocery shopping, laundry and housework, and at this time of year, there's the absolute necessity of keeping up with the test cricket.

That's not the point though, is it? It's not about what I have or haven't been doing. It's that he doesn't care enough to ask.

"Who's my first appointment this morning? Can you remind me?"

You see? When it comes down to it, I'm his receptionist. That's all.

I put down the white pot and slip around to the other side of my desk, starting up the appointments application, which only takes a moment to fill my screen.

Robson has his own version of this on his computer, which synchronises with mine, but he probably hasn't switched it on yet.

"It's Joan Evans." I look up and he nods his head.

"Oh, yes. Did you manage to squeeze her in for a double appointment?"

"Yes. Luckily you didn't have anyone else booked in until nine forty-five, so she's coming at ten past."

"Excellent. At least if we over-run, no-one's going to be upset about it."

"That depends how long you over-run by."

He smiles, and the butterflies take flight again. "It shouldn't be too bad. I've just got to give her the results of her blood tests."

I know this already. It's why he asked me to call her on Thursday of last week to make the appointment.

"You're obviously concerned about how she's going to react, though." Otherwise, why did he allocate the extra time?

"It's not terrible news, but I want to talk through what she can do to prevent things from getting worse. I need to give her some time and let her know I'll be here if she needs me."

I gaze up at him, wishing he cared about me like he cares about his patients, but as he turns away, the smile still etched on his face, I know I'm asking too much.

Chapter Two

Robson

I hold my breath, subduing the groan that's building in my throat until I get into my office, and have firmly closed the door behind me. Then I lean back against it and push my fingers through my hair. I know it'll look much more messed up than I like it to be during working hours, but I honestly don't care.

"Oh… God…" My voice is a strangled whisper, and I struggle against the nervous tension that's racing through my body, clenching my fists a few times.

Millie looks so beautiful today.

I almost feel guilty for thinking that, because Millie looks beautiful every day.

Except today is different.

Unable to sleep, just out of childish excitement at the thought of seeing her again after a weekend spent by myself, I'd been sitting at my desk, the door closed, and when I heard her arrive, I plucked up the courage to go out and talk to her. Don't get me wrong; she's my receptionist. I talk to her all the time. But it's only ever about work. Today, I'd decided, I was finally going to act on my instincts, and talk about her instead. It had taken me most of

Saturday and Sunday to work out how to go about it, and in the end, I'd reached the conclusion that all I had to do was simply to ask if she'd had a good weekend. It was lame, I know. But the problem is, I know next to nothing about her... including if she's single. Asking about her weekend felt like a good way of fishing, without appearing to be deep sea diving.

Of course, I hadn't expected that I'd wander outside and be met by a vision... by an angel, in my own reception.

I've grown accustomed to seeing her in black trousers and buttoned up blouses, and even though the sight of her always takes my breath away, I suppose I regarded that as something of a 'uniform'. I hadn't realised what a dress would do to her... that her legs would be so shapely... so sexy.

I know now, though.

I'm used to her trousers hugging her hips, but there's something about the pale pink dress she's wearing today... about the way it clings to every contour of her body.

"Stop it."

I push myself off of the door and walk over to my desk, sitting down. My computer only takes a minute to start up, but I use that time to think about Millie, because no matter how much I know I shouldn't, I can't seem to stop myself.

Even her hair looks extra special today. It's dark brown, and I imagine it must be quite long, but it's hard to tell, because she always puts it up, usually in some kind of bun or ponytail. I'm doing her a huge disservice there, though. I'm not experienced enough with women's hair to understand how she achieves the styles she wears, but they look stunning. Today, she's surpassed herself. At the back of her head, she's created a kind of twisted ponytail. It's not a plait. Even I know what a plait is, and this isn't it. This is different. It's elegant and sophisticated... especially as she's somehow threaded a pale pink ribbon through the twist, so it also looks delicate and feminine, too... just like Millie.

I shake my head, turning my seat. It's confined within a U-shaped desk, the base of which lies along the window ledge, and I lean over it, gazing out across the gravelled front garden, onto Bell Road. I shouldn't be letting myself get so easily distracted... not when I have responsibilities. That's the thing with being a GP in a small village like this. People rely on you. They don't expect you to lose your head, just because you've lost your heart.

I have, though.

And that's a problem. In all kinds of ways.

First, it's impossible to ignore the fact that Millie's eight years younger than me. I noticed that on her CV when she came for her interview, right before she walked into my office and captured my heart.

I know that, having lost my heart, I probably shouldn't have employed her, but I can honestly say, hand on stolen heart, she was the best candidate for the job. Besides which, I needed a receptionist in a hurry.

Millie's predecessor, Sophie, had only lasted two months before we'd both decided this really wasn't the job for her. Prior to that, the role had been filled by Cora, who I'd inherited from my forerunner as GP in Porthgarrion. She'd been here since I was a child myself, but retirement beckoned. I could remember her giving out stickers to well-behaved children, and frowning over the top of her glasses at the naughty ones. To be honest, I'd always been a little frightened of her. She exuded efficiency, but lacked any accompanying pathos. When she announced she was leaving, I felt like it was a heaven-sent opportunity to make my mark on the practice at last. In the years that I'd been working here, I'd adhered to Cora's ways, which involved doing things as they'd always been done. Now I had the chance to make some changes.

The problem was, I employed Sophie.

On paper, she looked good.

In person, she didn't look too bad. She was in her early fifties and suffering from empty-nest syndrome, her two sons having gone away to university. As a golf widow, she was looking for something to do with her time, and she seemed to have the requisite skills. I thought I'd landed on my feet…. until I realised her main purpose in life was gossip.

I don't have anything against gossips, per se. Porthgarrion is full of them, and even if Sophie wasn't from the village itself, the principle remained the same.

Gossips are fine. Sometimes they're even useful. The problem is, employing one, when you're the village GP.

I didn't actually catch her discussing patients, or their illnesses, but it felt like it was only a matter of time.

It was clear she didn't enjoy the job, any more than I enjoyed employing her, and we both admitted defeat quite quickly.

What I hadn't seen coming was that her husband would book them a holiday.

"It's the most romantic thing he's done in years," she gushed, standing on the other side of my desk.

"It sounds lovely."

She smiled. "I know. To be honest, I'm still in shock." I wasn't sure why she was telling me, until she bit her bottom lip, stepped just a little closer and said, "We're going on Saturday."

"This Saturday?"

"Yes."

"Two days from now?"

"Yes."

"How long for?"

"Three weeks," she said, her eyes sparkling. "Isn't it marvellous?"

We'd only agreed about her leaving my employ the previous Friday, and now it appeared the rest of her notice period was going to be spent on a beach in the south of France.

I didn't feel like arguing. To be honest, I was glad to see the back of her.

Of course, I was then left with the problem of finding a replacement… fast.

I placed an advertisement, and six candidates applied.

By the time I saw Millie, late on that Thursday evening, I was beginning to despair.

None of the other applicants had been suitable, but there was no way I could manage without a receptionist for much longer. It had only been four days, and I was already going quietly insane.

That was when Millie walked in.

She was wearing black trousers and a white blouse, buttoned right up to the neck, her hair tied behind her head in a loose arrangement, with two strands framing her face. She wore a little make-up, but not much, and as she approached my desk, I struggled to find my voice.

I spent the next thirty minutes doing my best to be professional. I'd deliberately moved the chair the candidates were sitting on, so it was the other side of the main part of my desk… the part that faces the door. It felt like a good idea when I was awaiting the first arrival, and it had worked well until then, as a means of keeping things a bit more formal. With Millie, though, I kept wishing I could move around to her side, grab the spare chair that I always keep against the wall, and sit next to her, just so I could see whether the light was playing tricks, or whether she really had amber-coloured eyes.

She answered all my questions with a shy, even deferential tone of voice, and at the end of her interview, when she stood again, she held out her hand. I took it, feeling her soft skin against mine… and I think that was when I knew for sure I was in trouble.

I had nothing else to do that day, so I went through to the kitchen at the back of the house and poured myself a glass of wine. It was warm enough to sit outside, and I took my wine with me, perching on a chair, unable to settle, my head full of images of the most perfect woman I'd ever seen.

Out of all the candidates, she was by far and away the best, and I had no-one else lined up. I faced a choice; either wait and find someone different, or employ Millie, knowing I'd fallen for her. My heart did a little flip at the thought of seeing her every day. It was trampled on, though, by the loud note of warning that rang out in my head, reminding me it wasn't an altogether sane idea to employ someone you're in love with. Especially when love is alien territory, like it is for me.

I'm not inexperienced with women, but love? I've never been there before… not even anywhere close.

So, how could I identify my feelings for Millie with such ease? I have absolutely no idea.

I can't put my finger on the 'how', or the 'why'.

All I can say is, I knew. It was an instinct… the same one I get sometimes when I know a patient isn't telling me everything about their symptoms, because they're scared of what I might say to them.

Those are the kind of instincts that can't be ignored.

So I turned a deaf ear to the voice in my head and called Millie the next morning to offer her the job.

She started working for me the very next week and by the end of her first day, I was already wishing I'd paid more attention to that voice.

It wasn't that she was no good at her job. Far from it; she was excellent.

It wasn't that she was difficult to get along with. On the contrary; she couldn't have been more friendly.

The problem was, I couldn't think straight.

Every time she came into my office, or I went out into the reception, I felt like every nerve ending in my body was on fire with a longing to hold her in my arms and kiss her.

Things haven't improved since. Whenever she's within touching distance, it takes a herculean effort not to let my hands wander over her hourglass figure, lingering especially over her hips... the hips her pale pink dress was just hugging to perfection. It takes all my willpower not to bend my head and kiss her, not to tell her I'm in love with her as my lips caress hers.

How can I, though? Aside from the age gap between us, I'm her boss.

I have to do the right thing.

It seems I also like to punish myself while I'm about it.

What other reason could there be for finding excuses to spend more time with her than is strictly necessary?

I don't know why I bother, though. It's not like she even notices my existence... not in the way I want her to. She's professional, polite and kind. But as for anything else? Forget it.

As far as romance goes, I might as well be invisible.

I turn my chair around again, focusing on my computer screen and my appointments for the day, shaking my head. It was a little pathetic of me to ask Millie who I was seeing first this morning. I could easily have come in here and looked it up for myself. I'd chickened out of asking how her weekend had gone, too distracted by the sight of her in that dress. But it was another of those situations where I was looking for a reason to spend time with her. It may only have been a few minutes, but I'll take whatever I can get, even if walking away from her leaves me feeling more and more empty every time.

I scan the names, starting with Joan Evans. She came in last week, saying she felt tired. That was it... just 'tired'.

My instincts told me she wasn't hiding anything… and that didn't help, because just being 'tired' gave me far too much room for manoeuvre, in terms of a potential diagnosis.

I asked a few questions, which got me nowhere. She had no other symptoms, hadn't changed her routine, was getting plenty of sleep… was eating regularly. Joan is fifty-two. I hadn't seen her for quite some time and was bound to ask the obvious question… was she experiencing any signs of being peri-menopausal? She laughed, and told me she'd been there, done that, and bought the t-shirt.

"I had my last period nearly two years ago," she said. "And while most women would hate me for saying this, I don't know what all the fuss is about."

I guess that explained why I was none the wiser. She hadn't been to see me with any problems about the latest change in her life, and in a way I was relieved by that. Not because she'd found it all such a breeze, but because it meant I could rule out the 'easy' option. GPs have a reputation for doing that sometimes, especially with women. So, we're accused of blaming periods, pregnancy, childbirth, the menopause… anything, rather than looking a little deeper to find the real problem.

And sometimes, some of us are guilty.

That said, being a GP is a little like being a detective. When the obvious lets us down, we need clues, and these can occasionally be provided by blood tests, so I took some blood and sent it away, ordering a whole raft of tests. To be honest, I'd expected them to come back within normal ranges… because that's what often happens in these cases, and as the GP, you're left staring into a dark abyss of uncertainty. However, that wasn't what happened this time, and now I've got to break the news to Joan. In a way, it's good. I know what's wrong now, and can advise her on what to do about it. The downside is, I don't think

Joan was expecting this result, any more than I was, which means it's hard to know how she's going to react.

I glance further down the list of patients, seeing a few familiar names, most of whom are coming in for follow-up appointments, a smile crossing my lips when I see the name 'Rachel Pedrick'.

She's due in at twelve-thirty, which makes her my last appointment before lunch.

That's something to look forward to, at least.

Rachel is thirty-eight weeks pregnant, and she usually sees the community midwife. Except Margaret's on annual leave, so today, Rachel's been booked in to see me. To be honest, I'd probably have seen her around now, anyway, just to confirm that everything is going to plan, that she hasn't got any worries or things she needs to discuss. Living in a small village like this, I can sometimes end up delivering babies, and that means I need to be familiar with mum, and what she wants, should the need arise.

Of course, I'm already fairly familiar with Rachel. We've been friends all our lives. We went to school together, grew up together, got drunk together… and on one such occasion, a few years ago, we came very close to sleeping together. Nothing came of it in the end. We were so drunk, I can't remember which one of us called a halt to the proceedings, or whether it was a mutual decision. Rachel's always maintained it was, although it's not something we talk about very often.

Do I regret not seeing things through?

No.

Rachel and I make far better friends than lovers. That's not to say she's not a beautiful woman, but we're very different people, and I know I'm not the man for her. Jack Turner is… and that's just as well, because he's the man she's engaged to, as well as being the father of her unborn child.

"Excuse me."

I look up at the sound of Millie's voice. She's standing in the doorway, holding a bright green vase with an orange flower in it, and I suck in a breath, wishing I could be the man for her.

"Yes?"

She comes into the room, approaching my desk. "I thought I'd have room on my window sill for four of these, but I don't, and I wondered if you'd like one."

No-one's ever given me a flower before, and I smile, nodding my head. "Thank you."

I mustn't read anything into her gesture. She's just disposing of an excess vase, not proposing, and I watch as she sets it down on my desk.

"Mrs Evans is due any minute," she says, looking down at me with a quizzical expression on her face.

"Yes, I know."

"Don't you think you should straighten your tie?"

"Oh… yes." I quickly fasten the top button of my shirt and pull up my tie. "Is that okay?"

She smiles. "It'll do."

I could kick myself. What I should have done then was to make a mess of straightening my tie. That would have given Millie the chance to lean over and put it right, and me the opportunity to kiss her. Of course, that's assuming she wouldn't have simply told me my tie was still crooked, and thought of me as an idiot, who can't even dress himself properly.

I study the vase for a moment, trying to forget about ties, kisses and lost opportunities, then look up at her. "How do you feel about brightening this place up a bit?"

"How do *I* feel?"

"Yes." I look around my functional surgery, with its white walls, grey linoleum floor and black or grey furnishings, contrasting them with the bright orange flower Millie's just brought in, and I shake my head. "We need some colour in here, don't we?"

"What are you suggesting?"

"Well… we can hardly paint the walls red. People might think we were trying to hide the bloodstains…" She giggles and suddenly I can't breathe. I'm not exactly clutching my chest and reaching for a defibrillator, but I have to cough to recover, and Millie frowns at me.

"Are you all right?"

"Yes, I'm fine." I'm far from 'fine', but I manage to sound convincing and I open my mouth to ask if she's got any decorating ideas, just to keep her in the room a little longer, when the front door opens and I glance over Millie's shoulder to see Joan Evans coming in. "Think about it," I whisper under my breath. "If you have any thoughts that aren't too psychedelic, let me know."

She nods her head, walking backwards to the door, and stepping aside to let Joan Evans come in before she leaves, silently closing the door behind her.

"Doctor Carew," Joan says, sitting down in the chair that's always at the end of my desk during surgery hours. Unlike when I'm interviewing prospective receptionists, I don't want the barrier of a desk – or anything else – between me and my patients. I want them to feel like I'm approachable… that they can tell me anything and everything.

"Mrs Evans. How are you?"

I smile as I'm talking, not just to put her at ease, but because it always strikes me as funny that people become so formal when they set foot in my office.

When I go into the Harbour Store, which Joan owns with her husband Bryn, she calls me 'Robson', and I call her 'Joan'. But here, we're 'Doctor Carew', and 'Mrs Evans'.

So much for being approachable…

"Not too bad."

I nod my head, calling up her notes on my screen.

"I've had the blood test results back," I say, clicking on them, and she raises her eyebrows. "Most of them are absolutely fine."

"Most of them?"

"Yes. One of the tests we ran was to see if there was any evidence of diabetes, and I'm afraid…"

"I've got diabetes?" She interrupts me before I can give her the result, her face paling.

"Not yet. You're pre-diabetic."

"What's the difference?"

"In your case, not very much. Your result was borderline, so we need to act quickly if we're going to prevent you from tipping over into full-blown diabetes."

She stares at me, blinking, dumbfounded, and I move my chair a little closer. "H—How can I be diabetic? I don't feel unwell, and I'm not overweight."

She's not… but then she's not actually diabetic… not yet.

"Is there any family history of diabetes? That might be the deciding factor, rather than your weight."

"I don't know. I was adopted when I was six weeks old."

"And you don't know anything about your birth parents?"

She shakes her head. "No. I never wanted to find them."

"I see." She's still in shock and I reach out, putting my hand on her arm. "It's going to be okay."

"Is it? People die from diabetes."

"People die from the effects of poorly controlled or untreated diabetes. We're not going to let that happen to you. You're not diabetic yet… and if we do this right, you won't be."

She sucks in a breath. "What do we have to do?"

"Make some changes… not big ones, I don't think, but hopefully they'll be enough to nip it in the bud."

"What sort of changes? It's not like I eat lots of sweets, or anything like that."

I lean back again, releasing her arm. "I'm sure you don't, but why don't you take me through a typical day's diet, and we'll see what we can change?"

She frowns, like she's thinking. "Well… we always have toast and marmalade for breakfast, with a couple of cups of tea."

"Any sugar in the tea?"

"No. I gave it up years ago."

"Good. Go on."

"Then we have sandwiches for lunch."

"What do you have in your sandwiches?"

"Cheese and pickle, more often than not. That's Bryn's favourite." I nod my head and she continues, "We like to have a couple of biscuits with our afternoon tea."

"Okay. And for dinner?"

"It varies, but it's always something quick. Bryn's a meat and two veg kind of man… as long as one of the veg is a potato, and I like pasta, so it's usually one or the other."

Thinking about Bryn's last health check, which was roughly six months ago, I don't think my plans will do him any harm either. He's bordering on obese, if you believe in the BMI charts, and while I'm not an avid follower of such things, he could do with losing some weight.

"There are plenty of things we can change there," I say, trying to sound enthusiastic. "There's nothing wrong with having a slice of toast in the morning, as long as it's wholegrain… but maybe cut out the marmalade and have it with scrambled eggs, or mushrooms, or a couple of grilled tomatoes. If you were feeling particularly healthy, you could try some Greek yogurt, with some fresh berries, or a homemade granola?"

"Can you honestly see Bryn eating granola?"

"You never know, he might like it."

She shrugs her shoulders. "What about the sandwich at lunchtime? Is that all right?"

"Not really… not if you're having bread for breakfast. Maybe you could try having a salad? In this heat, it would be quite nice."

"And what about in the winter?"

"You could try soup?"

"I suppose so."

"I'd try to cut out the biscuits, if I were you, and as for the evening meals, there's nothing wrong with pasta, or meat and two veg, but maybe add a bit of variety… try a stir-fry, or perhaps some stuffed peppers. What we're trying to do here is control your carbohydrate intake… not cut it out altogether, but keep it well managed."

"You mean, it's not just about eating sweet things… or not eating them?"

"Not at all."

I get up, going over to the filing cabinet in the corner and opening the bottom drawer. In the third file back are some booklets, and I pull one out, bringing it back to Joan and sitting on the edge of my desk.

"This will give you the basic information you need to know, and there's a list of websites and books on the back, a couple of which are really helpful." I point to them. "They'll help with portion sizes and understanding carbohydrates. The websites have some recipe sections you might find useful, too."

"So, I just need to eat a little differently?"

"Hmm… and take some exercise."

She frowns. "Exercise?"

"Yes. I'm not talking about anything drastic. You don't have to run a marathon or join a gym. Just take a walk along the harbour for twenty minutes every evening. You'll be amazed by how much difference that makes."

"I'll have to drag Bryn out with me."

I smile, nodding my head. "It won't do him any harm."

"And if I do all this, I won't need to take insulin."

"You're a long way from needing insulin. But you can't afford to be complacent. If you don't start watching what you eat and taking some form of regular exercise, then your results will only get worse over time, and you'll end up on medication."

"It's worth a try, then."

"Definitely. And you're not on your own. Encourage Bryn to join in and do it with you."

"Oh, I will… don't worry."

"And I'll be here to help if you need me." I stand, signalling the end of her appointment, and she gets to her feet, clutching the booklet and looking up at me.

"Thank you so much, Doctor."

"You don't have to thank me. Just make an appointment with Millie to come back in a month's time."

"To repeat the blood tests?"

"No. We'll just have a chat then, and see how you're getting on. I'll keep seeing you for the next few months, and then we'll repeat the blood tests once these changes have had a chance to take effect."

She nods her head and steps towards the door. "I'm really grateful, Doctor."

I smile, feeling embarrassed by her profuse gratitude, and she opens the door, passing through it, and closing it again behind her.

I sit, making some notes on her file, smiling when the notification pops up on my screen that Mrs Joan Evans is booked in for an appointment on the eighth of August.

It's hard to believe we're that far through the year already. I remember when I was younger, the summer holidays always seemed to go on forever. Now, they're gone in the blink of an eye.

I close Joan Evans's file and sit back in my seat, just as there's a knocking on my door.

"Come in."

The door opens, and Millie appears, bearing a grey cup. God… even the cups are grey. We really must do something about that… and the walls.

She smiles, walking over, and puts the cup on my desk.

"I thought you might like a coffee."

"I could murder one, thank you."

"Mrs Evans was just singing your praises."

"Was she?"

"Yes."

I gaze up at her, wishing she'd find something – anything – about me worthy of praise. I wouldn't care what it was. It could be that I'm an okay doctor, or that I have reasonable taste in ties. I'd take anything, and I'd cling to it, if it meant I didn't have to feel so empty, and so lonely without her.

Chapter Three

Millie

"If it's okay with you, I'll pop out and get my lunch."

Robson's got up from behind his desk and is helping Rachel Pedrick into her seat. He's not normally so solicitous, but she is very pregnant… and she's also a good friend of his. I found that out a while ago, when she came in to see him and had to wait because he was running late. I kept apologising, and she told me she didn't mind, and revealed that they'd been to school together, and that her call was as much for social reasons as a professional one. Rachel is beautiful, and I'll admit, I felt a little jealous then. I stared across the room, studying her light blonde hair and flawless features, until she told me she'd come to invite Robson to have dinner with her and her fiancé the following weekend. I realised I was being silly then.

I had nothing to be jealous of… not because Rachel was already spoken for, but because Robson's my boss, not my boyfriend.

"Of course," he says, bringing me back to my senses. "Just lock the door on the way out, will you? The last thing we need is people just wandering in and out if you're not here."

I nod my head, closing the door to his surgery, and grab my handbag from behind my desk, letting myself out through the front door, and locking it as instructed.

I don't double-check it, like I would if I were at home… but that's because the habit hasn't made it this far yet. And, of course, it's not my house. Although, the way Robson asked me about decorating it earlier, I started to wonder. I had to pinch myself when I got outside his office, just as a reminder that he was looking for my input as his receptionist; he wasn't asking me to move in with him… more's the pity. It was his office he was talking about decorating, not his home.

I still don't really know what he's got in mind. To start with, it sounded like he expected me to grab a paintbrush and a set of overalls and get on with it. Who knows? Maybe he does. Don't get me wrong, I wouldn't mind helping him decorate, if that's what he's got in mind. Frankly, I'd do anything that meant we could spend more time together. But I don't know if that's what he was suggesting. He asked for my ideas, making it clear they couldn't be too wild… and I wondered if that was his way of saying the vases were too brightly coloured. I couldn't be sure, and I didn't get the chance to ask, because Mrs Evans arrived, and we haven't had five minutes to ourselves since… not that I know how I'd ask him, anyway.

I guess I'll just have to come up with some ideas and see what he makes of them.

Then I might find out exactly how hands-on he expects me to get with the actual decorating.

It's sweltering out here and I stick to the shaded sided of the road, at least until I get out onto the harbour, where there's no shade to be had. The sun beating down on my skin feels like it's burning as I walk, and I rush to the baker's. I was going to stay out for my full lunch hour, but I think I'll just buy a sandwich and take it back to work with me. At least it's relatively cool in the office, and I won't get sunburned sitting at my desk.

There are only three people in front of me, but one of them has a list, which is always worrying if you're in a hurry. I'm not… not really, and I wait in line, thinking about Robson, which isn't unusual for me.

He seemed embarrassed earlier when I told him Mrs Evans had been singing his praises. I thought that was sweet, although I don't know why he blushed. It's a common occurrence. His patients always seem happy with him, but come to think of it, I suppose it's the first time I've ever told him in as many words. I wonder if I should do it more often. After all, it would probably be nice for him to know what his patients think. I'd never be brave enough to tell him what I think… but then, I doubt he cares.

It's my turn at last, and I ask for a tuna and sweetcorn sandwich. The lady behind the counter serves me with a smile, taking the five-pound note I give her, and returning my change.

"Would you like a bag?"

"No, thanks. I'm going straight back to work."

"I don't blame you. It's too hot out there today."

"I know. I was just thinking that."

She rolls her eyes as I move towards the door. "We're never happy, are we? We complain when it rains and we complain when it's too hot."

She has a point and I chuckle, stepping out onto the pavement, straight into someone who's walking along, right by the door.

"I'm sorry." I turn awkwardly as I'm speaking, almost falling over my own feet, and feel a pair of firm hands grab my elbows, holding me up.

"Careful."

The man has a deep voice, not to mention a solid, muscular chest, and I look up into a pair of deep blue eyes, set in a handsome face. I can feel myself blush and quickly step back.

"Thank you."

"Don't mention it." He smiles, dimples appearing in his cheeks, and I glance up at his thick blond hair as he stands upright, revealing himself to be ludicrously tall. "Are you okay?"

"Yes, I'm fine."

"Can I walk you to wherever you're going?"

"No. Honestly… I'm okay."

"Maybe you are, but I'd feel terrible if you fell again, and I wasn't there."

I step back a little further. "I didn't fall. I just tripped, and it isn't something I make a habit of."

I want to tell him that, if he'd allowed a little more space, rather than walking right by the shop door, none of this would have happened, but it seems unreasonable to blame him for my clumsiness.

"Why don't I come with you anyway, just to be on the safe side?"

"I'm sure you've got better things to do."

He tips his head to one side, and puts his forefinger up to his lips, like he's pretending to think. "Nope. Can't think of a single thing. So… which way are we going?"

He's not going to take 'no' for an answer, and it's the middle of the day. The harbour is crowded. I'll be perfectly safe, and besides, I've got to stop seeing men as the enemy. My brother isn't; my father isn't. Robson isn't, although I'm not entirely sure what Robson is. My boss, I guess. He certainly doesn't seem to want to be anything else.

"This way," I say. "I work around the corner, in Bell Road."

"Okay. Let's go."

I start walking and he falls into step beside me, which gives me time to take in his board shorts and white t-shirt that clings to every contoured muscle. He's wearing flip-flops and looks every inch a holiday-maker.

"What's your name?" he asks, as we pass the florist's.

"Millie."

He smiles. "That's pretty. Just like you."

That's about the corniest thing I've ever heard, but I can't say that. He'd probably be mortified. "Thank you."

"I'm Fraser," he says, even though I haven't asked. "Fraser Johnson."

We walk on a little further, going past the fish and chip shop, which is surprisingly busy, considering how hot it is, although it's nowhere near as busy as the ice cream parlour, which has a queue leaching out onto the pavement.

"Do you live around here?" Fraser asks.

I would I have thought it was obvious that I do, considering I've already told him I work here, but maybe he's assumed I live outside of the village. "Yes, I do." I'm not about to tell him where, though.

He nods his head. "It's a nice place."

"Are you here on holiday?"

"No." I'm surprised, but I do my best to hide it. "Although I don't live here either. I'm just here for the summer. I've taken a job at the surf school."

"You surf?"

"Yes. I love it, and even if I say so myself, I'm pretty good at it."

He grins, and I wonder how old he is. He looks about my age, which means he must be in his early twenties. I suppose he might still be at university, depending on the length of his course, and whether he took a gap year. It would explain why he's only here for the summer.

We turn into Bell Road.

"You work up here?"

"Yes."

"At the hotel?"

"No, at the doctor's surgery."

He turns, frowning down at me. "You're a doctor?"

I wonder about that university education now. How on earth could he think I'd be a doctor at my age? Unless I look older than I am, of course. I'm not sure how I feel about that, and rather than picking him up on it, just in case, I simply shake my head.

"No. I'm the doctor's receptionist."

"Oh. I see."

We get to the gate and I open it. "Thank you for walking me back."

"It was my pleasure. I don't suppose you're free tonight, are you?"

My stomach twists into a knot, my palms sweating, and I feel like something heavy just landed on my chest. It's been ages since I've been in this position and I don't know what to say... how to behave.

"T—Tonight?"

"Yes. We could meet at the pub, if you think you can get there without falling over."

He smiles, presumably to help me relax... or maybe to encourage me to say 'yes'.

"I hardly ever fall over." I didn't today, although he seems to have forgotten that already.

"Well, if you'd feel safer, I could come and meet you here?"

We both glance up at the building and I notice Robson standing by the window in my office. He's looking straight at me, although he quickly turns away, and I realise, in one of those lightbulb moments, that pining for him is getting me nowhere.

He's not interested in me romantically, and the sooner I wake up to that and stop daydreaming, the better. After all, if he was interested, he'd have said something by now, wouldn't he?

I need to forget about him as anything other than my boss… or I do, if I want to get over my past, and get a life of my own. And Fraser is as good a place to start as any.

"No, it's fine. I'll meet you at the pub."

He nods his head, smiling. "What time?"

"I finish work at six, so…"

"It must be fate. I finish at six, too." It doesn't feel like fate. Six o'clock seems like a fairly standard time to end the working day, but I don't say anything and after a second or two, he adds, "Shall we say six-thirty?"

"Okay."

I step through the gate, closing it with him on the other side, although he leans over slightly.

"I'm looking forward to it already."

I smile and nod my head, which seems polite. I can hardly say 'me too', because that would be a lie. It's not that I'm dreading it. I'm just ambivalent.

We're going out for drinks. We're not getting married. In fact, I doubt I'll see him again after tonight. He said he's only here for the summer, so there's no point in taking this seriously. In a way, that's what makes it the perfect idea. We can keep it very casual, and I can dip my toe into the water again without fear of repercussions.

This is just what I need.

And as for Robson?

Robson who?

Chapter Four

Robson

I sit down again, Rachel safely seated, and stare at the door Millie's just shut behind her, waiting a few seconds until I hear the front door close.

There's a perverse part of me that actually relaxes, because she's not here anymore. In her absence, I can rest assured she's not about to walk through the door, or ask me a question I can't answer because my mouth won't coordinate with my brain. She can't make my heart skip a beat when I'm least expecting it, either. I'm safe.

Except I'm not, because I miss her, and she's only been gone for thirty seconds.

"Hello?" Rachel clicks her fingers in front of my face. "Is anyone at home?"

"Yes. Sorry."

"Don't apologise." I look up and see the smile on her face, noticing that she's tied her long blonde hair into a ponytail. It's nothing like as fancy as Millie's, but Rachel's pregnant, and has probably done it for convenience, more than style. "I hadn't realised there was anything going on between you two."

"Who two?"

"You and your beautiful receptionist."

I feel myself blush. "There isn't."

She frowns, although it quickly clears. "Oh… but you'd like there to be. Is that it?"

"Yes." I sigh, unable to help myself and Rachel shifts awkwardly in her seat, trying to move it closer, which isn't an easy feat when you're nearly nine months pregnant. In the end, she gives up and just leans back, looking at me, and straightening her blue and white striped dress. It's made of stretchy t-shirt material, but at the moment it seems to be stretching in all the wrong directions, if Rachel's struggles are anything to go by. I give her a minute to settle. "Why didn't you warn me?"

"Warn you about what?" Her frown returns.

"About love… and how much it hurts."

"It doesn't have to hurt."

"It does when the woman you're in love with doesn't even know you exist."

Rachel raises her eyebrows, and she rests her hands on top of her bump, studying me. "Are you sure about that?"

"Absolutely positive. Millie knows I exist as her boss, but beyond that…"

She tilts her head, like she knows something I don't. "That's isn't how I saw it."

"Saw what?"

"Millie. Just now."

I perform the task Rachel can't and edge my seat forward. "Really? Tell me what you saw."

"A young woman whose face lit up when she looked at you… that's all."

I feel my shoulders drop. Somehow, I'd hoped for more. "She was probably just pleased it's lunchtime."

"Stop putting yourself down, will you? It's not who you are."

"Are you telling me I'm big-headed?"

"No. But you're never normally so negative." It's true. I'm not. I'm very much a glass half full kind of person. "And besides, it's my job to give you pep talks. Even if you weren't my best friend, you're the one who kept telling me to have a little faith in myself when I was nervous about Jack and his ex. It's payback time."

"Oh? Is that what you call it?"

"Yes. I've got nothing to worry about anymore. Not since Lucy got married and…"

"Hang on a second." I hold up my hand and she stops talking. "You've never had anything to worry about, regardless of whether Jack's ex tied the knot, because he loves you, not her."

"I know. I'm just making the point. My love life is pretty damn perfect, so I can help with yours now."

"Can you?"

"Well… I can't make everything right, necessarily, but I can listen."

She has a point. I'm always telling people to talk through their problems, so maybe I should heed my own advice for once.

"I don't know what to say to her."

Rachel smiles, shaking her head. "Have you tried asking her out?"

"Asking her out? Are you mad?"

"No. Isn't that what you'd normally do if you wanted to date someone?"

"Yes, but…"

"But what?"

"Not only is she eight years my junior, she works for me."

"And the problem here is…?"

"Obvious to most people."

"Not to me, it's not. I know you. If it's not an old-fashioned thing to say these days, I think you're an honourable man."

"Why… thanks."

"No, I'm serious."

"Does it seem honourable that I spend most of my time fantasising about someone so young, who's also in my paid employment?"

"I didn't say you were a saint… or that you have to be. And anyway, she's not that young. If there are eight years between you, that makes her twenty-three… not seventeen."

"I know, but…"

She shakes her head. "Stop saying 'but' all the time. You're being silly, Rob."

"Thanks for the support."

"You don't need support. You need to stop making excuses and take your chances. Just because Millie works for you doesn't mean you can't ask her out. It happens all the time, and as long as you're not using your position to gain an advantage over her, it's fine."

"I'd never do something like that."

"I know you wouldn't. I'm just pointing out the obvious, while telling you that the age gap is irrelevant."

"You don't think everyone in the village is going to accuse me of having an early mid-life crisis?"

She laughs, throwing her head back. "I don't think there's any such thing, is there? And who cares what other people think? Gemma and Tom have got ten years between them, and I think the age gap is even bigger for Laura and Rory. Hell, Jack's six years older than me, and we're going to be parents any day now."

"Hmm… speaking of which, I suppose we'd better focus on the fairly obvious bump in the room."

"Stop changing the subject."

"I'm not."

"Yes, you are." She sits forward as best she can. "Are you going to ask her out?"

"I don't know. I'll think about it."

"Seriously? You'll think about it? How do you expect to get anywhere if all you do is think?"

"It's not all I do."

"Oh?"

I reach for my blood pressure monitor. "I dream about her, too."

Rachel holds up her hand. "Okay. Stop talking. I may be your best friend, but I don't need to hear about the content of your dreams."

"No, you don't. And I wouldn't tell you, anyway."

She chuckles and I join in, wrapping the cuff around her arm. "Is this your way of shutting me up?"

"Yes."

She sits in silence while the cuff inflates, the numbers counting up on the monitor, and going a lot higher than I'd expected, or than I'd like. Finally, it reaches its peak, and the numbers count down again, stopping at 156/105. I clear my throat, switching off the machine, and Rachel holds out her arm.

"We'll just leave that on for now and test it again in a few minutes."

"Oh… okay." She puts her arm down again, resting it on my desk.

"How have you been feeling since your last appointment?"

I check her records on my screen, noticing that her blood pressure on her previous visit was a much more reasonable 122/75, and I shift my chair slightly, looking down at her ankles, which are noticeably swollen.

"I'm more tired than I have been," she says. "But I don't think the heat is helping. It's so much harder to sleep."

"Are you able to rest during the day?"

"Yes. I've stopped working now."

I nod my head. "Do you put your feet up, or do you just sit down in a chair?"

"I just sit in a chair, when I'm not cooking."

"Cooking isn't resting, Rachel."

"It's not working either. And besides, I wanted to stock up the freezer before the baby's born."

"Why? Because Jack can't cook? We both know perfectly well he can."

"Yes. Better than me."

"I didn't say that, but you don't need to feed the five thousand."

"I'm not trying to." She narrows her eyes at me. "Maybe I'm just nesting."

"Maybe you are. But do you think you could nest with your feet up?"

"Probably."

"Good. I'd be very grateful."

I press the button on the blood pressure monitor again and wait, feeling more nervous this time. I have good cause. The reading has gone up. It's 158/109.

I remove the cuff and wrap it back up, shoving the machine to one side.

"Is the baby still moving around a fair amount?"

"Yes. She seems to think my bladder is a football."

"In which case, you shouldn't have too much difficulty giving me a urine sample."

She frowns. "Now?"

"Yes. Now. You're pregnant. Don't tell me you can't pee to order." She giggles and, despite my worries, I manage a smile, handing her a pot from my bottom drawer. "If you'd rather use the bathroom in the house, instead of the one in the hall outside, just go through."

"Would you mind?"

"Not at all."

She leaves the room and I let out a sigh, rubbing my hands down my face. I hadn't expected this, and I gather the equipment I need for when Rachel gets back, entering her blood pressure readings onto her records.

It doesn't take her very long, and when she returns, I make a point of studying her ankles again. They look even more swollen now she's standing and I get to my feet, taking her hand, and cast my eyes over her fingers. They're also a little puffy, and as I sit her down, I move my chair even closer to hers.

"Give me the pot."

She does as I say and I dip the tester strip into it, holding it there for a moment or two, and then pulling it out again.

"I always think it's fascinating how quickly the little squares change colour," she says, although I ignore her for a moment, checking them against the printed ones on the outside of the pot. I'm looking for protein, but luckily Rachel's sample seems to be okay, and I get up, going over to the basin to wash my hands. "Is something wrong?" she asks, worried by my silence, perhaps.

"It doesn't look like it. I was concerned about pre-eclampsia, but…"

I turn, noting the pallor of her cheeks, and rush back, sitting down again. Rachel stares up at me, blinking back tears. "Th— That's dangerous, isn't it?"

"It can be, which is why I'm going to be extra cautious and take some blood."

She clamps her hands around her bump. "Where from?"

"Your arm," I say, and she relaxes, just slightly

"Okay."

"I'm going to send it away for an urgent test, to get a really accurate reading of your protein levels. Your urine is okay, but I'm concerned that your blood pressure has shot up, and your ankles and fingers are swollen."

I put on some latex gloves and take the blood, labelling up the vial, and then I remove the gloves, wash my hands again, and sit back down, taking Rachel's hand in mine.

"Rob…"

I can hear her fear. I can see it too, and I shift forward on my seat. "It's okay, Rachel. I've got you. I won't let anything happen to you or your baby. Okay?" She nods her head. "I want you to go straight home and put your feet up. If you feel sick, or you get a headache, or any kind of visual disturbance, I want you to call me straight away. I don't care if it's the middle of the night… call me. Do you hear?"

"Y—You're scaring me, Rob."

"I don't want to. But I need you to take me seriously, and listen to what I've said."

"I—If it's pre-eclampsia, what happens next?"

"The only cure is to deliver the baby." Her eyes widen. "It's okay. At thirty-eight weeks, delivery carries very few risks." I help her to her feet, guiding her to the door. "Remember what I've said. Go home, put your feet up on the sofa… and don't worry."

"I can do the first two things. The third one might take a little more strength than I've got."

"I'm probably just over-reacting, because it's you."

She takes a deep breath, looking so scared, and I put my arms around her, pulling her in for a hug.

"Thank you," she whispers, her voice croaking.

"I'll call you as soon as I get the test results. It won't be until tomorrow, but in the meantime, just rest. Okay?"

She nods her head, and I open the front door, letting her out.

She's in a bit of a daze and I wonder if I should offer to see her home, but before I can open my mouth, she pulls her phone from her bag. I know she's calling Jack. Just like I know he'll drop everything and come home to her, and I smile as watch her walk away, talking avidly. Knowing that Jack will be there for her doesn't mean I won't. But I'm her friend and her doctor. I'm not her lover, or the father of the baby she's carrying. Our roles are very different.

I close the door, stepping back into my office, where I sit down at my desk again, making a note to speak to Margaret when she gets back about monitoring Rachel's blood pressure. I can do it myself for now, and Margaret can take over when she returns from her holiday. Even if Rachel's test results are okay, we'll still need to keep an eye on her, and I make a second note to call her later, just to check she's okay.

I open the top drawer of the small filing cabinet under my desk, to find I've run out of sample bags. The spares are kept in Millie's office, in one of the cupboards, and I wander through, finding them straight away. As I come back, I glance at the flowers on Millie's window sill. They really brighten the place up, and I smile, wondering what she made of me asking her to come up with ideas for redecorating this place. It's about time we did it, and I'd like for her to feel involved... not just because she works here, but because I want her to feel like she belongs here with me.

I wonder what she'd make of my house, too. It's at the back of the property, and the door to it is behind me. It's never locked, but to my knowledge, Millie's never stepped through it. She's never needed to, and has never asked, either.

That makes me wonder if Rachel was right... whether Millie's face really does light up when she sees me. If so, I need to do something about it. The question is, what?

Dinner seems the obvious answer. It's where I'd normally start when dating someone. Dinner and conversation. I've always been a slow-burner with women; taking my time to get to know them before committing to anything more intimate, and while my reactions to Millie might be a little different from anything I've felt before, I see no reason to change. I want her to feel safe with me; to trust me, and if it takes a while to build that, then I won't mind in the slightest… as long as we can be together.

So… dinner it is.

Unless that's too formal.

We spend all day being formal with each other, and as well as trusting me, and feeling safe in my company, I want her to feel relaxed, too.

Perhaps lunch would be better…

I could invite her to have lunch with me tomorrow, couldn't I? I could even cook us something here. That way, she'd get to see where I live, we'd get some time to ourselves to talk, and she'd get to see me as someone other than her boss.

All I need to do is to work out how to ask her.

A movement outside catches my eye, and I look up, seeing Millie approach the house. She's walking beside a very tall man, with a mop of blond hair and more muscles than I've ever dreamed of possessing. He's gazing down at her, saying something, which reaches me as a muffled whisper through the open window. They stop outside the gate, and Millie opens it, although I still can't hear what they're saying. They seem deep in conversation, though, and the man smiles, one of those smiles that only film stars have, with dimples forming in his cheeks, and a vice-like grip of fear claws at my heart.

How can any normal man hope to compete against that?

Millie turns, the two of them looking at the house, although Millie's eyes seem to fix on me. Damn… she's seen me. I step away from the window, taking the sample bag back into my office. As I sit at my desk, I tell myself I'm not going to look out of the window. I'm not going to spy on her...

But I can't help it.

I turn my chair, leaning back slightly, and see that Millie and her young man are still talking. He's nodding his head and smiling, and after a few moments more, Millie steps into the garden, closing the gate.

The man leans over and I wonder if he's going to kiss her, and how I'll react.

Will I go out there and tell him to back off? Of course not. What reason would I have? I have no claim over her.

The thought of another man's lips on hers, though...

I clench my fists, then unclench them, repeating the process over and over, watching Millie nod her head. The man smiles again – damn him – then says something else, and turns, walking away, with a spring in his step.

I can't blame him for that. I'd have a spring in my step if I was Millie's boyfriend.

There's no chance of that now, though. He may not have kissed her – thank God – but the way he was looking at her was incendiary... and what woman in her right mind is going to say 'no' to a man who looks like a god?

The front door opens and I wish now that I'd thought to close the one to my office. I only have a matter of seconds to move my chair back, so I'm facing Millie, when she glances into my room.

"You're back early."

I can't think of anything else to say, and regardless of her conversation outside, she's only been gone for half an hour.

"I know. It's too hot out there."

"I see. I... um... I didn't realise you had a boyfriend." The words tumble out of my mouth. Millie's eyes widen and I wonder if I've overstepped the mark. As her boss, I almost certainly have, but I need to know. It's possible I mis-read the signs, isn't it? It's feasible they're just friends...

"His name's Fraser," she says, dashing my hopes. "He's teaching at the surf school."

"So he's just a summer visitor?"

"Yes."

I'm surprised. Millie doesn't seem the kind of woman who'd get involved with someone who wasn't going to stick around. But I guess that just goes to show I don't know her, any more than she knows me.

She turns towards her office, our conversation over, but I call her back and she steps closer, watching as I bag up Rachel's blood sample.

"I need you to send this off for urgent testing, please."

She takes it from me. "Oh. Okay." She glances at the name on the label and looks back at me, raising her eyebrows. I don't comment. Rachel's medical issues are personal and I'm not about to discuss them... especially not now.

Okay, so I know I can trust Millie not to repeat anything I tell her, and if she really wanted to, she could look up Rachel's notes, anyway. But that's not the point. The point is, I feel like everything's just changed between us.

Not only is she with someone else, but having seen him, I've realised that, if she goes for men like Fraser, she's never going to give me a second glance.

I suppose I knew that all along. I've felt invisible since the moment we met, after all.

But that doesn't make it any easier... not when faced with the reality of seeing the kind of man she likes, and knowing that can never be me.

Chapter Five

Millie

I'd never have thought it could be so difficult to hold a conversation.

But it seems I was wrong.

Unless, of course, 'conversation' counts as being talked at for the better part of an hour, in which case, Fraser is an expert at it.

From the moment I walked in through the door of the pub, feeling a little nervous about being out for the first time in so long, he's done nothing but talk. To start with, I put it down to nerves, wondering if he felt the same way I did, and his anxiety was coming out as incessant chatter. Then I realised, he just likes the sound of his own voice… and didn't intend shutting up anytime soon.

I keep wishing I'd been able to say 'no' to him when he asked me to join him this evening. I know I used Robson's disinterest as an excuse in my own head… but did that mean I had to say 'yes' to the first man who asked?

No, of course it didn't.

I could have waited… not for Robson, of course, but for someone… anyone, who's capable of taking a breath between sentences. Someone who's sole topic of conversation isn't surfing…

To think, I could have been at home, learning new ways of styling my hair. I know that sounds dull, but anything would be better than this, and it's something that's kept me occupied for hours, studying online videos and practising the styles the women on them manage to make look so easy. To be honest, even watching videos of paint drying would have been more entertaining than this.

My only saving grace is that we're sitting on the terrace, so I can gaze at the harbour, rather than feeling confined by the four walls of the pub, and Fraser's non-stop talking.

"… I'm thinking of entering again this year," he says, although I'm not sure what he's talking about. He was just telling me about a surfing competition somewhere, so it could be to do with that. "I came really close to winning it last year, and if the waves are anything like as good, I should be in with a chance."

I nod my head, finishing my drink.

"The competition's named after Eddie Aikau," he says. "He was a famous lifeguard and surfer in Hawaii… and my inspiration."

"I see."

He picks up his pint glass. "I first became a lifeguard when I was at college and then picked up a surfboard the following summer." He sighs, his eyes resting on the amber liquid nestling at the bottom of his glass. "It was like love at first sight. I belong on a board… you know?"

Not particularly.

He swallows the last of his lager, putting down the glass and then looks at mine. "Can I get you another drink?"

"No, thanks. I've got an early start. I should probably get home."

"Oh… okay." I get up and he copies me. "I'll walk you home."

"I'm fine… really."

"It's no trouble."

I nod my head, giving in gracefully, and he follows me back through the pub and out of the front door.

It's still very warm, and he walks beside me, up Church Lane, past St. Mary's Road and into Chapel Mews, all the while telling me about how Sam, who owns the surf school, had seen him in a competition at Newquay, and asked him to join his staff for the summer.

"I could hardly say 'no'," he says, with a smile. "But I can't wait to get back out on the circuit again."

How could I have thought he was at university?

I feel like such a fool.

"This is me," I say, relieved to reach my front door. Fraser glances up, nodding his head. "Thanks for the drink."

"You're welcome."

He gazes down at me and I wonder if he's going to kiss me. I don't want him to, and am just thinking up excuses when he steps back.

"I'll see you soon."

I nod, unwilling to commit, but relieved that he didn't kiss me or ask for a second date. 'See you soon', isn't definite. It's like 'see you around', and I wonder if he found me as boring as I found him. I couldn't disguise my lack of interest in surfing, and outside of that, he had nothing to talk about.

Still… at least I've only wasted just over an hour of my life.

I let myself in, climbing up the stairs, and open the door to my flat. It's stuffy and I quickly throw open the only two windows there are; one at the front and one at the back. The bathroom doesn't have a window, unfortunately, and being up here in the eaves of the house, even with the windows open, it still feels horribly hot.

I kick off my shoes, putting down my handbag, and wish now that I'd fended off Robson's question a little better.

When I got in from buying my lunch, I hadn't expected him to ask about my 'boyfriend', and while I know I ought to have denied the connection, and explained that Fraser and I had only just met, I didn't do any such thing. Not that it really matters, but the problem is, he's now under the impression that I've got a boyfriend, when I don't have any such thing…

I'm not for one second suggesting that my availability is going to change Robson's mind and suddenly make him decide to ask me out. Let's face it, I've been available ever since we first met, and he's not shown the slightest interest. But I don't want him to think I go out with men like Fraser… when what I really want is to go out with Robson.

I flop down onto the small, cream-coloured sofa and look around the room. I keep it tidy in here, because it's not my flat. It's owned by a friend of my parents, who very kindly said I could make use of it 'for the time being'. I don't know how long 'for the time being' is, but I suspect he took pity on me, when he heard my story, because he's charging me almost nothing by way of rent.

That said, the place is tiny. It comprises one room, with a door that leads to the bathroom. In here, there's just about enough space to swing a cat, providing you don't get too enthusiastic about it. The kitchen occupies the rear corner, and opposite it is my bed, hidden from view by a folding screen. The sofa on which I'm sitting is between the two, facing the wall-mounted television, which I turn on, just to take my mind off of Robson for a while.

Flicking through the channels, I find the highlights of today's cricket match, and put down the remote, twisting in my seat so I can put my feet up.

Today was the last day of the test match between England and New Zealand, and although it ended in a draw, it was quite exciting. I've been keeping up with the run of play on my phone throughout the day, making sure it was hidden from Robson, in case he objected.

The highlights might lack the thrill of watching the match live, especially when I know the outcome, but the English batting performance is outstanding. It's a shame they couldn't have done this in the first innings. If they had, they'd have won the test, hands down.

The programme's only on for an hour, and when it's finished, I feel cool enough to heat up some of yesterday's left-over pasta in the microwave, pouring myself a glass of chilled water to go with it.

There's nothing else I particularly want to watch on the television, so I switch it off, and while my dinner cools a little, I grab my phone from my handbag and connect a call to my brother, Ellis.

It's not that late, and he won't mind me eating while we talk.

"Hi, Millie." His voice rings out through the flat as I put him onto speaker, placing the phone on the arm of the sofa, while I sit down, picking up my bowl of pasta and resting it on my lap.

"Hello."

"How are you?"

"I'm fine. I've just been watching the cricket."

"And it made you think of me?" I can hear the smile in his voice, and it makes my lips twitch upwards, too.

"Yes, as it happens."

"I know. I used to be good enough to play for England..." His voice fades and we both wait to see who'll laugh first. It's me, unable to stop myself.

"You keep telling yourself that. You were a half-decent medium-paced bowler, and as a middle-order batsman, you did okay."

"Yes, as long as we remember I was only ever playing at a local level. Anything above that, I'd have been out of my depth."

"I don't suppose you've played much lately, have you?"

"It's not the most popular sport up here, no."

I'm reminded of how far apart we are. The east coast of Scotland sounds like another world away, but it's perfect for a marine biologist… even one who got his degree in Cornwall.

"How's work?" I ask, munching on my pasta.

"Busy, but good. What about you?"

"The same."

"What have you been up to, other than working?"

I take a breath, finishing my mouthful, and put down my fork. "I've just been out on a date."

"Just? As in tonight?"

"Yes."

"But it's only twenty to nine. Why are you back home already?"

"Because the man I went out with was so boring."

Ellis laughs. "You bailed on him?"

"Not really. I just said 'no', when he asked if I wanted a second drink. I honestly didn't think I could listen to any more surfing talk."

"The guy was a surfer?"

"Yes. Well… I think he said he was a lifeguard first, and then he got into surfing. To be honest, I wasn't paying very much attention."

"Did he at least walk you home?"

"Yes. You don't have to worry… although it's still daylight, so I wasn't in any danger."

I can hear his sigh. "Okay, so we'll write him off as boring, but well-mannered."

"I guess."

"And now, having taken the plunge, you can move on."

"If only it was that easy."

"It is, Millie. Not all men are going to be like Damian. And just because this surfer wasn't your type doesn't mean there won't be someone else."

"I know." I already work with the only 'someone else' I'll ever be interested in.

"So, who else is down there?"

"A lot of tourists, at the moment."

"Hmm… probably best to avoid them. I'm not sure you'd be very good at a long-distance relationship."

"No, neither am I."

"I'm sure someone will turn up… and I'm really pleased you said 'yes', when this guy asked you out."

"How do you know I didn't ask him?"

"Because that would have required a personality transplant."

I chuckle and roll my eyes, even though he can't see me. "I haven't mentioned anything to Mum and Dad about going out with Fraser tonight, and I don't intend to."

"Okay. Is that your way of asking me to keep quiet?"

"Yes. You know what'll happen if they find out. They'll be on the phone, checking up, making sure I'm all right."

"It's only because they care, Millie."

"I know. But you care, and you don't feel the need to keep tabs on me."

"I still worry about you."

I take a deep breath. "There's no need."

"You're my little sister, and after what happened…"

"I'm trying to put it behind me, Ellis. That's why telling Mum and Dad would be a mistake. I'd rather work things out for myself… at least for now."

"And tell them about it when you're engaged to someone?"

"No. But I don't want every single date to be scrutinised and checked up on."

"Your secret's safe with me," he says.

"Thank you."

I know Mum and Dad wouldn't mean to fuss, but they'd do it anyway, and that's the last thing I need when I'm trying so hard to live a normal life.

Whatever that is.

Chapter Six

Robson

I feel absolutely dreadful this morning.

I don't need a doctor, or even to be a doctor, to work out why.

Lack of sleep will do that to the best of people.

And why the lack of sleep?

That would be because of the hours I spent lying awake, torturing myself about Millie and her boyfriend. I was tormented by the guy's bulging muscles, knowing I could never hope to compete. Keeping myself in shape is one thing. Standing with my head held high alongside a cool surfing dude is something else altogether.

I know my limitations, and in him, I've met them.

I look up at the sound of knocking on my door. It'll be Millie. No-one else is here, and I call out, "Come in," while sitting up and trying to look busy.

She opens the door, smiling, a cup of coffee in her hand. As usual, my breath catches in my throat at the sight of her. She's wearing another of those dresses, like the one she had on yesterday, only this time it's cream in colour, and has four buttons down the front. They don't serve any purpose, other than to embellish the bodice of the dress... and why not? Her hair is styled in a sexy, messy kind of bun, tied up behind her head, with a few strands framing her face, and the more I look at her, the more I realise I'm going to have to find some way of distracting myself, if I'm going to stay sane.

"I've just made a cup, and thought you might like one," she says, putting it down on my desk.

"Thank you." I glance at my screen, desperate for something to talk about that doesn't involve whatever she was doing last night. "I'm not seeing anyone until ten today."

"No. It's much quieter."

It is compared to yesterday, but I'm too tired to complain… although it might be better to be busy. At least that way, I'd have less time to think about Millie.

"Have you sent out all the clinic reminders yet?"

"The asthma ones are all done. I finished those yesterday. I'm almost there on the diabetes ones, too, so I'm just left with the blood pressure checks."

"That's good. Hopefully, there won't be too many."

She nods her head. "Can I just ask… how long do the diabetes check up appointments have to be? There haven't been any since I started – not until now – but I suppose people might start calling to book in before the end of the week, and I don't want to get it wrong."

"For diabetes, you'll need to make two appointments. The first one should be thirty minutes long, and the second one needs to be about a week later, and roughly twenty minutes."

"That's to give them the results of their blood tests?"

"Yes. And discuss their medication and diet, if necessary."

My computer pings and I glance at the screen, noting that it's Rachel's test results.

"Was there anything else?" I say, looking back at Millie.

"No." She frowns, and I wish I could take back my words. They sounded dismissive, which I didn't intend them to be. Before I can apologise, she turns and walks towards the door.

"Thanks for the coffee."

She looks over her shoulder, managing a slight smile, and closes the door behind her.

"Damn," I mutter under my breath, and click on Rachel's results, taking a moment to study them. I might be feeling downhearted about Millie, but I can't help smiling. Rachel's protein levels are perfectly acceptable, and I sit back for a moment, feeling relieved. I know she and Jack will be, too, and I pick up my mobile from the desk and flip it over in my hand, recalling the conversation I had with Jack yesterday evening.

I hadn't called him. I'd called Rachel, just to make sure she was feeling okay, but it was Jack who answered, explaining that she was resting upstairs.

"She phoned at lunchtime in such a panic, I had to come home," he said, and I could hear the worry in his voice.

"Sorry. That was probably my fault. I'd reiterated to her that she needed to rest, and I may have overdone it. Her blood pressure was high, and her ankles were swollen. Even though there was no protein in her urine, there's still a risk of pre-eclampsia."

"I know. Rachel told me when I got home and then spent thirty minutes looking it up on the Internet."

"Oh, God."

Jack laughed then. "It's okay. I took her phone away from her in the end and made her go upstairs to rest."

"And she did as she was told?"

"For once… yes, she did. So, don't feel guilty. Whatever you said, it worked."

I'd have talked for longer, but I heard Rachel calling him in the background, and I let him go. Now, though, at least I can phone with better news.

I connect a call to Rachel, knowing she'll want to hear the news firsthand, and am surprised when Jack answers again.

"Is Rachel okay?" I ask, without bothering to say 'hello'.

"She's fine. I'm just wary of letting her near the Internet, in case she mis-diagnoses herself with something."

I smile, shaking my head. "You don't need to worry. I've got the test results back, and you can stand down. Everything's normal. There's no sign of pre-eclampsia at this stage."

"Why are her ankles so swollen?" he asks.

"Probably because of the heat."

"And her blood pressure?"

"That's harder to say. It could be a lack of sleep. It could be all sorts of things. I'll come down at lunchtime and test it again."

"Are you sure?"

"I'm positive. Will you be there? I don't want Rachel getting up if she doesn't have to."

"No. That's fine. I'm working from home for the time being."

Somehow, that doesn't surprise me. It's the kind of thing Jack would do... but then, he'd do anything for Rachel. Just like I'd do anything for Millie, given half a chance.

"I'll see you sometime between twelve-thirty and one. I can't be more precise. It depends on how my morning surgery goes."

"That's not a problem. We're not going anywhere."

"I'm glad to hear it."

He chuckles and we both hang up.

My last patient of the morning is Anna Goddard.

She's quite new to the village, and has only been to see me once before. That was not long after she first moved here. She was suffering from a rash on her arms, and although that was easily treated, I noticed at the time, she seemed a little down in the dumps.

"Miss Goddard... how can I help?"

She smiles, a slightly shy smile, which doesn't touch her light brown eyes, getting comfortable in the chair at the end of my desk. When I first met her, I was thrown by the fact that she looks nothing like her brother, the hotel manager, Stephen Goddard. But Rachel informed me they're only half brother and sister, so that may account for the fact that his colouring is a lot darker than hers.

"I've done something to my wrist."

She puts it up on the desk, and I glance down, unable to see anything obviously wrong with it.

"May I?" I say, reaching out, and she nods her head as I take her hand, turning it over to examine the other side. There's still nothing visible, and I gently flex it, which makes her wince. "You haven't fallen, or banged it?"

"No. Nothing like that." She pulls her hand away, letting it rest in her lap.

"Are there any times of day when it hurts more?"

"It's always stiff in the mornings, and just seems to get gradually more painful as the day goes on. Usually, by the evening, there's some swelling as well."

I nod my head. "My first instinct is to wonder about a repetitive strain injury."

"Caused by what?" She frowns at me.

"You work for Ben Atkins, don't you?"

"Yes."

"Which I imagine involves a fair amount of typing?"

She nods her head. "It's pretty non-stop at the moment."

"In which case, that could be the answer."

"But I like my job. I don't want to give it up. It's the only excuse I have to get out of the house and see other people." She blushes, and I wonder if she meant to say that.

"No-one said you have to give up your job. You might just have to make a few adjustments, that's all. Paracetamol or ibuprofen will help with the pain, and you can apply a cold pack to it for around twenty minutes two or three times a day as well."

"Okay."

"And maybe ask Ben if he can get you a wrist rest for your keyboard. It takes away some of the strain, if you're typing a lot." She nods. "Don't be tempted to rest your wrist too much, though. That can actually do more harm than good."

"I see."

"Come back again in a couple of weeks, and if there's no improvement, I'll book you an X-ray at the hospital." I sit back, studying her for a moment. "Is everything else okay?" She stares at me like she doesn't understand the question. "Are you settling in down here?"

"Oh. Yes, thank you."

"You said you're meeting new people?"

"Not meeting them, as such. I see people at work."

"So, you're not venturing out in the evenings?"

She shakes her head. "When I first moved here last year, my brother had grand ideas about taking me out and introducing me to everyone in the village. But he always gets waylaid by work." She smiles. "I don't blame him. He loves his job, and he's very good at it. I'm just…"

"You're feeling lonely?" I guess, and she blinks a few times.

"I don't know if lonely is the right word. I'm not looking for a relationship or anything like that." Her eyes wander to the window, misting slightly, and I wonder if she's been hurt before. It certainly looks that way. "I—I wondered about getting a dog," she says a little randomly. "That way I'd have an excuse to go out… to take it for walks, you know?" I nod my head as she turns back to face me. "I even spoke to Ben about whether he'd allow me to take it in to work, because it seemed unfair to get and dog and leave the poor thing by itself all day."

"And what did he say?"

"That he didn't mind, as long as it was well-behaved."

"In which case…?"

She shrugs her shoulders. "After I spoke to him, I remembered, my flat is rented. The last place I lived in, there was a definite 'no pets' policy."

"And here? What does your lease say?"

"It doesn't mention pets at all, but the place is immaculate, so I can't imagine my landlady is going to allow them."

"Why don't you speak to her? Laura Quick is very understanding. Tell her what you've told me. She'll listen, and I'm sure she'll do what she can."

Her eyes brighten. "Do you think?"

"It's certainly worth asking."

Her whole face lights up, and she stands. "I'll do that… thank you, Doctor."

"You're welcome."

She leaves, and I type her notes onto her record, looking up when I hear a knocking on my door. It's Millie again, and she steps inside.

"I'm just going to lunch. Do you want me to lock the door?"

"No, thanks. I've got to go out myself in a minute, so I'll lock it when I leave."

"Oh… okay."

She doesn't ask where I'm going, but she probably doesn't care, and she turns, leaving my office and the building, closing the door softly behind her. I glance out of the window, but there's no sign of her boyfriend – thank goodness – and once I've finished typing up Anna Goddard's notes, I grab my bag, opening it to check I've got everything I need, and then I pick up my keys and head out of the door, locking it behind me.

The sun is scorching, and I'd rather take my walk to Rachel and Jack's at a more leisurely pace… and I would, if I wasn't so worried about seeing Millie with her boyfriend. He may not have collected her from the surgery today, but I imagine they'll have met up somewhere, and I'm not sure I'm strong enough to see them together.

In fact, I know I'm not.

I keep my head down, making it to St. Mary's Road in just over five minutes.

Jack's car is parked outside the house, and I walk up to the front door, knocking on it, and waiting a few seconds until Jack appears, a smile forming on his lips. His dark blond hair seems slightly more messy than usual and he's wearing shorts and a t-shirt, which isn't his usual work attire. These are the advantages of working from home, I suppose.

"Hi, Robson." He steps aside, letting me in, and I pause for a moment to catch my breath.

"It's nice and cool in here."

"Yes. I've got every window in the house open, so it's just about bearable."

"It's rapidly becoming unbearable outside."

"Can I get you a drink?"

"A glass of water would be lovely."

He leads me through to the kitchen at the back of the house, and I wait while he fetches a glass, filling it with iced water from the fridge, before handing it over. I drink it down in one go, and he smiles. "You were thirsty."

I'm not about to admit the reason for that… which is that I almost ran here. Instead, I just smile and hand him back the glass. "Thanks."

"I'd better take you up to Rachel. She'll have heard you arrive, and if we're not careful, she'll come down to find out what the delay is."

I chuckle, following him up the stairs and through the door on the left.

Rachel is sitting up in bed, the pillows behind her. She's wearing a dress that's similar to the one she had on yesterday, her hair tied up in a ponytail, and she's holding a hand-held fan about three inches from her face, which is rosy, to put it mildly.

I decide against commenting on the heat and glance around the room, noting the duck-egg blue walls, and pine furniture... not to mention the fact that the bed seems bigger than her old one.

"You've redecorated," I say, going around the bed to Rachel's side. I glance back at Jack, who frowns at me, and I smile. "Don't panic. My knowledge of Rachel's bedroom is limited to me having carried her up here a couple of times, when she's had too much to drink."

His face clears, and we both look down at Rachel, who rolls her eyes. "The chance would be a fine thing these days."

Jack sits on the bed, leaning over and resting his hand on her thigh. "Not long now, sweetheart."

"Hmm..." She turns to him. "If we ever do this again, we're going to time it better, so I can give birth in the depths of winter."

"Whatever you say."

I put my bag on top of the chest of drawers, taking out the blood pressure monitor and I wait while Rachel transfers the fan to her other hand, so I can put the cuff around her arm. We all wait in silence while it inflates, the tension building as it slowly deflates again. The numbers seem to take ages to settle, but when they do, I nod my head.

"And?" Rachel says, her voice laced with impatience.

"It's one four six over ninety-two."

"Which means?" Jack asks, and I turn to him.

"It's lower than yesterday, but still higher than I'd like." I look back down at Rachel. "I take it baby's still moving?"

"God, yes. She kept me awake most of last night."

"In which case, try to get some rest today."

"My ankles seem a little less swollen," she says and I look down as she wiggles her feet.

"Yes, they are, but that's no reason for you to get up and start running around."

"Running? I can't remember the last time I ran."

She shifts on the bed, and I smile. "I know it's frustrating, having to stay up here, and it's probably warmer, too, so you can go downstairs, if you want, but you must keep resting... okay? I'm still concerned about your blood pressure, so I don't want to hear you've been on your feet all day."

"She won't be," Jack says before Rachel can get a word out, and she narrows her eyes at him, although her lips are twisting into a loving smile. "I'm going to carry on working from home for now, just to make sure she behaves herself."

"Good. I'll come by every day to check your blood pressure, and when Margaret gets back from her annual leave, she'll take over."

"Do you do this for all your patients?" Jack asks, and I nod my head, winking at him. He grins and I pack away the blood pressure monitor, sitting down on the edge of the bed and taking Rachel's hand in mine.

"Now... I want you to listen to me."

"Yes, Doctor."

"I'm serious, Rachel."

"I'm listening."

"If you're worried about anything, or you feel unwell, or the baby doesn't seem as active as usual, I want you to call me. Do you understand?"

"Yes, I do."

"I'm not saying this to scare you, but because you're my best friend and I love you. Okay?"

She nods her head. "I love you, too."

"I know." I glance up at Jack, half expecting to see a scowl on his face, but I'm greeted with a smile, which I return.

"I'll show you out, shall I, Robson?" he says.

"I can find my own way."

"No, it's okay." I sense he wants to say something, and wonder if I misinterpreted that smile. I hope not. The last thing Rachel needs is Jack getting jealous when he has no cause.

I get up, closing my bag, and after saying, "Goodbye," to Rachel, I follow Jack down the stairs. He leads me to the front door, pausing before he opens it.

"She'll be okay, won't she?" he says, lowering his voice, and I realise his reason for talking has nothing to do with that smile, or with my words to Rachel.

"She'll be fine. Just keep an eye on her and call me if you're worried. I'm only ever five minutes away." He nods his head.

"Is there any way she could hear the baby's heartbeat? Rachel's worried sick that something's wrong, even though the baby's kicking pretty much all the time."

"I don't have a monitor at the surgery. The community midwives all have their own."

"Oh, I see… and with Margaret being away…" He lets his voice fade and I reach out, placing my hand on his upper arm.

"It's okay. I'll contact Sue."

"Who's Sue?"

"Rachel won't have met her before, but she's the midwife for the next village along the coast. She's covering emergencies for Margaret while she's away. I'll ask her to pop over this afternoon, just to check the baby's heartbeat."

"Could you?"

"Of course. Sue's lovely. She won't mind. I can't say when it'll be, but…"

"We'll be here whenever it is," he says with a smile as he opens the door.

I step out and turn. "I'll come back tomorrow, but call if you need me."

He nods. "I got that message loud and clear."

"No… I meant, if *you* need me. I know you're worried."

"I'm terrified, actually."

"You don't need to be. If I thought there was any real danger to Rachel or the baby, I'd have admitted her to hospital. I'm just being over-cautious, because it's Rachel."

"And because you love her?"

"Yes. But not in the same way as you."

He smiles. "It's okay. I'm not jealous."

"You've got nothing to be jealous of."

"I know. I get that your feelings for Rachel are different to mine, but in any case, Rachel told me."

"Told you what?"

He steps outside, his foot over the threshold. "About you and your receptionist."

"Oh, I see."

"You didn't mind her telling me?"

"No. Although there's nothing to tell. It seems Millie's already got a boyfriend, so…"

His face falls. "I didn't realise."

"Neither did I until yesterday, just after Rachel left my surgery, and I saw Millie with her burly surfer. Seeing them together made it clear to me I'm not her type."

"I'm sorry, Rob." I shrug my shoulders, unable to think of anything to say, and he steps a little closer. "That thing you were saying just now about calling, if I need someone to talk to?"

"Yes?"

"It works both ways. Rachel's not the only friend you've got at this address."

"I know. Thanks, Jack. Now, get back to your fiancée before she comes looking for you."

He grins and nods his head, and I step out onto the street, feeling the heat of the sun beating down on my back.

I've been at Rachel's for nearly half an hour, and I could do with something to eat and a cup of tea, so I stride quickly back towards the harbour, making my way past the shops. Glancing up ahead, I notice Dan Moyle coming out of the florist's shop. I haven't seen him for a while, and I'd swear his hair gets more and more blond with every summer. He's laughing, looking back into the shop, presumably talking to Gemma, and as he steps down onto the pavement, he loses his footing, falling awkwardly.

Despite the heat, I run forward, reaching him at the same time as Gemma comes out of the shop. He's just getting to his feet, although he's clutching his arm, and I put down my bag, taking hold of it.

"Where does it hurt?"

"My wrist," he says. "I landed on it, although it was my bum that took most of the impact."

"Do you want to come back inside?" Gemma offers, standing on the other side of him.

"No, I'm fine."

I let go of his arm, picking up my bag. "Why don't you come to the surgery with me? I can take a proper look at you there."

He hesitates, flexing his arm and pulling a pained face. "Okay, Doc."

He leans over, kissing Gemma on her cheek, and she smiles up at him. "Call me later, just so I know you're okay?" she says, and he nods his head, falling into step beside me as we make our way along the harbour towards Bell Road.

"I feel like such an idiot," he says.

"That'll teach you to do two things at once."

"Walking and talking, you mean?" He smiles at me.

"Yes. Men aren't built for multi-tasking."

We get back to the surgery quite quickly and I let us in through the front door, closing it behind us. There's no sign of Millie, but I can't think about that now. I can't think about where she might be, or what she might be doing, and instead I show Dan into my room.

"Take a seat and I'll have a look at your wrist." He does as I say and I pull up my chair, making a thorough examination. "You're working at the surf school, aren't you?"

"Yes," he says, watching, as I manipulate his hand, twisting it one way and then the other.

"Does that hurt?" I ask, and he shakes his head.

"No, it's fine."

"Good. Do you know someone called Fraser?" Millie didn't tell me his surname, but I doubt there are too many 'Frasers' working at the school.

Dan looks up at me, raising his eyebrows. "How do you know him?"

"I don't, but he's dating my receptionist."

I see a moment of disappointment, bordering on anger, fleetingly cross Dan's face. "For crying out loud."

"What's wrong?" I sit forward a little further, letting go of his hand.

"I thought I was bad with women, but Fraser's only been here about three weeks, and I think that must be the fourth or fifth girl he's been out with." He rolls his eyes, shaking his head at the same time, and lets his hand fall from my desk into his lap. "I wouldn't mind so much, but he's a dreadful surfer… completely talentless. He can talk a good wave, but he couldn't ride one if his life depended on it. He keeps telling people he's going to The Eddie, but he's not."

"I'm sorry, Dan, but I don't have a clue what you're talking about. What's The Eddie?"

He leans forward, resting his elbow on my desk. "The Eddie is a big surfing event in Hawaii. It's held in honour of Eddie Aikau, who was a famous lifeguard and surfer at Waimea Bay. He was lost at sea, and in the mid-eighties, they started running 'The Eddie' in his memory."

"I see… and how do you know Fraser won't be going?"

"Because it's invitation only. I was invited last year, but it didn't happen. They've invited me back again this year, but there's no saying it'll run."

"Why not?"

"The waves have to be perfect… and that doesn't happen very often. In all the years they've been holding the event, it's taken place less than a dozen times so far."

"Heavens. How 'perfect' do these waves have to be, then?"

He smiles. "There's a stipulation that they have to be thirty feet high."

"Excuse me? Did you say thirty feet?"

"Yes."

"You ride waves that are thirty feet high?"

"Of course. That's the whole point. Eddie Aikau was renowned for going out to rescue people in seas that no-one else would tackle. 'Eddie would go' became a byword for the kind of waves he'd be willing to take on, when others would rather stand and watch. That's why the event is invitation only. The organisers have to know you're capable."

"And you are?"

"If I wasn't, they'd never let me enter… which is how I know Fraser won't be there. Aside from the fact that they publish a list of the surfers who are invited, and his name isn't on it, Fraser couldn't ride anything higher than about five feet… not and stay upright, anyway."

"Don't you ever get scared?"

"What of?"

"Surfing… the size of the waves?"

"Scared? No. You have to respect the waves, but you can't fear them. It's a strange feeling, but when you're on a board, you feel kind of joined to the water… like it's a part of you. You know the danger it poses, and you're constantly aware of that, but there's a kind of mutual understanding between you. You won't overstep the mark, and it'll let you be. The moment you take it for granted, or think you know too much, it'll bite you."

"Well… unfortunately, I don't think you'll be getting on a board for a while."

He frowns at me. "Seriously?"

I nod my head. "You've sprained your wrist."

"Oh, God. Sam won't like that."

"Maybe not, but your boss will just have to lump it."

He sighs, pushing his fingers back through his hair, staring at his damaged wrist. "How long will I have to rest it?"

"It's hard to be precise. The secret to getting better quickly is RICE."

"You want me to eat rice?"

I laugh, shaking my head. "No. R stands for rest, I stands for ice, C is for compression and E for elevate. You need to rest it as much as possible, put ice on it two to three times a day for twenty minutes, and keep it raised. You can wrap it in a bandage, or elasticated support, but don't keep that on all the time, and once it stops hurting enough that you can move it, I've got some exercises you can do."

I get up, going to the filing cabinet and open the second drawer down, pulling a sheet of paper from a file near the back, and bringing it over to Dan.

"These should help. But don't try doing them straight away. Take some paracetamol or ibuprofen if you need pain relief over the next few days."

"When will I be able to surf again?"

"That's going to be very much up to you. You'll need to feel confident that your wrist will be take the strain… but I'd say probably somewhere around a month should do it. And if you get any pain in between times, or it doesn't seem to be healing, come back and see me."

"I dread to think what Sam's going to say."

"There's not very much he can say. You didn't do it on purpose, did you?"

"No. He'll probably stick me in the office and take over my lessons himself."

"He won't get Fraser to help a bit more?"

Dan chuckles, shaking his head. "I think he'd rather close the surf school than do that."

"Oh?"

"I told you Fraser was talentless, and I wasn't kidding. Sam's got him handing out boards and going through safety checks. It's about all he's capable of."

I want to smile. In fact, I want to laugh, but I hold in my childish reaction. "You never know, Sam might quite enjoy the chance to get in the water, especially in this weather."

"He might. I won't."

He stands up, just as the front door opens, and Millie steps inside. I didn't bother to close the door to my room, and both Dan and I glance over in her direction.

"Do you want me to shut this?" she says, nodding to the door.

"No, I'm just leaving." Dan smiles at her, and she smiles back, going into the reception. He turns back to me. "I assume that's your receptionist?"

"Yes."

He nods. "Fraser may be useless in the water, but he clearly has excellent taste in women."

I know.

I don't say that out loud, and instead, I show him to the door.

"Thanks for your help, Doc," he says.

"Any time."

Once he's gone outside, I leave the door on the latch for afternoon surgery, and wander into the reception, my hands buried in my pockets.

"You weren't due to see him, were you?" Millie says, checking her computer screen.

"No. He fell over outside the florist's when I was on my way back from visiting Rachel."

"Oh. Is he okay?"

"Yes, he's fine. He's just sprained his wrist." I wonder if I should mention that he's a surfer… and that he knows Fraser. Would it be wise to let her know her boyfriend has a reputation with women? Or would that come across as the outpourings of a jealous man, desperate to interfere in her relationship?

Probably.

"Your next appointment is due in five minutes," she says, and I snap to attention.

I can't tell her anything. Even if I had time. It wouldn't be fair. Fraser may have played the field a little since he's been here, but who's to say he wasn't just trying to find the right girl? Who's to say he hasn't now… in Millie? It's not my place to intrude in that.

No matter what he's done in the past, people can change.

They do it all the time.

I just wish I could fall out of love with Millie, so this didn't have to hurt so much.

The problem is, hell would have to freeze over first.

Chapter Seven

Millie

It's been a long day.

I guess that's because we haven't had so many patients today. Robson warned me it can get like this during the summer holidays. I remember asking him why and the smile on his face when he explained that even the locals go away, so there are fewer of them around in the summer months, and that people are just less sick.

"Winter's always worse for colds, coughs, flu, chest infections…" His voice faded, but I got the feeling he could have listed another dozen or so ailments that were worse in the winter than the summer, and I felt a little embarrassed for not realising myself. "We get the odd holidaymaker who needs a doctor, but usually, if something happens with someone who's on holiday down here, it tends to be more of an emergency, and they'll either call an ambulance or get themselves to the hospital in Truro."

Despite being less busy, I had a nice lunch today. Having bought my sandwich, I decided against coming back to the surgery. I knew Robson was going to call on Rachel Pedrick, and didn't want to sit here in the reception by myself, so I went and sat in the churchyard. That might sound like an odd place to choose, but it's lovely and quiet there, and I found a shady spot under a tree where I could sit, hidden away from the village. It was calm and cool, and peaceful, and I thoroughly enjoyed that half hour's break. It gave me time to think… which, of course, meant my mind was full of Robson, although I devoted a little time to the redecorating conundrum and even came up with a solution.

I'd have put it to him, too… except he had a patient with him when I got back, and that made me feel guilty for not being here. I'd been off enjoying myself, but it seemed like he was forever on duty.

Looking back, though, I'm not sure what I could have done. Robson didn't need my help. He seemed to be managing very well without me.

As usual.

I check the time on my computer screen, sighing with relief that it's five to six. I can start packing up for the day. My relief isn't born out of a desire to go home to my empty flat; it's the result of a heartfelt need for a shower and a change of clothes. I might have opened the window as wide as possible, and had a fan on my desk, pointing directly at me, but there's still no air today.

My computer takes a few minutes to shut down, and while it does, I close the window, turning off the fan, and gather my things together, leaving them on the desk, while I wander into Robson's office. The door is open, but I knock on the frame and he looks up.

"I'm going home."

"Oh… okay."

I suddenly remember the thoughts that occurred to me when I was at the churchyard… the ones that I forgot all about when

I came back here and found him with that young man who'd fallen and hurt his wrist.

"Have you got a minute?" I ask, going further into Robson's room.

"Of course." He puts down the pen he was holding and sits back, looking up at me.

"It's just that I've been giving some thought to the colour scheme."

He frowns, like he doesn't understand. "Colour scheme?"

"Yes. You said about redecorating?"

"Oh… yes."

His reaction makes me wonder yet again whether he's less interested in my opinions and more interested in me helping with the actual painting, but I move a little closer to his desk, anyway.

"I—I was thinking about blues and greens. I know the colours of the sea have been done to death around here, but I had lunch in the churchyard today, and there was some moss on one of the graves. It was a lovely green… really soothing. I'm sure there would be a complimentary blue that would go with it."

"You went to the churchyard for lunch?" He's smiling, although I'm not sure why.

"Yes." Has he not heard a word I've said about paint, and moss, and colours?

"Why?"

"Because it's really shady up there, and it's quiet, too."

"And that's where Fraser took you?"

"Fraser? I didn't go with Fraser. I went by myself."

He blinks… twice, and then sits forward. "Y—You were saying… about the moss?"

So he was listening, after all. "Yes. It was this really kind of earthy green, and I thought we could paint the fireplace in my room that colour, and then do the fireplace in here a muted kind of blue."

"And the other walls?" he says, looking around his surgery.

"Maybe a really, really pale version of each colour… so they're only just off-white?"

He nods his head slowly, his smile widening. "I like the sound of that."

"It's just an idea. You don't have to…"

He holds up his hand, and I stop talking. "No. I like it."

I can't help feeling pleased with myself, and I back up towards the door. "Goodnight, then."

He nods his head. "Goodnight."

I go back to the reception, picking up my handbag from my desk. When I come back, Robson is standing in the doorway to his office, leaning against the frame, his hands in his pockets. He looks gorgeous, and I struggle to stop my eyes from wandering.

"Have a nice evening," he says.

"I'm not doing anything special."

"Oh?"

He smiles, which seems odd to me, and I shake my head, wishing he'd take the bait and ask me to do something with him. He's not going to, though. I can tell from the look on his face. And why would he? He thinks Fraser is my boyfriend.

If only I'd set him straight when I had the chance…

He leans over and opens the door, pushing it back for me. I grab it, switching the latch, and look up at him as I pass through onto the doorstep.

"See you tomorrow."

He nods his head. "See you tomorrow, Millie."

He closes the door behind me, and I feel my shoulders drop, making my way down the path to the gate.

It all feels so hopeless. How can I get Robson to take an interest? How can I even get him to see that I'm not going out with Fraser? I can hardly bring it up in conversation, can I? It would sound so odd for me to just blurt out that Fraser isn't my boyfriend, when I didn't bother to deny it before. He'd think I was mad. Could I maybe say we broke up? I guess I could... although I'm not sure how I'd start that conversation either.

I close the gate, letting out a long sigh.

Basically, I've taken a situation that was already impossible, and made it worse.

Well done, Millie.

I stroll down Bell Road, feeling despondent, wondering if I should confide in Ellis... whether he'd have any words of wisdom for me. I'm not even sure how I'd go about telling him, but I feel a little lost, and maybe a male perspective would help.

It couldn't hurt.

I'll call him when I get home, and maybe try to bring the conversation around to my predicament... and how to resolve it.

"Hello."

I jump at the sound of the familiar male voice and step back, almost falling into the road. Fraser reaches out, grabbing me, and pulls me back.

"Careful, Millie."

"What are you doing here?"

We both speak at the same time, and I shake myself free of his grasp.

"I was just coming to find you," he says.

"Why? I wasn't lost." I'm struggling to hide my fear, and burying it beneath anger seems like a good idea.

He laughs, which wasn't the response I'd hoped for. I'd wanted him to be affronted, but he just grins at me. "I know. But I forgot to take your number last night, and I was going to see if you wanted to come out with me again. Then I remembered you saying you finished at six, so..."

"So you thought you'd come and jump out at me?"

"I didn't jump out at you."

It felt like it, but maybe that's more to do with me and my history than anything he's done wrong, and I take a breath, letting it out slowly. "Sorry. I just wasn't expecting to see you there."

"That's okay. At least I was here to save you from falling… again."

I want to tell him that the only reason I was in danger of falling was because he scared me half to death, but it doesn't seem worth harping on about.

"Hmm… so you were."

"What do you feel like doing?" he says, taking it for granted that I have nothing better to do than be bored rigid by his surfing stories for a second evening.

"I'm sorry… I've got plans."

He frowns, staring down at me. "You have?"

"Yes." His expression says he expects more of an explanation, but he's not going to get one. Aside from the fact that I don't have any plans to explain, I don't feel as though I should have to tell him every intricate detail of my life just because he bought me a drink in the pub yesterday. It implies there's something between us which I haven't acknowledged yet… and don't intend to.

After a moment or two, once it's become clear I'm not going to add anything, he shrugs his shoulders. "Okay. In that case, I'll see you home."

Again, he's making assumptions, but I don't know how to get out of this one. I could say I'm meeting someone, but I get the feeling he'd insist on accompanying me, and then he'd see through my lie. At least this way, he can just walk me home and that will be that.

I nod my head and take a pace forward, letting him fall into step beside me.

"Have you had a good day?" he asks, as we come up to the florist's. I'd been enjoying the silence, but I suppose nothing lasts forever…

"Not bad. It wasn't that busy, but…"

"Mine was," he says, interrupting me. "One of the other instructors at the surf school fell over at lunchtime and sprained his wrist, so I'm having to take charge of all his classes. It's an enormous responsibility, but… you know…" He puffs out his chest in a self-important way and I want to scream at him that nothing he does makes a difference to the world. I'm sure surfing is great fun. I get that he has to behave responsibly, and teach people the rights and wrongs of safe surfing. But does he save lives? Does he stop them from being in pain? Does he help them when they're at their lowest ebb? Of course he doesn't. I don't want to belittle him, or what he does, but he's not Robson, and I wish now, more than ever, that it was him walking beside me.

Still, it seems polite to make conversation.

"I think I saw your friend. He was at the surgery when I got back from lunch."

Fraser frowns, tensing slightly, and looks down at me. "Oh?"

"Yes. I didn't talk to him. He was just leaving."

"I see." He relaxes, and we turn the corner into Church Lane, going past the police station, towards the Italian restaurant. I usually cross over here, and I stop to check the traffic, just as I feel Fraser grab me from behind.

"What are you doing?"

"What do you think?"

His voice is a harsh whisper against my ear and I freeze, which makes the next part of his plan oh, so easy. He drags me to the other side of the restaurant, down an alleyway I hadn't even noticed was there, stopping about halfway down. There are boxes and crates lining one side, but he ignores them, pushing me up against the rough brick wall.

"P—Please, Fraser… please don't."

He ignores me, a smile touching his lips, as he bends, covering my mouth with his. I don't respond, but he neither notices, nor cares. His hands are everywhere… touching… groping. I feel him pulling up my dress, and suddenly, I leave the here and now, losing myself in the past…

Beer-laden breath, a body stronger than mine. Damian's cajoling words… "You want it, really. Stop teasing." Except I didn't want it. I didn't want him. I was screaming at him to stop, begging him to leave me alone.

I turn my head, breaking Fraser's kiss, and I open my mouth. There should be a scream, like the one that pierced the air of Damien's flat, but nothing comes out, and Fraser reaches up, clasping my chin, turning my head to face him, his tongue darting too far into my mouth before his lips can catch up with it.

I gag, wanting to be sick, my stomach roiling, and I push against him, my fists raining on his shoulders. He grabs them, holding them above my head, hard against the wall. I feel the scratch of rough brick, and yelp as he holds them there with one of his, yanking my dress up again. It's around my hips, bunched, and I feel his hand moving between us, my heart beating so fast in my chest, I know I'm going to faint. Would that be a good thing? Would it stop him? Should I pretend to faint, anyway?

"What the hell's going on?"

Fraser leaps back, glancing to his left, and I turn too, seeing a man in a white jacket, standing by an open door further down the alleyway. It wasn't open before, so I presume he's just stepped out for some reason. He looks to be about forty years old, with dark hair and even darker eyes, and he's got them fixed on Fraser.

"What are you doing?"

"Nothing. Mind your own business. Can't you see we're busy?"

Busy? I glance in the other direction, seeing that the end of the alleyway is just fifteen or twenty feet away, and I take my chance, pushing myself off the wall and running. I can hear the man talking, and Fraser's shouted responses, and I turn to see he's coming after me.

He's following me...

I know I daren't go home. My road is too quiet... too anonymous, so when I get to the end of the alleyway, I turn left, heading back towards the harbour, panic driving me on.

"Whoa... where are you going?"

I run straight into a very tall man, and I look up, seeing that I'm right outside the police station, and the man who's currently blocking the path is dressed in black... or maybe it's dark blue. Who knows? Who cares? The point is, he's a policeman.

"Help me... please help me."

He glances down, and I follow his line of sight, quickly adjusting my dress, which has lowered itself far enough to cover my knickers... but only just. I pull it down further and look back up at him. I don't know his name, but I think he's the policeman who's married to the lady in the flower shop. Gemma, wasn't it? I might have little faith in the police force, but I know he won't hurt me.

Thank God.

"Tell me what's happened?" he says, with a soft, kind, yet urgent voice.

I point back up the hill, turning to see Fraser walking away in the opposite direction, towards the main road. He must have seen me with the policeman and decided to make his escape. He glances over his shoulder, picking up his pace, his walk becoming a run.

"Th—That man…" I squeeze out the words, and then burst into tears. The policeman doesn't touch me, thank goodness. He looks down at me, worry filling his face.

"What did he do to you?" I shake my head, making it clear I don't want to talk, and he nods. "Okay. You don't have to say anything now, if you don't want to. Can I get someone to help you?" he says. "A friend? The doctor?"

"No." My response is too loud, too hasty, but Robson is the last person I need to see right now.

"Okay." He holds up his hands. "Where do you live?"

I suck in a breath, struggling against my tears. "In Chapel Mews."

He nods his head. "Let me see you home."

Home. Yes. That's where I need to be. I'll be safe there now. "Yes, please."

He still doesn't touch me, but somehow he turns me around, so we're facing up the hill. There's no sign of Fraser, but that's hardly surprising.

I put one foot in front of the other, aware of the tall policeman beside me, feeling the protective force of him, even though he's keeping his distance.

It only takes a few minutes to get to my front door, during which neither of us utters a word. I have none, and I don't think he knows what to say, either. Once we reach the house, I pull out my key and he turns to me.

"Do you want me to come in with you?"

I think about it for a moment, but shake my head. "No. I'll be fine." I'm not sure I'll ever be 'fine' again, but I want to be by myself. "Thank you for helping, though… and for seeing me home."

"You're sure there's nothing more you want me to do?"

"No. Honestly."

He nods his head, stepping back and watching while I unlock the door.

Once inside, I run up the stairs and let myself into my flat, collapsing onto the floor, before the door's even shut. Then I curl into a ball, hugging my knees to my chest, tears rolling down my cheeks.

How? How can it be happening again?

Chapter Eight

Robson

It's too hot to cook yet, so I'm sitting outside on the patio at the back of the house. I love it out here, surrounded by potted shrubs, with a view down the garden. It's not the biggest plot in the land, but it's enough for me. I have a small patch of lawn, with beds on either side, mostly filled with yet more shrubs. I'm not a great one for flowers… not because I don't like them, but because I find they require more time and attention than I'm willing to give.

This part of the garden is shaded and cool, and I lean back, putting my feet up on the low wall in front of me, and I let my head rock back. My hair is still a little damp from my shower, and I've changed into shorts and a t-shirt, a glass of chilled white wine on the table beside me.

The sky above is still clear blue, with not a cloud in sight, but to be honest, if the heavens opened and it poured with rain, I think I'd just sit here and wallow in it. There's a heavy, sultry atmosphere, although I'm not sure it's caused entirely by the weather.

My mood is partially to blame… or at least my thoughts about Millie.

Because I didn't have very many patients to see this afternoon, I spent a lot of time thinking about her, wishing I'd taken my chances sooner. It's too late for regrets, I know that... but that doesn't make it any easier.

I think that was why I felt so tongue-tied when she came into my office to say goodbye this evening. It's probably also why I'd forgotten about the colour scheme I'd asked her to think about... and why I sounded so vacant when she brought it up.

She didn't know I'd only said that to make conversation, but the thought that she'd given it some time made me smile. Almost as much as the idea of her having lunch in the churchyard. It seemed like an odd venue, but once she explained that she'd gone there for the solitude – and without Fraser – my heart skipped a beat. Of course, I realised I was over-interpreting. So what if they didn't meet for lunch? It didn't mean anything. It was probably just that he couldn't get away from work.

Was I surprised by her choice of colours?

Not really. If I'd given the matter any thought myself, I'd almost certainly have come up with something similar, and I liked the fact that our tastes seem to align.

It made me smile. Although nowhere near as much as when she said she wasn't doing anything tonight.

Did that mean she and Fraser had broken up?

Or did it mean I was desperate?

The latter. Probably. Which was why I let her out of the front door. I was scared I might take matters into my own hands and kiss her.

I've thought of little else since... picturing my hands on her cheeks, my lips hovering over hers, our eyes meeting... and then the horror on her face as she realises I'm about to kiss her.

"Damn," I mutter under my breath, taking a sip of wine.

Why can't I just get over this?

Other people do.

The problem is, I don't know how.

I've had plenty of girlfriends in the past, but I've never been touched by love before. Now I have, and the irony hasn't escaped me that the woman I love is unattainable.

How do people endure this… this agony?

And why do they bother?

I shake my head, realisation dawning…

Because it's not always painful. For some people, it's magical. Look at Rachel and Jack… and my parents. They've been married for thirty-three years, and are still so much like newlyweds, it can get embarrassing.

I take another sip of wine, almost spilling it as the doorbell rings.

I've set it up so it echoes loudly throughout the house and garden, because even though I have regular surgery hours, things happen at all times of the day and night, which means I'm never not available.

I put down my glass and get up, wandering through the house to the surgery door, which I pull open, surprised to find Tom Hughes standing there in full uniform. He's a little out of breath and looks up at me.

"What's wrong?" I ask. Something is, or he wouldn't be here.

"It might be nothing."

"If it's nothing, why are you here?"

I step aside, inviting him in with a wave of my hand, and he walks across the threshold. I notice the beads of sweat on his forehead, closing the door behind him.

"Did you just run here?"

"Yes. I didn't know what else to do."

Okay. I'm getting a little concerned now. "Tell me what's happened."

"I'm at a bit of a loss. Rory and Laura have gone to visit her father for the evening, and your dad mentioned something about taking your mum over to Padstow for dinner…"

"He did?"

"Yes."

"You know more about what they're doing than I do." Although it sounds like the kind of romantic thing my dad would do… just on a whim. "Did you need to speak to one of them, then? I'm sure they'll have their phones…"

"That's just it," he says, interrupting me. "I don't know what to do. The last thing I want is to call either Rory or your dad and drag them back here, if there's no need." He sighs. "If this had happened back in Wimbledon, we'd have had a specialist team… or at the very least, I'd have been able to involve a female officer. As it is, Naomi's on annual leave, and…"

"Naomi's one of the Special Constables, isn't she?"

"Yes, but like I say, she's not here, and…"

"Tom." He stops talking and looks down at me. I might be over six feet tall, but Tom is even taller, and I look up into his worried eyes. "Whatever has happened, if it's a police matter, I suggest you call Rory."

"Except I'm not sure it is a police matter. I need to find out, somehow. She seemed upset, but…"

"Who seemed upset? For a policeman, you're not making very much sense, you know?"

He nods his head. "Sorry. I'll start from the beginning."

"I think that would be wise."

He takes a breath. "I was just locking up the station. Your dad and Rory had left early, and I'd just put the keys in my pocket when I heard footsteps coming from up the hill. I turned, and this young woman ran straight into me."

"Okay."

"No, she wasn't okay. That's the point. She was… dishevelled, to put it mildly. Her dress was rucked up, and her hair was all over the place. She looked absolutely terrified. I asked if she was okay, and she just said 'help me'."

I stand up straighter, paying more attention. "What had happened to her?"

"It wasn't immediately obvious, until I saw a young man come out of the alleyway… you know, the one by the Italian restaurant?"

"Yes. Had she come from the alleyway, too?"

"I don't know. I didn't see where she came from, but I think it's a reasonable assumption. For all I know, whatever had gone on between them could have been completely innocent, or at least consensual."

"If it was, why was she asking for help?"

"Precisely. And why did the man run away?"

"He ran?"

"Yes. The minute he saw me."

"So whatever was going on probably wasn't consensual."

"Probably not. I thought about running after him, but it seemed more important to look after the young lady. In any case, I got a good look at him, and I'd know him again, if I saw him." I nod my head. "Anyway, I asked what had happened, and she made it clear she didn't want to talk. She just stared at me, shaking her head, like words were impossible. That got me worried. I felt out of my depth. I've never been involved in a rape case before. Like I say, where I'm from, there are specialist teams to deal with anything like that, and I know it's a failing on my part, but I didn't know what to do… or what to say. I suggested she might like to talk to a friend or a doctor, but she said she didn't. So I offered to walk her home. The thing is, though, if she has been raped – and I can't be sure she has – we need to know."

"And that's where I come in?"

He shrugs his shoulders. "It's where someone needs to come in. She's declined my offer of any help, but I can't just let it go, can I?"

"No, you can't."

"Equally, I don't want to get all official on the poor woman, if it was just a misunderstanding."

I nod my head. "No… I can see that. What was she like on the walk back to her house?"

"It wasn't really long enough to say. She only lives in Chapel Mews. When we got there, she wouldn't let me in. She just…"

"Hang on. Did you say Chapel Mews?"

"Yes. Why?"

"Can you describe her to me?"

"Around five foot seven, dark hair, brown eyes…"

"What was she wearing?" I ask, my heart pounding.

"A cream dress."

I nudge him aside, opening the door to my surgery, and going inside. I'm at the filing cabinet within seconds, yanking open the top drawer, and pulling out a file from halfway back.

"What number in Chapel Mews did she live at?" I ask, opening the file.

"Number twelve. It's one of those houses that's been converted into flats."

I glance down at the document in front of me, my chest hollowing and terror filling the void. "It's Millie," I whisper, letting the file drop to the floor.

"Who's Millie?"

I turn to see Tom standing over by the door still.

"Millie Adams. My receptionist." I run, pushing past him, out into the hallway, stopping dead. "My keys. Where are my damn keys?"

"Where do you normally keep them?"

I stare at him, my mind a blank, and then it comes to me… I left them in the kitchen. Without a word, I rush through to the reception and into the back of the house, grabbing the keys, and running back.

"Pull the door closed when you leave," I call out, yanking open the front door, and hurrying through it.

I don't wait for Tom's reply. I can't.

Millie might have said she didn't need a doctor, but she does. She needs me.

Chapter Nine

Millie

I can't stop crying.

Whenever I draw breath, more tears gather and fall, and although I'd have thought the well would have long since run dry, it seems not.

Lying on the floor is getting uncomfortable, though. My arms ache, and my back is stiff. I'd like a shower, too. It might help me feel clean.

Okay… 'clean' is an unrealistic hope. 'Cleaner' is a possibility.

To achieve that, I'll have to get up… and just the thought of that is a little daunting. It has to be done, though, and I release my knees, flexing my arms as I straighten my legs, and then I roll over, kneeling up, and slowly getting to my feet. I place my hand against the wall for support, while I adjust to being upright, and then I let go, jumping out of my skin when someone knocks on my door.

My stomach churns, my palms sweating.

It's Fraser. I know it is.

How did he get in through the main door?

What does it matter? He's here now.

I bend, reaching into my handbag, and pull out my phone, my fingers shaking as I turn it on and step back a little, feeling the need to put some space between me and my enemy. I can hardly breathe, but I click on the phone icon, trembling as my finger hovers over the 'nine'.

"Millie? Are you in there?"

That's not Fraser's voice. It's Robson's. My hand falls to my side, my phone slipping to the floor.

"Y—Yes?"

"Can you open the door?"

Can I? I don't know. The thought of facing him is humiliating, but the thought of staying here all by myself, thinking about what's happened, and going over and over it in my mind, is even worse.

I tiptoe to the door, opening it a crack, and peer out. Robson's standing there, looking so worried, it hurts, although he manages a half-hearted smile. His hair seems even messier than usual, and he's slightly out of breath.

Something's different – other than his hair – and I take a moment to realise that he's not wearing his usual trousers and shirt, but is in shorts and a t-shirt, with casual canvas shoes on his feet.

"Tom came to see me," he says, and I'm struck by how quiet his voice is.

"Who's Tom?"

"PC Tom Hughes. He's the man who brought you home." He's also the man I practically threw myself at outside the police station. I imagine Robson is aware of that, if the policeman called Tom has told him what happened, but I don't feel like mentioning it myself.

"Oh, I see."

"I know you told him you didn't want to see a doctor, but I'm not your doctor, anyway. That's not why I'm here, Millie. I'm here as a friend."

His words stab at the lump in my throat and I can't swallow around it. Instead, I burst into tears, yet again, covering my face with my hands, my body shaking as I lean back against the wall for support. I've never needed a friend more than I do now, but before I can get any words out, Robson slips silently inside my flat, closing the door behind him.

I'm aware of him standing fairly close, and I lower my hands, looking up at him.

"Do you want to sit down?" he says and I nod my head, noticing he's holding my phone in his hand. He must have picked it up while I was crying. He doesn't offer it to me, and doesn't touch me, thank God. Instead, he just waits while I slowly make my way into the flat, following behind. Once I've sat on the sofa, he puts my phone on the table in front of me and glances around. Then he disappears into the bathroom, returning with a new toilet roll. He must have found it on the shelf and as he approaches, he hands it to me.

"I don't have any tissues," I whisper, and he smiles.

"It doesn't matter."

I don't suppose it does.

I tear off a few sheets of toilet paper and wipe my eyes and nose while he takes a seat beside me, and although my couch is so small there's not much of a gap between us, I'm okay with that.

"Can you tell me what happened?" he asks and I turn my head, looking up at him.

"Tonight, you mean?"

He doesn't know this is about so much more than what happened on the way home from work, but I suppose that's as good a place to start as any.

"Yes. Tom said there was a man involved."

"It wasn't just any man. It was Fraser."

His eyes widen, his face paling slightly. "Your boyfriend?"

I shake my head. "He's not my boyfriend."

"Well, obviously not after this, but…"

"No. I mean, he never was."

He frowns. "But I thought…"

"I know, but… no…"

He nods his head, as though to tell me there's no need for further explanations, and I feel my shoulders sag with relief. I've been such a fool, in so many ways.

"What did he do to you, Millie?"

"He jumped out at me."

"By the restaurant?"

"No. He was waiting for me at the end of Bell Road. At least, that's what it felt like. He said he was coming to meet me at the surgery, but now I look back, I'm sure he'd been standing there all along."

He clasps his hands together on his lap. "He was waiting for you?"

"Yes, I think so. I wasn't concentrating on him at the time. I was thinking about something else…" I blush, recalling my thoughts, which were about Robson, and the situation I'd got myself into, and whether I was going to call Ellis to talk it through with him. None of that seems very relevant now, and I look down at my dress, seeing some grey marks on my skirt, and brushing at them with the middle finger of my right hand, to no effect.

"Millie?"

"Yes?" I turn and look at Robson again.

"What happened after he jumped out at you?"

"I almost fell into the road and he grabbed hold of me. He made a thing about having saved me again…"

"Again?"

"Yes." I nod my head. "That's how we met yesterday. I almost tripped over him coming out of the baker's."

"Are you telling me that was the first time you met him?"

"Yes. He insisted on walking me back to work, and then asked me to have a drink with him last night. I agreed, although I didn't stay for very long."

"Why not?"

"Because I didn't like him, if I'm being honest. He was so full of himself."

"I see. And after he'd scared the living daylights out of you at the end of Bell Road, and then pretended to save you… what did he do next?"

"He asked if I wanted to go out with him again tonight. I—I was angry with him for frightening me like that, and I wasn't in the mood for listening to more of his boring stories, so I told him I was busy, even though I wasn't."

"Okay."

"And that was when he offered to walk me home. Unfortunately, I couldn't think of a single reason to say 'no'. Not one that sounded reasonable, anyway, so we started walking. We talked a little… which is to say, he talked and I pretended to listen." He smiles and I try to smile back, almost getting there. "He was being very pompous about something to do with the surf school, but I wasn't interested. I was rushing home, so I could get away from him. I went to cross Church Lane and he… and he…" My voice cracks and I'm overcome with tears once more, shaking my head and turning away from Robson.

"Millie… it's okay. You're safe now."

"Am I?" I turn back and he nods.

"Yes, you are." He says those words with such conviction, I believe him, and I swallow hard, tearing off some more toilet paper to wipe my eyes again.

"He grabbed me from behind. Things are a little hazy after that, but I remember asking what he was doing." I look up into Robson's eyes, surprised by the anguish I see reflected back at me, although I can't think about that right now. "That was a stupid question, really, wasn't it?"

"No. What did he say? Did he answer you?"

"Yes. He said, 'What do you think?' I knew then what he was going to do." My nose is running and I raise the tissue, my hand shaking as I wipe it. "He dragged me along the alleyway beside the restaurant, and about half-way down, he stopped and pushed me up against the wall. He kissed me then… or tried to. And he was touching me, pulling my dress up. I tried to scream, but my voice wouldn't work, and even though I was punching his shoulders, trying to stop him, he just kept going. He grabbed my hands…" I look down at them, seeing the grazes on the side of my wrists. They're deeper than I thought, and there's blood on my arms, which I hadn't noticed before.

Robson reaches over, his hand hovering above mine. "May I?" he says and I look up, nodding my head. He takes my hand in his, and I'm surprised by how soft his fingers are, as he turns it over and examines my wrist, putting it down and repeating the process with the other one. "Do you have clean tea towels?" he asks.

"Yes. In the drawer underneath the draining board."

He gets up, striding over to the kitchen, and I watch as he pulls open the drawer and delves inside, retrieving two striped t-towels, which he then runs under the cold tap, until they're soaking. He wrings them both out, and folds them into strips, returning to me.

"This might sting a little," he says, sitting down and taking my left hand in his, wrapping one of the cool, damp t-towels around it before he does the same with my right wrist. "We'll leave those on for a while and then I'll take another look."

"Okay."

He sits back and takes a deep breath. "Do you want to carry on, or do you need a break?"

"There's not much more to tell. He had to pull my dress up again, because it had slipped down, and it was then that the man came out."

"The man?" Robson frowns at me. "What man?"

"The man from the restaurant. I don't know who he was. He was wearing a white jacket, so I suppose he might have been a chef or something. Whoever he was, his arrival gave me the chance to run. So I did."

"Right into Tom?"

"Yes. Thank God."

"Amen to that."

He sits forward, turning in his seat, and then looks down at his hands for a second before he raises his face, his eyes fixing on mine. "This isn't easy for you Millie, and I know you'd rather just forget all about it, but I need to know… is there anything you haven't told me?"

"Are you asking if he raped me?"

"Yes, I suppose I am. That, or anything else…"

"He didn't do anything I haven't told you. I promise. He kissed me. He groped me. That was all."

"All?" He shakes his head. "Don't say that. Don't belittle what he did."

"Believe me, I'm not. I'm just grateful it's not as bad as last time." I close my eyes, wishing I'd thought before speaking, and when I open them again, it's easy to see that Robson's face has paled, his brow furrowing as he tilts his head.

"Last time?"

"Yes."

"What does that mean?"

I stare at him for a moment, wondering if I should try to find a way not to tell him the truth. But how can I? I've put the words out there now. I can hardly take them back. And I'm not sure I want to… not with Robson.

"It means this has happened before… only last time it was worse."

It was also different. Very different.

I know that now, even if parts of it feel the same. The differences are there. I just need to keep them in my sights, and remember them.

He shifts a little closer on the sofa. I half expect to feel alarmed by that, but I don't. In fact, I feel the opposite. I feel safe…. comforted by his presence, and although I'm incapable of moving, I lean over in his direction, just slightly.

"Worse?" he whispers, in the softest of voices, like he can't quite believe I said that.

"Yes."

He pushes his fingers back through his hair, messing it up even more than it already was. "Do you want to tell me about it?"

I hesitate, unsure of how to answer him. "I—It's not something I talk about very often."

"I can understand that. It probably feels easier not to, but it might help if you did… especially after what's happened tonight. You don't have to talk to me, though. I can refer you to someone, if you like?"

"How? You're not my GP."

He smiles, although it doesn't touch his eyes. "I know, but that doesn't mean I can't recommend someone who can help you."

I shake my head, the thought of sharing my darkest secret with a stranger, filling me with dread. "I'm not sure talking any more is going to help. Not in the way you mean, anyway."

"Why not?"

"I had months and months of counselling after it happened, and I was still a nervous wreck. I honestly don't think it got me anywhere."

He nods his head, doing me the favour of believing in my uncertainties, rather than trying to persuade me to do something

I'm not convinced about. I had enough of that the last time, from my doctor, my parents…. and even from Ellis, all of whom spent ages trying to persuade me I'd get 'better', if I just talked about it. I couldn't see how repeating the same things over and over was going to make me feel safer. It didn't stop me from wanting to hide away, or from blaming myself for what had happened.

"That's okay." Robson's voice interrupts my thoughts… my memories. "You don't have to talk, if you don't want to."

A strange thing happens as he utters those words. It's as though, in being given permission to stay silent and keep it to myself, I want to do the opposite, and do the very thing he's been suggesting. Call me contrary, if you like, but I suddenly want to talk.

"C—Can I tell you about it?" I say, stuttering over my words. "Not as a doctor, but as a friend?"

He smiles again, this time in a way that makes his eyes sparkle. "Of course you can. I feel it's only fair to warn you I'm still going to treat whatever you tell me with the same level of confidence that I would have done if I were your doctor, but you can tell me anything you want."

I nod my head, lowering it, and studying the front of my dress. There are a couple of blood stains I hadn't noticed before, and all along the hem, there's a dirt mark. I don't know where that came from, but I use my thumbnail, trying to scratch it out of the fabric.

I'm not sure where to start my story, but I suppose I have to go back to when I was at university… to where it all began…

Chapter Ten

Robson

I keep completely still, watching while Millie scrapes her thumbnail along the hem of her skirt. She's trying to rub away the dirt along its edge, but I don't think she'll have much luck. It's fairly well ingrained. She touched the small bloodstains just now, which I'm guessing came from the wounds on her wrists. She doesn't seem to be bleeding anywhere else, although she hasn't noticed the tear in the seam at the side of her dress yet, and I'm not going to point it out. I'm guessing that's from where Fraser pulled it up, and it shows how rough he must have been, to split the seam like that.

That thought makes me angry, but I bury it, focusing on the fact that she asked if she could talk to me... as a friend.

I feel like I'm here in so many capacities. First and foremost, I suppose I have to be professional. She's been assaulted. I have to be a doctor; to make sure she's okay. She seems physically unharmed, apart from her wrists. As for her mental and emotional wellbeing... I think only time will tell.

Putting aside my professional responsibilities, though, I'm here because I'm in love with her, and as such, the last half an hour has been a rollercoaster. The idea of her being hurt in any way, by anyone, is more than I can handle. The thought of what might have been is too much for me. If that man hadn't come out of the restaurant, I dread to think what could have happened, and it's taking all my self-control not to react to that.

I want to hold her, to wrap her up and keep her safe, but I know that being touched by any man is almost certainly the last thing she needs.

And in any case, it's not about what I want. It's not about me.

It's about being here for her. It's about listening to her story… the one she wants to tell me as a friend.

Because even though I love her more than life, I'll take friendship. I'll take anything, if it helps her.

So, I'm hiding my feelings… including my euphoria that Fraser wasn't her boyfriend. I'm holding back the myriad of unanswered questions, and I'm focusing instead on Millie's tear-streaked face as she opens her mouth, sighs deeply and starts to talk…

"I was in my third year at uni when it happened."

I frown, feeling confused. "University? I didn't even realise you'd gone. It wasn't on your CV, was it?" I know it wasn't. I studied her CV closely, and I'd have remembered something like that.

"No. I don't put it on there, because I never finished my degree… and because I don't like answering questions about that time."

"I see. What were you studying?" She looks up. "Sorry. That's a question, isn't it?"

She smiles. "It's okay. I was reading Law." I nod my head, unsurprised. It's the kind of thing I would have expected Millie to study. "I was about to take my finals," she says, getting back to her story.

"So, it was two years ago?"

She nods. "Just over. It was early April… and the circumstances were very different to tonight."

"In what way?"

"The man who… who did what he did… I'd been going out with him for about four months."

"He was your boyfriend?"

"Y—Yes. My first boyfriend. His name was D—Damian."

She's struggling and although I know I can't move any closer to her on this tiny sofa without touching her, I twist around a little in my seat, so I'm facing her, hoping it might make her feel more at ease.

"What was he studying?" I ask.

"He was reading Law, too. I wouldn't say we'd been friends for the entire time we'd been at university, but we'd certainly been nodding acquaintances."

"And he asked you out?"

"Yes. At a Christmas party. I'd never really thought about having a boyfriend before then. I'd always been really serious about my studies, right back to when I was at school and college, and I suppose from that perspective, his timing couldn't have been much worse, with finals looming. Even so…"

"You liked him?"

"Yes, I did. He seemed to have similar ambitions to me. We'd both got placements, at a reasonably big law firm in Southampton."

"You were going to be working at the same company?"

"Sort of. We had training contracts. That's how you become qualified, you see? It takes two years after you've finished your degree."

"I see. So, it's a bit like becoming a doctor. There's an element of on-the-job training."

"Yes. The fact that our placements were at the same office wasn't as much of a coincidence as it sounds. We were at university in Hampshire, and it was standard practice to apply to as many law practices as possible. Four of us from my intake were going to the same firm to complete our training."

"So you hadn't applied to the same places because you were together and wanted to keep it that way?"

"No. When we did the applications, we weren't even seeing each other." I nod my head, and she dips hers, like she's embarrassed. "He was as serious about his studies as I was, and although I know it sounds really dull, we even went to the extent of agreeing on a schedule."

"What for?"

"Dating each other." She looks up, her cheeks pinking. "We worked out our study requirements, and fitted in seeing each other around them. That was my idea, because I didn't want to mess up my degree when I was so close to completing it. I was predicted to get a First, too… and the thought of letting myself down over a boy…" Her voice fades and she shakes her head.

"I presume he agreed with you, though?"

She looks up. "Oh, yes. He thought it was a good idea, and we both reasoned we'd have plenty of time to be together after we'd taken our finals."

"So you were looking at having a long-term relationship?"

"Yes. We talked about what we were going to do during the summer."

"Deciding on what?"

"Nothing. We didn't reach any decisions, but we talked about travelling… probably in Europe." She looks down again, although I catch sight of her biting on her lip. "We didn't go into details… like sleeping arrangements. We just talked about the countries we'd like to visit, or the cities, to be more precise." She takes a deep breath, but still doesn't look up. "I'll admit, the thought of going away with him had me in a quandary."

"Why?"

She tilts her head, glancing at me. "Because we'd spent so little time together. All we'd done was kiss, and hold hands, really."

"And you were nervous he'd want more?"

She shakes her head. "It wasn't that… or not just that. I was nervous, but I was also…"

"Also what?"

"I was kind of excited." She looks away, so I can't see her face anymore.

"There's nothing wrong with that, Millie. It was going to be an adventure." I notice her hands are shaking and although I want to reach out and hold them in my own, I can't. I daren't touch her, because I know her story won't end well.

"That's what I thought," she says, turning back and staring right at me. "I thought we'd finish our finals, pack up our rucksacks and go travelling together. I got this romantic notion in my head that we'd visit all the places we'd talked about, that we'd get to know each other a little better, and that eventually we might…" She lets her voice fade, and I know she won't be able to finish that sentence.

"You might do more than kissing and holding hands?"

"Yes. Don't get me wrong, I enjoyed kissing… or rather being kissed, and I wanted to do more than that, but I had this silly, romantic idea that I wanted to know him better first. I thought love should be a part of making love, and Damian had never mentioned the word."

"Did you love him?" I ask, dreading her answer.

"I thought I might be falling in love with him. He was very charismatic… very charming."

I hate him already, without her telling me what he did to her. "Did he know how you felt?"

"Not that I was aware of, and by the beginning of April, we were both too wrapped up in our finals to worry about anything else. We were studying hard, and barely had time to see each other at all, but one of his friends was celebrating his twenty-first birthday, and had decided to throw a party on the Friday evening. We toyed with not going, but in the end, we both needed a break, and we went along together."

"Did you have a good time?"

"No," she says, surprising me. "There were a lot of drugs floating around, which we avoided… but the alcohol was free-flowing, too…"

"And you didn't avoid that?"

"Not entirely. I had a few drinks, but Damian went overboard. It was like he'd decided to let his hair down after so much studying, and by ten-thirty, I was still just about sober enough to realise he was too drunk to stay there any longer."

"What did you do?"

"I got him back to his place, with the help of a taxi and a lot of gentle persuasion. He couldn't even get the key in the lock, so I did it for him, and then thought I'd better make him some coffee. He sat on the sofa, while I fixed him something to drink, and when I brought it back to him, he… he grabbed me." She stops talking, blinking hard, her eyes fixed on the window, although I'm not sure she's looking through it… just at it.

"You don't have to go into detail if you don't want to."

She shakes her head in a dazed kind of way. "He… He pulled me down onto the sofa, beside him, and he kissed me. I kissed him back, even though he tasted of stale beer. And then, the next thing I knew, I was on my back, and he was on top of me." She starts talking more quickly, like the words couldn't be stopped now, even if she wanted them to. "We'd never done anything like that before, but his hands were everywhere, all over me, and I knew this wasn't what I wanted at all. It wasn't how I'd imagined it would be. I told him to stop, and he laughed. He said he knew I'd worn a short dress just to tempt him." She stops, looking at me. "I—I hadn't. I'd worn it because we were going to a party. And in any case, it wasn't that short. It was just that Damian was used to seeing me in jeans and trousers. I hardly ever wore skirts. I tried to tell him the dress was for the party, but he didn't let me. He said he'd seen the look in my eyes. He kept calling me a tease, saying he knew I wanted it really, and I'd just been making him wait, playing hard to get… it was written all over my face, evidently. I yelled at him to get off of me, and that's when he clamped his hand over my mouth." I can see the fear in her eyes now. She's reliving the moment and I wish I could stop her, even though I know she needs to get this out. "I was crying, sobbing, trying to push him off, but he was strong… so much stronger than me. I couldn't… I couldn't…"

"Did he rape you?" I ask, hoping we can cut to the chase rather than prolonging this agony.

She shakes her head and I struggle not to sigh out my relief, even though I know her ordeal was terrifying, as it was. "I think he would have done," she says. "In fact, I'm sure of it. But he pulled his hand away from my mouth to undo his jeans and I screamed. The noise woke his flatmate. We didn't even know he was in, but he came out of his bedroom to see what was going on. Damian knelt up then, swearing at his friend, but releasing me in the process. I caught a glimpse of confusion on his friend's face. He could obviously see that something wasn't right. He stepped forward and started yelling at Damian, and although I felt a little safer with him there, and I knew Damian might come to his senses, I didn't want to hang around to find out. I realised I had a chance to escape, and that seemed more important than anything else. So, I slid out from underneath Damian, grabbed my bag from the coffee table and ran… just like tonight, really."

"Where did you run to?"

"Home. It wasn't that far away, and luckily my parents were on holiday. What I didn't realise until I got there was they'd arranged for my brother to come and visit… to check up on me, I think. He must have arrived while I was out, because he was there when I got back."

"Hang on," I say, interrupting her. "When you say you went home, you really mean 'home', as in your parents' place?"

"Yes. I was still living there. Call me pathetic, but I didn't feel ready to leave home, so I went to the local university, and took advantage of the free accommodation my mum and dad were willing to offer."

"And you have a brother? I didn't know about that." Although why I thought I would is beyond me.

"Yes." She manages a slight smile. "His name is Ellis. He's quite a bit older than me, and very protective. He took one look at my torn blouse and tear-streaked face, and wanted to know what had happened. So, I told him… at least part of it. It was enough for him to persuade me I needed to report it to the police."

"I'm glad to hear it."

She frowns, shaking her head, although I'm not sure why. "Ellis came with me, and they sat me in a room, and took a statement. They… they insisted on getting a doctor to examine me. I sent Ellis out of the room for that part, and then afterwards, they let me go home. It was the early hours of the morning by then, and I was exhausted, but he ran me a bath, and afterwards he stayed with me until I fell asleep. We spent the weekend just chilling out at the house, neither of us talking about what had happened, but on the Sunday afternoon, the police sergeant who'd taken my statement came round to the house. He sat in the living room, and told me, in front of my brother, that Damian had made his statement, and told them I'd consented to everything he'd done."

"Are you serious?"

"Absolutely."

"But what about his friend? The one who came out of his bedroom because he'd heard you screaming? I presume you'd told the police about him?"

"Of course. They'd spoken to him as well, and he'd told them he hadn't seen anything out of the ordinary. He'd maintained in his statement that he'd been woken up by the two of us, and had come out to find us having loud sex in the living room."

"Having sex?"

"Yes."

"But you hadn't been having sex… loud or otherwise."

"I know. I couldn't understand why Damian's friend was lying. He'd known what was happening was wrong. I could see it in his face, and he'd started shouting at Damian before I left. It was only much later that I found out that Damian's parents owned the flat they were both living in. I guess he was worried he'd be homeless if he didn't side with his friend."

"Or maybe Damian threatened him?"

She shrugs her shoulders. "I wouldn't have thought he was the threatening kind."

"Would you have thought him capable of sexual assault?"

"No."

I sigh, further words unnecessary. "Did the police believe them?"

"They didn't say. All they said was, it was Damian's word against mine. He was maintaining I'd consented, and that I 'liked it rough'."

She puts air quotes around those last three words, but I can't believe I heard them right. "I'm sorry?"

"He'd said in his statement that I enjoyed him being rough with me. It was evidently a game we used to play. That's what he told them. Ellis argued I was bruised. The doctor's examination had revealed marks on my arms and the insides of my legs, but they said that was consistent with Damian's story of me liking rough sex. Nobody paid any attention to the fact that I was still a virgin... so rough sex wasn't even a feature on my radar." She stops talking and looks up at me, blushing. "I'm sorry. I didn't mean for that to come out. It's just that it makes me so angry."

She sounds livid... understandably. "I don't blame you," I say. "And you've got nothing to be sorry for."

It's like she hasn't heard me, her eyes still fixed on mine, the rage still boiling beneath the surface. "The police said there wasn't a strong enough case to take it further."

"So they let it drop?"

She nods her head. "Of course, that meant I'd have to see Damian in my lectures. I couldn't face him... not knowing what he'd done to me. His lies just made it worse, and the thought of sitting in the same lecture hall as him, or bumping into him in a corridor... it was too much. Ellis said he'd come with me to see my tutor, and I arranged a meeting with her on the Monday morning."

"What did she say?"

"That I needed to see the Vice Chancellor. It wasn't something she could get involved with."

"That was it?"

"Yes. I'd like to say she was sympathetic, but in reality, she just wanted to wash her hands of the whole thing and pass the buck."

"And what did the Vice Chancellor say? I'm assuming you went to see him... or her?"

"We did. Ellis was getting fed up by this stage. He'd had enough of all the bureaucracy, and he insisted on sitting down with the Vice Chancellor that day. We told him what had happened, in as much detail as I could bear, and he sat and listened, nodding his head, and then told me that, as the police had found no evidence against Damian, the university couldn't take any action. He said it would be detrimental to his education, and unfair to taint his future, based on something that couldn't be proved."

"This is like some kind of sick joke."

"I know… except it's not funny. It's anything but funny. I— I couldn't go back to uni after that. I was too scared to even think about being in the same space as him. So, I left, there and then, without finishing my degree." She sucks in a breath, stuttering as she lets it out, and as she does, she starts to cry. I desperately want to hold her, although I know she's not ready for that, and I have to sit and watch as her body shakes, tears dripping down onto her dress, leaching into the fabric. She sniffles and I pull some tissue from the toilet roll, holding it out to her, waiting until she takes it, dabs at her nose and eyes, and then looks up at me. "I'm sorry."

I shake my head. "Please… don't apologise." She wipes her nose again and takes a deep breath, rolling her shoulders. "What happened next?"

She frowns, like she's trying to remember. "Ellis had been due to go back to work, but he phoned his boss and took the rest of the week off, so he was there when my parents came back from their holiday. He helped me explain it to them, because I knew I couldn't do it by myself."

"How did they react?"

"They were angry… mostly at Damian, but also at the university, and the police. They told Ellis off for not contacting them, but I reasoned there wouldn't have been any point. What could they have done, other than spend a fortune changing their flights?"

"They could have been with you, I suppose."

She tilts her head, one way and then the other. "I know, but I'm not sure they understood."

"Understood what?"

"That in the end, I just wanted to forget about it. They didn't understand that, every time they brought it up, I had to re-live the whole thing, over and over. It was worse after Ellis went back to work. He'd been a kind of buffer for me, but once I was alone with them, their need to wrap me up in cotton wool, while also seeking revenge on my behalf, became overwhelming."

"What did they do?"

"They didn't *do* anything, but only because I wouldn't let them. It was like a constant battle, though."

"Over what?"

"Everything. Initially, they spent ages trying to persuade me to defer for a year and then go back to uni to take my finals. There was no way I ever wanted to set foot in that university again, but even when they suggested I could go somewhere else, I had to explain that the idea of living away from home right at that point in time was too frightening."

"Of course it was. You needed your family."

She nods her head. "You can see it. I could see it. But they couldn't. They weren't being unkind. I think they were just trying to be practical… and weren't thinking through the consequences. I resolved the situation by getting a job."

"Doing what?"

She sighs. "I made the mistake of going to work for a local firm of solicitors. It was just a clerical job, but I shouldn't have taken it. Every day was a reminder of what I'd tried and failed to do."

"You didn't fail." How can she think that?

"Didn't I? Damian got his degree. He's probably a fully fledged solicitor by now. That's what I wanted… but I couldn't do it, because I was too weak."

I take the risk and move closer. "Don't you dare say that. You weren't weak." I close my eyes, just to regain some control. "None of this was your fault."

"I'd been made to feel like it was. Damian had said I'd wanted it, and to a certain extent, he wasn't wrong, was he? I had thought about what it might be like." She stops talking and raises her hand, biting on her thumbnail for a second before she lowers it again. "I—I've never told anyone the entire story before... not even Ellis. I've never revealed the part about wanting to do more than kiss. It makes me feel ashamed."

"Why? You've got nothing to be ashamed of, Millie. Wanting to be loved isn't a crime. Wanting to have sex isn't a sin, either. They're both perfectly natural feelings."

"Are they?"

"Yes."

"Then why does this keep happening to me? I've only ever dated two men, and on both occasions..." Her voice fades to a whisper, and I have to clench my fists to stop myself from reaching out and hugging her.

"It's not supposed to be like this, Millie. I promise."

"So I was just unlucky, was I?"

"Yes. Very."

She stares at me for a long moment. "I suppose I was lucky, too. At least someone was there to interrupt... to stop it from being worse than it already was."

"That's a good way of looking at it."

"I know. That's what I kept telling myself after Damian... that even if his friend hadn't stood up and told the truth, at least he'd been there to stop Damian from raping me. He'd given me a means of escape."

"Exactly. You can't let yourself become a victim."

"That was what I thought. Not straight away, you understand. It took me a while to come around to that way of thinking, but when I did, I decided I needed to move away… to start again somewhere else. All the while I was living at home, my parents were never going to let me forget. They brought it up far too often, and I needed to leave it in the past."

"Is that why you moved here?"

She nods her head. "It was Ellis's idea, really. He'd studied down here…"

"Studied what?" I ask, wanting to make this more of a general conversation, for her sake and mine. I want to get to know her, so I can understand her better… so I can help her more.

"Marine biology. He hadn't lived in Porthgarrion. In fact, he'd never heard of it, but he suggested moving to Cornwall, and then a friend of my parents said I could use his flat."

I look around at the living room we're sitting in. "This place?"

"Yes. My parents' friend usually rents it out to holidaymakers, but he'd been having trouble finding people who wanted to stay here, because it's so small. He hadn't been able to decide whether to put it back up for this year at a lower price, or sell it, or rent it out on a more long-term basis, and when my dad mentioned to him that I might be moving down here, he suggested I could live here for the time being, while I found my feet, and he decided what to do. I wasn't about to say 'no'. It felt like fate giving me a nudge, and when I found your advert for a receptionist, it seemed like the nudge had become a fully fledged shove. Becoming a doctor's receptionist may not have been my life's ambition, but it felt like a fresh start." She blushes, pursing her lips and then biting the bottom one. "I'm sorry," she says. "That sounded very ungrateful."

"What on earth do you think you have to be grateful for?"

"You gave me a job."

"Yes. Because you were the best candidate." That's not a lie, although I can hardly tell her my other reason for employing her… especially not now.

She blinks a couple of times, and I wonder if she's going to cry. She doesn't, but she sucks in a slightly stuttered breath and murmurs, "Thank you."

"For employing you?"

"No. For listening."

"You don't have to thank me for anything, Millie."

She sits back, her body sagging, like she's relieved that's over. I know I am, although there's a part of me wondering if she'll want to leave Porthgarrion now… if the memories of what Fraser did will be too much for her to want to stay. I can't ask her that, though. Not yet.

"I could really use a shower," she says, like she's talking to herself. "I feel so grubby."

I sit forward slightly, looking back at her. "You're not going to involve the police, then? Because, if you are, you should hold off on that shower."

She shakes her head. "After what happened last time, there's no way I'm doing anything official. I know the policeman who helped me is a friend of yours and I'm sure he's very kind, but I can't go down that route again."

"That's okay. No-one's going to make you do anything you're not comfortable with." I stop talking, take a breath, and then say, "There are different levels of police involvement, though, Millie. Will you at least agree to leave it with me?"

She shrugs her shoulders. "I suppose… as long as no-one expects me to make a statement, or listen to Fraser Johnson tell a pack of lies about me."

She's been burned, and I can't expect her to walk back into the fire again. No-one can. I nod my head and hold out my hand. She looks up at me quizzically, and I smile. "If you're going to shower, I need to take a look at your wrists."

She nods, offering her right hand, and I unwrap the tea towel, revealing the grazes down the inside of her wrist. There are a couple of deeper gashes, but the wet tea towel has cleaned them up reasonably well. I reach for her left hand, but don't take it until she holds it out, offering it to me, and after removing the towel from that, see that it's not as bad as the wound on the right.

"You should be fine to shower. Do you have a first-aid kit?"

"Yes. It's in the cupboard under the sink."

"Okay. I'll see what I can find in it."

I get to my feet, which makes her jump, and she looks up at me with something like fear in her eyes.

"You're going to do that now?"

"No. I'll check it out while you're in the shower. If you like, I could make you a cup of tea, while I'm about it."

"Oh… that sounds lovely."

I hold out my hand and she takes it, just for long enough that I can pull her to her feet. Then she lets go again, which is fair enough. I wasn't looking for anything, and I think she's knows that. I think she trusts me enough to let me stay a while… and to help her.

At least, I hope she does.

Because I'm not going anywhere.

Chapter Eleven

Millie

The shower feels cleansing… cathartic, even.

Or maybe I just feel that way because I've told Robson everything, and he didn't freak out.

That was the first time I've ever told anyone the entire story of what happened with Damian. I hadn't intended to go into so much detail, or reveal how I'd thought and felt at the time, but when I was talking, it seemed wrong to hold back.

I'd held back from Ellis, unwilling to admit to him that I'd been thinking about having sex with my boyfriend, because it's not the sort of thing you discuss with your big brother, is it? And, in any case, I always wondered if I was partly to blame. I kept thinking back, trying to work out if I'd led Damian on in some way. We'd never actually talked about taking our relationship further… not even when we were making our tentative plans to travel around Europe. But he'd said he knew it was what I wanted. He could see it in my eyes.

See what, though?

I don't know exactly.

But that doubt in my mind, and the fear that other people would blame me too, has always made me reticent to tell the whole story... until tonight.

I think I realised, as I was telling Robson about what Fraser had done to me, that what happened today was different. How could I have been to blame for what he did? I'd only gone out with him once, and our date had lasted for roughly an hour. He couldn't possibly have interpreted anything I said or did as an invitation to take things further. I'd been as dismissive as I could, without being rude. It made me think that perhaps some men are just made like that... not just Fraser, but Damian, too.

Maybe I wasn't to blame for either incident?

I can't say for sure yet, but I think it was that knowledge that made me want to open up to Robson... that and the fact that I knew I had to be honest with him.

Why?

Because I think honesty is important in a relationship, and that's what I want to have with him... one day. God knows how, given everything that's happened, but I do.

It won't be easy, but I know now, beyond any shadow of a doubt, that I love Robson, and when all is said and done, you don't lie to the person you love, do you?

How do I know I love him?

Given my inexperience, it's a fair question.

It's not because he sat and listened to my story without flinching or judging me. It's not because he's been so kind and helpful and supportive... and not even because he makes me feel safer than anyone I've ever known.

It's just because he's Robson.

I think I've always loved him – deep down – but something changed tonight. I saw him differently. The look in his eyes was like nothing I've ever seen before. There was anger, pain, sorrow… and something else. Something I couldn't identify, but which gave me hope.

And I need hope now, more than ever.

I've always thought I was invisible to him… but now I'm not so sure.

I turn, letting the water fall over my face.

Am I reacting to the situation? Is that what this is? Am I seeking solace, looking for love and reassurance – and hope – in the man who's shown me such tenderness over the last hour or so?

Am I seeing things that aren't there?

I shake my head. No. I don't think so.

I can't doubt my own feelings. They were there before, even if I hadn't fully acknowledged them.

As for Robson? I don't know how he feels. Not exactly. I just know he's a good and genuine man.

I wish I'd acted sooner; buried my insecurities and shyness, and found a way to let him know how I feel about him. If I had, I might have saved myself from yet another nightmare experience.

I look down, noticing that my hands are trembling, and I shake them, water splashing off the tiles. I refuse to be beaten by this, despite my tears. Damian and Fraser, and what they did, won't turn me into a victim. Robson's words struck a chord when he said that. Bouncing back from this won't be easy… not when I'd barely recovered from what Damian did. It's going to be hard not to feel like I'm being persecuted. But I can't hide from what's happened either, any more than I can shy away from how it makes me feel. If I do, I'll end up having to leave Porthgarrion… and I can't think of anything I want to do less.

Because leaving Porthgarrion would mean leaving Robson.

And that would break my heart.

I climb out of the shower, my wrists stinging, and I glance down. The grazes are red and angry, although they're not bleeding, and I wrap myself in a towel, using another to dry my hair.

I knew I couldn't wander around the flat half-naked, so I brought some clothes in here with me, leaving them on the toilet seat, and I dry off quickly, feeling the need for that cup of tea now. My leggings stick slightly as I pull them on, and I wish I'd chosen shorts now. At least I was sensible enough to pick out a t-shirt, and once I've got my bra on, I pull it over my head, straightening it out, and I glance up at myself in the mirror. It's still a little misted, but I can make out that my hair is a mess, and grab my brush from the shelf.

After a few minutes, I'm as presentable as I'm going to be, and I fold up the towels, leaving them over the rail, and pick up my dress and underwear from the floor. I don't want to keep any of these things, and I roll them up into a ball, clutching it in my hand as I open the door.

The aroma of onions and garlic hits my nostrils, and my stomach grumbles. I've got no idea what time it is, but it's almost dark, so it must be late, and I haven't eaten since about twelve-thirty.

I'm hungry.

I don't know where the smell is coming from, but it's going to drive me insane… especially as I'm too tired to think about cooking. The Italian restaurant isn't far away, and neither is the pub, but I don't normally smell anything from either establishment… so it must be one of the neighbours, I suppose.

I step out of the bathroom, stopping in my tracks when I see Robson standing over by the stove. He's got his back to me, but is clearly stirring something.

"What's that wonderful smell?" I ask, and he flips around, a wooden spoon in his right hand.

"I thought you could do with something to eat, as well as a cup of tea." He nods towards the sofa, and I follow the line of his gaze, seeing a steaming mug of tea on the table in front of it. Rather than going to take a drink, though, I wander over to him, putting my dress down on the work surface, and I stand on my tiptoes, peering over his shoulder. He's frying onions, garlic, and potatoes, and has some beaten eggs in a bowl. I step back slightly, resting my hip against the countertop beside the oven.

"What are you making?"

"It's a kind of Spanish omelette… or my version of one, anyway. Is that okay?"

"If it tastes as good as it smells, then yes. I hadn't realised how hungry I was until I smelt it cooking."

He stirs the mixture in the pan and then turns down the heat, a slight smile settling on his lips. "Do you know, I don't think I've ever seen you with your hair down before?"

"No, you probably haven't. But that would be another of my deep, dark secrets."

His smile fades. "It would?"

"Yes. You see, after what happened with Damian, I became a little reclusive for a while – which is another way of saying that, until I decided to get a job, I shut myself away and tried to pretend I didn't exist. To avoid climbing the walls, I used to spend ages trying to style my hair… only I wasn't very good at it."

"You could have fooled me. I've never seen anyone with hair that looks as beautiful as yours."

I can feel myself blush and look down at the space between us. "That's because I discovered the Internet, and the all the videos it contains, of people showing you how to style your hair. It's amazing how interesting plaits can be when you have nothing else going on in your life."

His smile returns, but only just, and he turns to face me. "Shall I look at your wrists?"

I hold them out to him, both together, wondering which of us is more embarrassed by that conversation; me for admitting to having spent far too much time learning to style my hair in the comfort of my own bedroom, or him for saying my hair was beautiful. His blush has faded now, although he keeps his head bent, and takes my right hand in his. "That one hurts more," I say, and he nods, studying it for a moment before he takes my left hand, gazing down at that one, too.

"I've found some antiseptic cream in your first-aid kit," he says, letting my hand go and stepping over to the draining board. He returns within a second or two with a tube of cream and a couple of bandages, putting them down on the work surface. "I'm going to put some on and bandage up your wrists, just to be on the safe side. I'll take another look at them tomorrow, if that's okay?"

"Of course. You can do it when I get to work, can't you?"

He frowns. "I wasn't expecting you to come in tomorrow, Millie. Not after what happened. I can pop down and take a look at your wrists in the morning. Take as much time off as…"

"I don't want time off. I want to come to work."

His frown deepens. "Are you sure about that?"

"Yes." *I want to be with you.* "I can't sit around here feeling sorry for myself."

"I think you'd be entitled."

I shake my head. "I'd rather keep busy, Robson."

His frown fades at last. "Okay. As long as you're sure."

"I'm positive."

He stirs the mixture in the pan again and picks up the tube of cream. "In that case, keep these bandages on overnight. Take them off in the morning when you shower, and I'll see how the grazes are looking when you get into work."

"Thank you."

He shakes his head. "Don't thank me."

"Why? Because you're just doing your job?"

He looks up at me, but doesn't say a word and, taking my right hand, he applies a thin layer of cream with the gentlest of touches. I watch him work, studying his face as he wraps the bandage around my wrist, checking it's not too tight. Once it's secured, he moves on to the left, repeating the process, and then he steps away. I hadn't realised how close he was standing, and I'm surprised by that. I'm surprised his presence didn't make me feel nervous… or even uncomfortable. Maybe that's because having him here feels right. It's as though he belongs…

He's certainly made himself at home in my kitchen, and that thought makes me smile… which in itself feels like a minor miracle.

"Are you going to stay and eat with me?" I ask, surprising myself with the invitation. I've clearly surprised him, too, and he replaces the lid on the cream, taking his time over it before he looks up at me.

"I don't have to. If you'd rather be alone, that's fine." He puts the cream down, picking up the wooden spoon again. "This tastes fantastic cold, so whatever you don't eat, you could always bring into work with you tomorrow for lunch."

"I could. Or you could stay and help me eat it now." He tilts his head, a smile tugging at the corners of his lips. "It seems unfair for you to cook my dinner and then leave."

"I don't mind, Millie. I'll do whatever makes you feel most comfortable."

You see? This is why I love him.

How could I not?

"Please… stay?"

His smile fills out into a grin as he nods his head, and my stomach knots with something more than hunger. I'm half tempted to lean in to him, to ask him to put his arms around me. I think I'd have to ask, too… not because he'd be unwilling, but because he's been so careful not to touch me without asking my permission. And I'm grateful for that.

"Why don't you go and drink your tea?" he says. "This won't take too much longer."

I do as he says, sitting down on the sofa and picking up the mug of warm tea. It tastes good, even if he has put sugar in it. Why would he do that? He's made enough cups of coffee at work to be aware of my tastes.

"Did you forget that I don't take sugar?"

He puts down the spoon and turns. "No. But sweet tea is excellent for shock."

"Is it?"

"Yes. Even if it doesn't taste very nice."

I giggle, surprising myself, and he smiles across at me, turning around again and picking up the bowl of beaten eggs.

I can hear the sizzle as they hit the pan and I watch his back as he stirs, turning in my seat and putting my feet up. It's strange, but I feel relaxed… so relaxed, I could happily drift off to sleep.

"Millie?"

I hear my name being spoken in a soft, familiar voice and I crack my eyes open to see Robson standing above me, a plate in one hand and a knife and fork in the other.

"God… I'm sorry. Did I fall asleep?"

I sit up properly, turning and putting my feet on the floor again as I take the plate from him.

"Let's just say you were dozing," he says with a smile.

He wanders back to the kitchen, returning with another plate, and sits beside me, resting it on his lap.

"This looks amazing." I stare down at the dish before me, studying the slice of omelette, with its richly coloured top, the aromas making my stomach growl. I cut into it, taking a bite, and close my eyes, soaking up the flavours. When I open them again, I turn my head to see Robson staring at me, smiling.

"Does it taste okay?"

"It tastes better than okay. It's wonderful."

He chuckles, shaking his head, like he doesn't believe me, and then takes a bite himself. "Hmm… not bad."

"It's just what I needed."

He stops chewing, just for a second, and then starts again, waiting until he's finished before he says, "Good."

He's made himself a cup of tea, too, and he takes a sip, leaving his cup on the arm of the sofa as he turns, taking another mouthful of omelette, and says, "Did you want to call your brother?"

I put down my fork, staring at him. "What for?"

"To tell him what's happened. He understood last time, and…"

I shake my head, and he stops talking. "I don't want to talk to anyone else. Although I was thinking of calling Ellis tonight, before this happened…"

"Was there a reason you were going to call him?"

I blush, recalling my thoughts as I left work, and how I'd planned to have a phone call with my brother, and somehow bring my feelings for Robson into the conversation. I'm not about to admit that now, though. "No. I just thought we could do with a catch-up." *Like the one we had last night, after my date with Fraser.*

Robson nods his head. "So, it wasn't anything to do with Damian?"

"No. Not at all." Although I remember Damian's name coming up in my last conversation with Ellis, now I come to think about it… when he told me that not all men would be the same as him. Based on my recent experience, I'm wondering if that's true…

I dismiss that thought, though. Robson's nothing like Damian or Fraser.

"You could still call him, couldn't you?"

"Why?"

"Because you need support, Millie."

He sounds worried, or at least concerned, and I turn in my seat, so I'm facing him. "Maybe I do, but I can't talk to him at the moment."

"Why not?"

"Because I can't hide this from him. He'll guess there's something wrong, and then I'll have to tell him… and he'll tell Mum and Dad. I can't cope with that. I can't talk to them. Any of them."

"You talked to me."

"I know, but you're different." I wonder if I should have said that, especially when I see the confusion in his eyes, and I know there's nothing I can say or do to ease that. There's no way I can explain what I mean… not right now.

"Because I'm a doctor?" His voice is barely a whisper in the stillness between us.

"No." That's all I can say and for a moment longer, he just looks at me, the confusion still there, until he nods his head. It's like earlier, when he accepted that I couldn't elaborate about Fraser not being my boyfriend. He seems to know that explanations are beyond me today.

"Okay. When I go, I'll leave you with my number. I don't know why you haven't got it already, but you haven't, have you?"

"No."

"I didn't think so. Anyway, I'll make sure you have before I go tonight, and that way, if you need to talk to someone, you can… even if it's in the middle of the night."

"The middle of the night?"

"Yes."

"But, I wouldn't…"

"No 'buts', Millie. If you need me, I want you to promise you'll call, no matter what time it is."

I wait for a second, but he doesn't take his eyes from mine and I realise how serious he is, and that he's not going to back down.

"Okay."

He nods his head and goes back to eating. I copy him, wondering if he's just being kind… just being a doctor…

The more I eat, the more tired I feel and by the time I've finished my omelette, I can barely keep my eyes open.

"You need to get some sleep," Robson says, taking my plate. I haven't yawned yet, although I'm struggling not to, but somehow he seems to know how tired I am, and he gets up, taking the plates with him to the kitchen.

"Let me help with that," I say, shifting forward on the sofa.

"No. You stay where you are. This won't take five minutes to clear away."

He makes quick work of washing up the dishes and the frying pan, and I smile as he wipes down the work surfaces, too, then frown when he picks up the notepad I always keep by the fridge, jotting something down on it.

"What's that you're writing?" I ask, and he looks up.

"My mobile number. You can put it on your phone later."

He replaces the notepad, checking around the kitchen, and then grabs my dress, bringing it over. I feel myself tense. "I was going to throw that away," I say, although the thought of touching it makes me want to be sick.

"Do you want me to do it for you?"

I almost sag with relief, but then recall my bra and knickers, which are rolled up within its folds. "M——My underwear is wrapped up inside it somewhere."

"Sorry." He holds it out, although I still can't bring myself to touch it. "I didn't realise."

"That's all right. I don't want to keep it, either. He may not have touched me that intimately, but it all feels tainted by him. I'll certainly never wear any of it again."

He sits, putting the dress on the floor beside him. "Hey... it's okay. I'll get rid of it all for you."

"Thank you."

He hesitates for a moment, and I half expect him to get up again... except he doesn't. He takes a breath, and says, "I know you don't want to talk to a counsellor, but if you change your mind, I can find one for you. Or if there's anything you need to see a GP about, I can help with that."

"How? I'm not registered with you. I'm not registered with anyone yet, but being as you're the only GP here..."

I let my voice fade as he shakes his head. "I don't think registering with me is the best idea."

"Oh?" I wonder why he offered to help, then.

"We're not supposed to see friends and family."

"I see. So what should I do then?"

"That all depends on whether you're planning on staying."

His cheeks turn a subtle shade of pink as he's speaking. I'm not sure why he's embarrassed, but he seems to be. "In Porthgarrion?" I ask, just to make sure.

"Yes. You left home after what happened with Damian. If the memories of what Fraser did are too much..."

"This is different," I say, interrupting him and he tilts his head to one side, like he doesn't understand. "Part of the reason I left was because my parents wouldn't let up. I know they meant well, but sometimes it felt like they were smothering me. I needed to get away. But I don't feel the same way now. Besides, you're the only person who knows what's happened."

"Tom knows."

"Not the full story. He doesn't know about Damian. So, unless you're planning on bringing this into every conversation we have…"

"I wouldn't dream of it." It's his turn to interrupt and once he has, and he's got my attention, he shifts just a little closer. "I'll talk to you about it, if you want me to. Or, to be more precise, I'll listen to whatever you need to say, but other than that, I'll do my best to keep a lid on the subject."

"In that case, can you tell me how to register with a GP, please?"

"I use the one in the next village, and he comes to me, if he needs to, so I guess you could always go there, too."

"Okay. It's not something I need to look into tomorrow, though, is it?"

"No. It can wait until you're ready. But if I can help at all, let me know."

"I will."

He picks up my dress from the floor and stands, although I notice he holds it behind him, shielding it from my view.

"I'll let you get to bed now, but don't forget to lock your door after I've gone."

"I won't."

I get up, following him to the front door, although as he opens it, I step back, unable to help the slight gasp that escapes my lips. Robson must have heard it too, because he turns, looking down at me.

"What's wrong, Millie?"

"I—I've just realised… I might be able to lock Fraser out of here, but what if he's waiting for me somewhere tomorrow? What if he's out there in the morning?" I step back a little further, unable to fight the fear that's bubbling inside me, threatening to turn me into that victim I'm so desperate not to become. "You got in through the main door this evening. What if he does the same thing? What if he's out there, waiting for you to leave, and he gets in here, and knocks…"

Robson comes right up to me, standing as close as he can without actually laying a finger on me, and looks down into my face. "Please, Millie… don't be scared. You're safe here."

"But…"

He shakes his head. "I only got in because the people from the flat downstairs were going out, and I told them I was the local doctor and had just come to see you on a house call."

"So you lied?"

"Sort of. I am a doctor, and I'm visiting you at home."

"Yes, but I'm not a patient, am I?"

"No, but it was close enough to the truth to get away with it." He takes a deep breath. "You mustn't worry about Fraser. He can't hurt you anymore. Okay? You'll be safe… I'll make sure of it." I don't know what he means by that, or how he thinks he can keep me safe, but I feel reassured by his words, and I nod my head. "Now… lock your door when I leave, stop worrying, and get some rest."

"Okay." He turns away, but I reach out and grab his arm. He swings back around, looking down at the connection, and then raises his face to mine. "Thank you," I murmur, letting him go.

"You're welcome."

At least he didn't tell me I didn't need to thank him. I think we both know I do.

He departs, pulling the door closed, and I lock it.

"Goodnight, Millie," he calls from the other side, and I smile.
"Goodnight."

Chapter Twelve

Robson

I get to the end of Chapel Mews and stop, turning back to look at Millie's house. The light is still on. I can see it in the window. Although as I stand, staring, wondering if I should have left her by herself, when she was clearly so scared, it goes out. She must have gone to bed… thank God.

I wait for another few minutes, but nothing happens, and I continue on my way, going out onto Church Lane, and down to the harbour. There's a breeze coming in off the sea, and I suck in great lungfuls of it, trying to breathe normally, although I doubt I'll ever do that again… not after tonight.

I knew it would be bad when Tom told me what he'd witnessed, and what Millie had said. When I arrived at Millie's flat, I realised how bad it was likely to be… just the state of her gave that away. What I hadn't expected was that tonight's assault wasn't her first.

How can that be?

How can two men, on two separate occasions, have treated her so badly?

And how can the system have treated her worse?

It makes my blood boil to think that the authorities failed her. Wasn't it bad enough that she'd endured the ordeal of being assaulted by a man she'd grown to trust... a man with whom she'd believed herself to be falling in love... with whom she'd harboured thoughts of sharing her body? Did she have to endure the degradation of being told no-one was going to do anything about it? No-one was going to help?

Their actions left her blaming herself, feeling responsible. Because of them, she gave up her ambitions, turned in on herself, relinquished the life she'd dreamt of.

Millie might not want to involve the police, and I can't blame her for that... but like I said to her, there are different levels of involvement, and I plan on tapping into them.

My father's a police officer. I've grown up around him and his colleagues. I know there are things that can be done which don't involve going down official routes... and that's what I intend talking through with Tom. He's the one who came knocking on my door, so I feel as though he's the best person to discuss it with. And besides, I'm not sure my father's the right man to go to. This is personal for me, and I know he'll see through that in the blink of an eye.

By the time I reach Bell Road, I've decided exactly what I'm going to do, and I sigh out my relief when I see the lights are still on at Tom and Gemma's house. It's fairly late now... but as he's clearly still up, I know he won't mind if I call on him.

I climb up the steps to the front door, knocking on it, and step back slightly, waiting.

Gemma answers, pulling the door right open when she sees it's me.

"Doctor Carew?"

"Call me Robson, please?"

"Sorry." She smiles and tilts her head, like she's waiting for me to say something, which isn't surprising.

"Is Tom at home?" I ask.

"Yes." She moves to one side. "Come in."

I duck my head, stepping over the threshold, and Gemma closes the door behind us, just as Tom comes out from the kitchen area at the back of the house. He's wearing jeans and a t-shirt, drying his hands on a tea towel, and he frowns when he sees me.

"Doctor?"

"Constable."

Gemma coughs, and we both look at her. "Is this one of those occasions when it would be better if I made myself scarce?"

Tom puts the tea towel over the back of one of the dining chairs and strides across the room, placing his hands on Gemma's waist and looking down into her eyes. "Would you mind?"

"Of course not. I'll go upstairs and read for a while."

He kisses the tip of her nose, releasing her, and she smiles at me before she runs up the stairs, disappearing from sight.

The moment she's gone, Tom turns to me.

"I take it this is about your receptionist?"

"Yes. I've just come from her place."

He looks down at my hand and I realise I'm still holding Millie's dress. "Is that for me?"

"No. These are the clothes Millie was wearing today, including her underwear. I said I'd dispose of them for her."

He frowns. "Dispose of them? I'm not sure I should let you do that. They could hold vital evidence."

"It's only evidence if she's going to report the crime."

"And she's not?"

"No."

"But there was a crime?"

"Yes."

He shakes his head, letting out a long sigh. "Shall we sit?" he says, and I follow him around his dark grey sofa, sitting beside him, Millie's dress clutched on my lap. The alcoves on either side of the fireplace are stacked with books, and he reaches for the remote control, turning off the television, which has been playing away to itself in the background, unnoticed by me until now.

The silence feels a little stifling, and I don't know how to break it. Tom saves me the trouble, asking, "What happened?"

"I went to see Millie, and she's… well, she's a mess. Or she was. I think she's a little better now. She seemed better when I left, compared to when I arrived."

"That's good."

"Yes. If anything about this can be called 'good'."

"I take it that what I witnessed wasn't consensual?"

"No. Far from it."

"Was she raped?"

"No. It didn't get that far. One of the chefs at the restaurant came out in the nick of time, giving Millie the chance to escape."

"The man I saw running away, he did something to her, though… right?"

"Oh, yes. He pinned her up against the wall and groped her. According to Millie, his hands were everywhere. She did everything she could to get him to stop, but he didn't want to know." Tom's face darkens, and I wonder if I looked like that when Millie told me her story.

"Is she hurt?"

"She's got some nasty grazes on her wrists from where he held her hands against the wall."

"None too gently," he says, and I nod my head.

"There are obviously the mental and emotional scars as well."

"Obviously." He sits forward, so he's perching on the edge of the sofa, and looks back at me. "What you've described is a sexual assault, Robson."

"I know."

"And yet, she doesn't want to report it?"

"No. She has her reasons, and they're good ones."

"Care to elaborate?"

I shake my head. "Even though I'm not be her GP, I'm going to treat what she told me tonight in confidence. So, I'm afraid you're going to have to take my word for it that her reasons are among the best there are."

He lets his head rock forward. "Okay. If you say so." He sits back again, resting his arm along the back of the sofa. "Thanks for finding out what happened. It can't have been easy for you." I frown, tilting my head, and he smiles. "Do you think I'm a fool, Robson? I get that you're a GP and that you care about your patients. I even get that Millie is your receptionist, and you care about your employees. But there was more to it than that. I saw the panic on your face when you realised who I was talking about earlier. She means something to you, doesn't she?"

"No. She doesn't mean something. She means everything."

He nods his head slowly. "Are you okay?"

"Me?"

"Yes. Like I said, this can't have been easy for you. I can't imagine how I'd feel if that had been Gemma."

"I hope you'll never have to find out."

"So do I. But if you need to talk, you know where I am."

"Thank you."

"I just wish there was more I could do."

"Well…"

He frowns. "Well, what?"

"There might be. Unofficially."

He lets his arm fall from the back of the sofa and turns to face me. "Unofficially? How? We don't even know who the man is."

"Yes, we do. His name's Fraser Johnson, and he works at the surf school."

Tom shoots to his feet. "How do you know this?"

"Because Millie went out with him last night. They had a drink together."

"Nothing else? They didn't…?"

"Would it matter, Tom? Even if he'd spent the night with her, doing everything both you and I can imagine, other than sleeping, that still wouldn't entitle him to do what he did… not if she didn't want it."

"I know. But if I'm going to pay him a visit – even unofficially – I need the facts."

"Which are, that they met for the first time yesterday lunchtime. He asked her for a drink at the pub, and Millie went along after work. They had one drink together and then she left because she found him too boring to stay for another one, and he took her home."

"That was last night?"

"Yes."

"And this evening?"

"He jumped out at her at the bottom of Bell Road."

"Jumped out at her?"

"That's what she said. He claimed he was coming to meet her from work, but she said it didn't feel like that. She said it felt like he was waiting for her."

"They hadn't arranged to meet up again?"

"No."

"He'll probably still try to claim he was coming to meet her, though."

"I don't doubt it."

"Did she agree to walk home with him?" he asks.

"Yes. She said she couldn't think of a reason not to… not on the spur of the moment, and then once they got to Church Lane, he pushed her down the alleyway by the restaurant and assaulted her."

"You know he's going to claim she was a willing participant, don't you? He'll use last night's date, and the fact that she'd agreed to let him walk her home on two occasions as evidence that they were in some kind of relationship."

"Even if they were, does that give him the right to do what he did?"

"No. You know it doesn't. We've just agreed on that."

"Exactly. And this isn't going to be an official visit, is it? So what does it matter if he comes up with far-fetched excuses?"

"It matters because I need to counter them with the truth. I'm going to pay him a visit tomorrow and I have no doubt he'll deny every word of this. If what I say to him is going to carry any weight, it needs to be accurate, so that regardless of how he responds, he knows deep down that I've got his number."

"What are you going to say, then?"

He shrugs his shoulders, a smile forming on his lips. "I don't know yet. I'll probably make it up as I go along."

"Be careful, won't you? I've seen this guy. He's built like a wall."

He chuckles. "Don't worry about it… or me. I can be very intimidating when I want to be."

I smile. "I was really hoping you'd say that."

I stand, tucking Millie's clothes under my left arm, and Tom looks down at my right hand as I hold it out to him. He offers his too, and we shake. "Thanks, Tom."

"No problem."

I turn, moving towards the door. "Sorry I interrupted your evening. Apologise to Gemma for me, won't you?"

"There's no need to apologise. I'll come and see you tomorrow, when I've been to the surf school."

"Okay."

I open the door, stepping out into the night.

"Oh, by the way," he says, and I stop, looking back at him, "I noticed a draught when I was at your place earlier."

"A draught?"

"Yes. I realised it must have been coming from somewhere, so I wandered in and found you'd left the patio door wide open. I brought in the wine glass you'd left on the table outside and locked the door before I left."

"Thanks. Where did you leave the key?"

"On the draining board." He rolls his eyes. "People around here have a habit of leaving their doors open all the time, but it's not one I can get into."

"Neither can I in normal circumstances… not with all the drugs I have on the premises."

"Hmm… that thought crossed my mind, too." He smiles. "You weren't yourself earlier, though, were you?"

"Not in the least."

I thank him again, making my way down the steps and giving him a wave as I walk up the hill to my house.

Letting myself in through the side door, I go down the hallway and straight into the living room at the back of the house. It's well-lit by the moonlight and I put my keys on the kitchen table and quickly drop Millie's clothes into the bin. Then I pour away the remains of my wine from earlier, putting the glass into the dishwasher before I wander into the other half of the room, sitting on the sofa in the darkness. I'm not in the mood for light. There's something about it that I know will feel too stark… too real.

It's a struggle just to breathe, but for a minute or two, I focus on that and nothing else.

The next breath in…

The next breath out.

My emotions are still in turmoil, as is my brain, but at least my heartbeat feels a little more regular, and I turn, lying back on the sofa and putting my feet up.

I'm still not sure that leaving Millie was the right thing to do, but I could hardly offer to stay with her in her tiny flat, could I?

Aside from the fact that her sofa was one of the smallest I've ever seen, and I'd never have been able to fit on it, her bed was in the same room, only hidden by a folding screen. I doubt she'd have felt any degree of privacy with me there, and in the circumstances, I imagine that would have made her feel very uncomfortable.

Still, I hate the thought of her lying in bed, feeling scared, and I wish now that I'd taken her phone number, as well as leaving her with my own.

"Of course... you idiot."

I get up, rushing through to the front of the house and into the surgery, opening my office door. Tom must have closed it earlier, before he left, because I'm pretty sure I didn't, but I ignore that, switch on the light, and go over to the filing cabinet, pulling open the top drawer to find Millie's CV. It's where I found her address earlier, and sure enough, beneath that is her mobile number.

I could call her, just to make sure she's okay.

I pull my phone from my pocket, adding her to my contacts list, and then hesitate before connecting the call.

Should I?

Should I speak to her, just to put my mind at rest? Or should I trust her to call me if she needs me?

She said she would, and I really ought to leave it at that. Calling her would be for my benefit, not hers... especially as she's hopefully fast asleep by now. I can't be that selfish.

Besides, one of the mistakes her parents made was to crowd her. I can understand why they did it. They love her. They wanted to help her then, like I do now. But it must have been hard for her, when all she wanted was to forget about what Damian had done.

Having me wake her to check she's okay is hardly conducive to forgetting, is it? It's conducive to a terrible night's sleep, and to her resenting me for interfering.

I put my phone back in my pocket and replace Millie's CV in the file, closing the drawer again.

I can't see any point in staying up, and I go through to the back of the house again, making my way up the stairs and into my bedroom. I've got an early start tomorrow, so I might as well get some rest.

My bedroom is at the back of the house, and the window is already open, just a crack. I open it wider, letting in the night air, and leave the door ajar too, hoping to cool the place off a little. It needs it, and once I've been to the bathroom, I come back and undress, putting my clothes into the laundry basket, and folding the duvet down to the end of the bed. I doubt I'll be needing it tonight, and once I've re-set my alarm, I lay down, naked, willing the breeze to work its magic.

It's too hot, but that's not the reason I can't sleep. My mind is racing, going over everything that's happened this evening… and not just to do with Millie's stories.

There was that little white lie I told her, for one thing. I wonder what would happen if she ever found out?

There's no reason she should, and I'm sure I'd be able to explain that I only had her best interests at heart when I told her she shouldn't register with me as her GP.

Okay… so that wasn't completely untrue. It is frowned upon for us to treat our friends and family, just like I said, but in small villages like this, where there's only one doctor, there's a lot of latitude. If I wasn't allowed to see my friends in a professional capacity, I'd have next to no patients at all. My parents are registered outside of the village, although they know I'll see them in an emergency… and when Millie asked me the question earlier this evening, I decided it would be better if she wasn't registered with me, either. My reason? It would be impossible for me to be impartial with her.

I've obviously never been in this situation before, and while I know seeing my friends and family is one thing, even I can appreciate that attending to the woman I love would be something else.

I turn over, wishing I could see her lying beside me. Not in the way I've wished for it before... but just so I could comfort her, and hold her, and reassure her that everything will be all right, even if it doesn't feel that way today.

At least I can console myself that she's not thinking about leaving the village. That question just fell out of my mouth while I was lying to her about not being able to register with me. It wasn't perhaps my finest hour – between the lies and the stupid question – but I had to know. I couldn't help myself. Her answer was reassuring, although as with everything else, I mustn't let myself get carried away. She might have reminded me I'm the only one who knows everything about what happened with Damian, but that doesn't mean she wants to make anything of it.

Especially now.

I still want her, just as much as I always did, but I'm aware I'm going to have to put my feelings on hold.

That's not a problem, though. I'll wait for as long as it takes...

Because I feel like I have something worth waiting for now.

Before, I felt hopeless, like I couldn't compete with the kind of man she spent her time with. Now, I'm not so sure. She wanted to speak to me... to confide in me. And when I asked her if that was because I'm a doctor, she said 'no'. She didn't elaborate, but I liked that.

It's left me with something to hope for.

I must have fallen asleep eventually, because my alarm wakes me with a start.

I glance out of the window at the pale blue sky. It looks as though it's going to be another warm day, and I get up, making my way to the bathroom.

I'm on a tight schedule this morning, even though it's half an hour earlier than when I usually get up. I race through the shower, coming back to the bedroom with a towel wrapped around my hips, and take a few minutes to sort out my clothes.

Despite the heat, I'll still wear trousers and a shirt, and I roll up the sleeves before laying it on the bed, so they'll look neater once it's on.

I'm essentially dry now, and I return to the bathroom to shave and brush my teeth, coming back to get dressed. Making the bed takes no time at all, considering I didn't use the duvet last night, and once that's done, I go downstairs and into the kitchen, putting a pod into the coffee machine, and some bread into the toaster.

With one eye on the clock, I eat my breakfast and drink my way through two cups of coffee, hoping I've timed this right.

I know when Millie gets to work, but I've got absolutely no idea what time she leaves home in the mornings. She may not come straight here. For all I know, she could go for a walk first, or do her shopping. She might even stop at the café for breakfast or a coffee on the way into work. Whatever her routine, I've got my fingers crossed I won't have missed her.

Once I've finished, I put my plate and cup into the dishwasher and grab my keys from the table where I left them last night.

It's still quite early, but that's fine. I don't mind waiting, and I leave the house, locking the door behind me, and make my way down Bell Road and out onto the harbour. Most of the shops are still closed… except for the baker's, and I smile, knowing that at least Rachel will be at home resting, rather than getting up at the crack of dawn like she used to. I'll check up on her later, just to make sure she's okay, although I'll have to fit the visit into my surgery hours, rather than going to see her at lunchtime, as I originally planned. Still, I'm sure I've got a couple of slots…

I get to Millie's flat by seven-thirty, and look up, smiling when I see the window is open at the front. That must mean she's still there. I think about knocking, but decide against it. I don't want her to feel like I'm hassling her, so I lean against the wall opposite her door, and I wait…

Chapter Thirteen

Millie

Considering everything that happened yesterday, I fully expected to lie awake half the night, reliving every second of every minute of what Fraser did to me. Exhaustion must have got the better of me, though, because I don't even remember getting into bed, and my alarm wakes me at ten to seven, just like it always does.

My first thought, when I turn over and stretch my arms above my head, is of Robson. A smile twitches at the corners of my lips when I recall the way he gazed into my eyes; the way he stared down at me when he told me I'd be safe. I think I knew that, if I needed him, he'd come; if I called, he'd be here. That was obviously enough to make me feel protected, because without that, I don't think I'd have slept at all.

As it is, although I won't go as far as to say I feel refreshed, I'll admit to feeling better than I thought I would.

I turn again, glancing out of the window, and a shadow of fear creeps over me. I shudder against it, but can't suppress it.

What if Fraser is out there, waiting for me?

What if he's lurking behind a wall, or a bush, like he was yesterday?

Robson might have said I was safe, but he's not here, is he? And Fraser could be. He could be right outside my front door.

"Oh, God…" My voice cracks, my bottom lip trembling, a claw of icy fear catching at my spine, making me shiver.

I can't do it. I can't go out there.

I might be naked, and the curtain might be open, but I get up anyway. Being on the second floor, there's no-one to see in through the windows, and I run around the screen and over to the sofa, picking up my phone from the table, where I left it last night.

I'll call Robson. I'll tell him I can't come in to work today. He said he wasn't expecting me to, so I'm sure it'll be okay. I go to my contacts list and scroll down to the letter 'R'. His name isn't there, and I tut at myself for being so stupid. Of course… I went straight to bed last night. I didn't put Robson's number into my phone.

I dash over to the kitchen, picking up the notepad, and gaze down at the digits, written in his familiar hand. He'll understand. I know he will. I dial the '0' and the '7' and then stop.

"What are you doing?"

The words come out of my mouth, filling the room with their unexpected volume. They startle me, but they have a point. What am I doing? Becoming a recluse again? That's what happened after Damian, at least for a few months, and I'm damned if I'm going to let it happen again. I moved here because my parents were treating me like a victim, and I wanted to escape that. So why allow myself to become one a second time? I told Robson I wouldn't, and I can't believe there are many more ways in which I could style my hair… none that warrant staying indoors to learn about them, anyway. In which case, I can't allow what Fraser did to change who I am. Or at least, who I want to be. Because I'm not going to deny I wasn't myself, even before this happened. I was still recovering… still trying to get back to being me. Can I really take such a backward step?

No, I can't.

I delete the two digits and go back to my contacts list, quickly adding Robson's number to it, and then I put the phone down and look around my tiny apartment. Okay, so it's not really 'mine'. It's just somewhere to live for a while, but it's the closest thing I have to a home of my own, and I'm not giving it up. I'm not leaving… or being driven out. I'm going to get showered, get dressed, and get on with it.

I stride through to the bathroom, stepping straight into the shower, and am just about to turn on the water, when I notice the bandages on my wrists, and recall Robson's instructions to remove them before taking a shower. I quickly do so, studying the grazes for a few moments and noting that they seem a little better this morning, and then I turn around, switching on the water.

I don't take long to shower, and once I'm out, I brush my teeth and dry my hair, braiding it simply for once. I'd normally do something much more elaborate than this, but my fingers won't stop shaking, and I know I'll only mess it up. Even so, once it's done, I have to smile, just slightly, as the memory of Robson's words creeps into my mind… 'I've never seen anyone with hair that looks as beautiful as yours.' I wonder for a second if I should undo the plait and make more of an effort to make it look 'beautiful'. But I know I'm too nervous. Even breathing is proving to be a challenge. Every time I get to the top of my breath, I stutter, like I've forgotten how to let go… how to relax enough to breathe out again. A simple plait is my limit and if that isn't 'beautiful' enough, there's not very much I can do about it. Not today.

I wander back to my bedroom area and pull out some underwear from my chest of drawers, putting it on, and then select a pair of black trousers and a white blouse, which buttons all the way up to the neck. It has long sleeves, too, and I know I'm going to roast, but there's no getting away from it… every time I put on a dress, something bad seems to happen.

I don't care how hot I get, I'm not making that mistake again.

The time is nearly eight o'clock, and ordinarily, I wouldn't need to rush, but it occurs to me that, if Fraser is thinking of accosting me, he'll probably assume I leave home at somewhere around eight-thirty. My best course of action is, therefore, to leave a little early. I make myself a quick cup of coffee and pour a bowl of cereal, although I eat less than half of it. My stomach is churning too much to cope with food.

Once I've cleared away my partially eaten breakfast, I close the windows and pick up my keys, handbag and phone, before making my way to the door. As I reach out to open it, my hand is shaking so badly, I clench it a couple of times.

"You can do this," I say under my breath. The harbour will be busy by now, and even if he is out there, he won't try something in broad daylight. You're safe…

A voice in my head reminds me that I thought I was safe with him last night. It was daylight then, too.

Still, I can't stand around here forever. I open the door, step out, and pull it closed again, locking it, double checking, and putting the keys into the pocket in my handbag. When I get to the top of the stairs, I stop and go back, trying the door, just to make sure it won't open, and then I check my handbag one more time, even though I know perfectly well my keys are there, cursing the fact that I can't relax.

The door is definitely locked, and I've got my keys. I can go. I hesitate for just one more second, and then bolt for the stairs before I can change my mind.

I run down as fast as I can, reaching the bottom, where the hallway seems dark, and I open the front door, the sunlight streaming in and blinding me for a moment. I step out, letting my eyes adjust as I close the door behind me, and then I turn and gasp when I see Robson leaning against the wall opposite.

He smiles, then pushes himself off the wall, coming straight over, although his smile slowly fades as he approaches.

"What are you doing here?" I look up into his weary face.

"I'm walking you to work." He's frowning now, looking down at me. "Don't you think you're going to get a little warm in those clothes? It's already boiling."

I shrug my shoulders, lowering my head slightly so I'm not looking at his face, but at the third button down on his shirt. He's not wearing his tie yet, and the top two buttons are open, revealing short, dark hairs… much darker than the hair on his head. "Maybe. But I only started wearing dresses at the beginning of this week, and look where it got me."

He takes a half step closer, and I look up just in time to see him shaking his head. "I thought we talked about this last night."

"Talked about what?" I don't remember discussing my clothes, other than when he offered to dispose of my dress for me.

"About not being a victim."

"I'm not."

"Really?" He raises his eyebrows, making me wonder what he'd have said if he'd seen me upstairs just now. "I told you, none of this is your fault. If you want to wear a dress, wear a dress. I'm sure you'll find it more comfortable in this heat." I hesitate, hearing his words, but feeling unsure whether I'm brave enough to see them through. He steps even closer, so I can smell his body wash, and he leans down a little and whispers, "You'll be safe, Millie… I promise." My breath catches, and I struggle to unleash it. This has nothing to do with fear, though. Not if the butterflies flitting around my stomach are anything to go by.

"Can you give me five minutes?"

He smiles, then checks his watch. "Take your time. My first patient isn't due for another three quarters of an hour."

I nod my head and turn around, pulling the keys from my bag and opening the front door again, before I dash up the stairs. By the time I reach the top floor, I'm out of breath and too hot for words, but I let myself into my flat, throwing my bag down onto the sofa, and going into the bedroom area, where I find a dress in my small wardrobe. It's a pale blue one that's very similar in style to the ones I wore yesterday and the day before, but this time without the decorative buttons, or the belt. That should make it slightly quicker to change into, and I strip out of my trousers and blouse, leaving them on the bed, and step into the dress, zipping it up. I have to change my shoes as well, from black ones into a pair of nude coloured heels, and then I pick up my bag and head out again.

I go through the same routine of double-checking the door, even after I've locked it, shaking my head at myself as I'm doing it, and then I rush down the stairs, pulling open the front door and blinking against the bright sunlight for the second time this morning.

My heart lurches in my chest when my eyes grow accustomed to the light, and I see there's no sign of Robson. He told me I had time, and I've been as quick as I can, so why would he have left?

I take a step out, feeling nervous... maybe more nervous than before, now I'm in a dress, and I wonder about going back and putting my trousers back on, just as Robson appears from beside me.

"That's better," he says, and I jump, letting out a startled yelp. "Sorry. Did I scare you?"

"Yes. I thought you'd gone."

"Of course not. I just decided to stand on this side of the road. There's a little more shade over here."

I move out onto the pavement and look up at him, my nerves calming as he reaches into the house and pulls the door closed for me.

I push against the lock to double check it, which makes him frown, and then we both turn, stepping off the pavement, and crossing to the other side of the road. He's right, it's hotter over here, but he buries his hands in his pockets and switches positions, walking on the outside, nearest to the kerb.

"How did you sleep?" he asks.

"Surprisingly well."

"So you weren't lying awake half the night, feeling scared?"

I shake my head. "No. Why? Were you?" I answer him in jest, but he doesn't reply and I turn, looking up at the serious expression on his face, stopping in my tracks on the corner of Church Lane. "Robson?" He looks down at me, and I step up to him. "You weren't really lying awake half the night, feeling scared, were you?"

He shrugs his shoulders. "I'm not sure if it was half the night exactly. I don't know when I fell asleep."

Did I hear that right? Can he really care that much? I reach out, my fingertips brushing against the short hairs on his forearm before they clutch around it, and I give him a gentle squeeze. "If I'd been awake half the night, I would have called you. Why didn't you call me?"

He smiles. "I thought about it."

"You did?"

"Yes, but…"

"Oh. I suppose you don't have my number, do you?"

He tilts his head, biting on the corner of his lip. "Yes, I do."

I let go of his arm, stepping back slightly. "How? I haven't given it to you."

"Not as such, but it's on your CV, and as of about ten-thirty last night, when I first thought about calling you, it's also on my phone." He moves closer, filling the gap I just created. "Is that too much? Am I being too intrusive?"

I shake my head. I hadn't expected him to say he'd added me to his contacts list, or gone out of his way to find my number on my CV, which must have been tucked away in his office, but I like the fact that he did. "No. It's not intrusive. It's good to know you can contact me now, if you're struggling to sleep."

He smiles, gazing into my eyes, and I feel a connection between us, like an unbreakable bond. I can't be imagining this, can I? It's as real as the heat on my back and the gentle breeze blowing against my face.

Still… given my track record with men, anything's possible.

Rather than making a fool of myself, I start walking again, and Robson quickly falls into step beside me. We're in Church Lane now and although I'd normally cross over by the Italian restaurant, I don't want to. Robson seems to sense my reluctance, and we stay on this side of the road, until we've passed the garage, only crossing opposite the police station.

"Okay?" he says, looking down at me.

I nod my head, reluctant to focus on last night, or even what just happened. I know I ought to tell him how frightened I just was, merely at the thought of going near the Italian restaurant, and that if I don't, it'll hang over me, but I can't talk about it. Instead, I say the first thing that comes into my head.

"Thank you for making dinner last night."

"That's okay. It was only an omelette."

"It was a very nice omelette. I didn't realise you could cook so well."

"I wouldn't call it cooking well, but I get by."

"Where did you learn?"

Am I fishing? Am I trying to find out about his past? Probably.

Has he noticed? It doesn't seem so. There's a smile on his face that suggests not.

"My mum taught me. Once I'd made it clear I wanted to train to become a doctor, she realised how long I was going to be away from home, and she gave me a crash course in fending for myself. Cooking wasn't the only talent I learned. She had me doing the washing and ironing, as well as some of the cleaning."

"Good for her."

"I'm not sure Dad agreed. He had to live on my cooking for about a month."

"It can't have been that bad."

"I didn't have to take either of them to the hospital with food poisoning, but some of my efforts were definitely better than others."

"Such as?"

"I still have nightmares about my attempt at a beef stroganoff." He shudders and I can't help chuckling, which is a surprise.

"Is there anything you really enjoy cooking?"

"Yes. Curry. I started off fairly tame, but now I like making up my own spice mixes, and experimenting."

"Experimenting?"

He nods his head. "You know? Living a little…"

"With curry?"

"Hmm… don't you like curry, then?"

"I'm not keen on really hot and spicy food, no."

"My curries aren't hot; they're just full of flavour… at least, I think they are. I'll have to make you one, and you can judge for yourself."

"Okay." I like the sound of that, and he smiles.

"What do you like to eat?" he asks, as we turn into Bell Road.

"I'm becoming a fan of Spanish omelettes, actually."

He laughs, and I join in.

When we get to the surgery, Robson lets us in through the front door, pocketing his keys and waiting while I go in ahead of him, then he puts the door on the latch and closes it.

"Do you want to open the window?" he says. "It's really stuffy in here already."

"Okay. And then I'll make us both a coffee, shall I?"

"The coffee can wait. Once you've done the window, come into my office for a minute." I glance up at him and he smiles. "I need to examine your wrists, remember?"

"Oh… yes."

How could I have forgotten?

Because I've been enjoying myself, I suppose… because he made me feel safe enough that I could relax and forget about everything.

He goes into his room, while I wander into mine, and I put my bag down behind my desk, opening the window. The gerberas are running low on water, and I make a mental note to top them up later, before I cross the hall and go into Robson's office.

He's leaning back on his desk, facing me, and he nods towards the chair, which he's moved so it's in front of his desk.

"Take a seat."

I do as he says, and he pushes himself off of the desk, crouching before me, and holds out his hand, waiting for me to put mine in his. When I do, he examines each of my wrists in turn.

"What do you think?" I ask. "I thought they were looking better."

"They are, and ideally, I'd rather we could leave them open, but I'm not sure you'll be able to type with them like this, will you?"

I hold out my hands, mimicking the actions of typing. "No. The desk is going to scrape the edge of the graze."

"I thought so." He stands, turning around, and picks up something from his desk. "I've got some slightly more potent cream, and some breathable dressings. They'll hopefully help you heal more quickly." He applies the cream, peeling the backing off of the dressings, and laying them carefully over the grazes, patting down the edges. "How does that feel?" he asks, examining his work.

"Fine, thank you."

"Good. Now, when you get home this evening, take them off again, so the air can get to the wounds."

"Should I have anything on them in bed?"

"No. I think they'll be fine as they are now, other than when you're working, so I'll dress them again in the morning."

"Are you sure?"

"Absolutely positive."

He gathers up all the rubbish, screwing it into a ball, and throws it into the wastepaper basket, returning the cream to a cabinet behind the door.

"Shall I make the coffee now?" I ask, and he turns, his hands in his pockets, and smiles at me.

"I can do it, if you like." I shake my head, letting out a sigh and he steps closer, raising his right hand and pushing it back through his hair. "Am I being annoyingly over-protective?"

I could hug him, just for asking… but I'm not going to. "Not annoyingly, no."

He smiles. "That's good to know."

For a moment, we just stare at each other. It doesn't feel like either of us is breathing. I'm pretty sure I'm not, and the air around us is so still, I'm certain I'd be able to hear if Robson was. The phone rings, and I startle back to reality.

"I'd better answer that."

He grabs my hand, stopping me from moving. "Let the answerphone pick it up. The surgery doesn't open for another fifteen minutes." I stand, gazing up at him, and he lowers his head, staring down at our hands, which are still joined, before he looks up at me again. "I wanted to say, if you need me today, just come in."

"But what if you have a patient with you?"

He shakes his head. "Let me rephrase that... if you need me today, regardless of what I'm doing, or who I'm with, just come in."

"I—I can't."

"Yes, you can." He moves closer. "I can't dismiss my patients, but I'll come out and talk to you, if that's what you need."

"I'm sure I'll be fine."

"I'm sure you will be, too. You're stronger than you think. But I'm just saying... I'm here."

I don't feel strong right now. I feel like I want to fall into his arms.

I've felt like that for a long time now... ever since I first met him, really. But this is the first time I've been absolutely certain that, if I did, he'd catch me.

Chapter Fourteen

Robson

I fold my hands on the desk, staring at Carter Edwards, while he fixes his eyes on the box of latex gloves on the window sill beyond me. I know that's what he's looking at, because he always does. Wherever I put the box, that's what his light blue eyes always focus on. It's a standard deflection technique employed by people who are avoiding eye contact. They simply choose something else to look at. In Carter's case, he's taken it to the next level, and will only ever look at one thing… but I've grown used to that now. Just like I've grown used to our tense and often one-sided conversations.

He speaks, but only when it suits him… like when he first arrives, and sits down in the chair at the end of my desk. He says, "Hello," and then tells me he wants a repeat prescription for his anti-depressants. After that, we go through the same rigmarole, where I ask if he's considered other kinds of therapy, and he asks me why I won't just give him the prescription he's asking for. He's not unkind about it. He's just dismissive.

"I can arrange for you to see a counsellor," I say, repeating what I said to him last month, and the month before.

"I'd rather just stick with what I know."

Even if it clearly isn't working.

"It'd do you good to talk with someone, rather than relying on medication."

He shakes his dark blond head, although he keeps his eyes fixed on the box of gloves.

"It would also do me good if you'd automate this process, so I didn't have to keep coming in to ask for a prescription, which we both know I need."

That's the longest sentence I think I've ever heard him utter, and I sit forward, letting out a sigh. "If I did that, you'd just order the medication online, pick it up from the pharmacy, and never speak to anyone."

"Precisely."

The stupid part about this is, I know I'll give in to him. I'll give him the prescription he's asking for, because it's the best offer I have. If he won't speak to anyone, there's little else in my arsenal... and he knows that, too.

"Will you at least think about some talking therapy?"

"What's the point? It won't work."

"How do you know? You've never tried it."

He stares at me, taking me by surprise. "How do you know I haven't?"

"Because it's not on your records."

He shakes his head, looking back at the box of gloves. "Private treatments get listed on your GP records, do they?"

"No... not necessarily. Are you saying you've been to see a private therapist?" He sits in silence, his lips pursed, making it clear he won't answer me. "Carter? Have you been to a private psychologist?"

"What does it matter? It didn't work."

"When was this?"

He sighs. "I can't remember." He can. I can see it in his eyes.

"Was it before you came to Porthgarrion?"

"Yes."

"That was a long time ago. Things change. People change. You might find it more useful now. I could find you someone to —"

"I'd rather just have my tablets, if it's all the same to you."

I shake my head and pull forward my keyboard, typing out the prescription, and printing it. There's no point in arguing any further. We both know that. He reaches out his tanned hand and takes the slip of paper from me, getting to his feet at the same time.

"Thank you, Doctor."

"If you change your mind, you know where I am."

He doesn't answer, and makes his way to the door. I know he'll be in a hurry to get back to the café. It's lunchtime, and he's taken time off to come here… but it's more than that. He wants to get away from me, just in case I find a chink in his armour.

I click into his record, scrolling back up through his history. Carter moved here roughly six years ago, before I even took over the practice, but there's a note that he was already taking Citalopram at the time. The records from his former GP mention a road traffic accident about a year before that, although I can't find anything that mentions him being treated for any serious injuries. Other than that, I can see no obvious reason for him being prescribed anti-depressants, and there isn't enough information on file for me to work it out. Ordinarily, I'd ask the patient, but Carter isn't talking… to anyone, it seems.

It's frustrating that I haven't been able to do more, and to an extent I feel as though I've failed him… yet again. But there's nothing I can do if he won't take my advice. All I can do is keep an eye on him. Which is why I won't automate his prescriptions.

At least this way, he has to come and see me once a month, so I can monitor how he is.

Fortunately, Carter is my last patient of the morning, and I've never been so pleased to get to the end of a surgery… not because it's been especially difficult, or even because I'm tired, after a fairly sleepless night. It's because I've been so distracted by thoughts of Millie all morning, I've struggled to concentrate.

Things definitely changed between us this morning.

I'm sure they did.

Was that because I let my guard down and admitted I was scared for her?

I don't know.

I only said that because I thought she might have been putting a brave face on things herself – or trying to – and I wanted her to know that fear is a perfectly natural reaction in her situation.

I think she understood. She put her hand on my arm, and there was a moment right about then, when we just stared at each other. I've never done that before… not with anyone. I've never just gazed into someone's eyes and completely lost myself. But I did then. And I think Millie did too.

I hope she did.

That might explain why she didn't get angry with me when I became over-protective. Not annoyingly over-protective, you understand. Just over-protective.

I think she'd realised by then how much I care for her.

Although that could just be wishful thinking on my part.

Mis-reading her reactions, or over-interpreting them, seems to be something I'm excelling at. I suppose I always was. The difference now is that my confusion is a much more pleasant experience. Don't get me wrong, I still feel as though I've got no idea what's going on between us… but at least I know now that something is. I don't claim to understand what that 'something' means. All I know is, she used to look away, and now she holds my gaze. She used to blush, and although she still does, it's now accompanied by a smile... or even a giggle. My mind is in a whirl, but I'm going along with the ride, hoping it leads to somewhere better... for both of us.

There's an element of uncertainty, which is worrying, but I'm trying to ignore that, to take each moment as it comes, and keep my eyes on the prize...

Millie.

I've still got one more task before I can break for lunch. I need to find time in my afternoon schedule to visit Rachel.

I pull up my appointments application, and look through it, finding a free slot at three-fifteen. Perfect. My next appointment after that isn't until four, so I'll have plenty of time to get to Rachel's, take her blood pressure, make sure she's okay and still resting, and get back here. I book her in, saving the appointment, and pick up my phone from my desk, flipping it around and going to my messages app.

Jack is in my contacts list and I type out a quick message to him.

— *Hi. Sorry to mess you around. Something's come up at work, and I won't be able to make it down there at lunchtime. I can fit in a visit at 3.15 this afternoon, though. Is that okay? Rob.*

He replies immediately, with a thumbs up, and I pocket my phone, going across the hall and into the reception, locking the front door en route. I know Millie will still be here, because she'd have told me if she was leaving, and sure enough, I find her sitting at her desk, gazing out of the window, with a worried expression on her face.

"Is something wrong?" She looks up, startled, and I feel guilty for not finding a more subtle way of announcing my presence. "Sorry. I didn't mean to frighten you."

She shakes her head. "You didn't." *Much.* "I was just thinking about going out to get some lunch." And feeling terrified by the prospect, I'd have said.

"I can come with you, if you want."

"I couldn't ask you to do that. You must have so many other things to do."

"Not at all." *I've cancelled the only thing that would have prevented me from spending the next hour with you.* "But if you'd prefer, we could stay here. I could make us some lunch… assuming you're brave enough to take a chance on my ham sandwiches?"

She smiles, with not a trace of a blush in sight. "Are they as good as your Spanish omelettes?"

I tip my head to my right and then my left. "That all depends on the bread, to be honest."

Her smile widens, and she nods her head. "I'll take the risk."

I move towards the back of the room. "Come on then. You can make the tea."

She gets up and follows me.

"I noticed you'd made an appointment to see Rachel Pedrick this afternoon," she says and I turn, walking backwards.

"Yes. I need to check her blood pressure."

"Isn't a house call like that something you'd normally squeeze into your lunch break?"

"It is." I get to the door and open it, waiting for her to pass through ahead of me. "But I'm busy today." Now she blushes, but rather than looking away, she gazes up at me, and I close the door again, smiling down at her, and then lead her down the hall into the living room.

"Goodness… this is lovely," she says from behind me and I turn, noting her wide eyes and slightly open lips.

"What did you expect? A dingy little back room with three weeks' worth of washing up piled in the sink and wallpaper peeling off the walls?"

She chuckles. "No. But I didn't expect this, either."

I have to admit, this space is a little out of keeping with the front of the house, and it's a lot more than a living room. I just call it that because it's where I live.

"Whoever converted the front of the house into a surgery – which I hasten to add was something that happened before I was even born – kept this as their living space."

"Like this?"

"No. When I moved in, it was divided into a kitchen and a separate living room. I had the wall knocked down to make one big space, and added the french doors. It would have been nice to have bi-folding doors all the way across the back, but to be honest, I couldn't afford them. I had some work done upstairs, too… and there were limits."

She shakes her head. "I think you made the right decision. This way, you get to throw the doors open in the summer, but in the winter, it's probably a lot more cosy than if you had a wall made of glass."

"Yes, it is. Especially when the fire's blazing."

She glances over at the log fire, which is currently lying empty, a few pillar candles sitting in front of it, just for decoration. "I can imagine."

"And speaking of throwing the doors open…" I grab the keys from the draining board where Tom left them last night, and open the doors, pushing them outwards and letting in the breeze. "That's better."

"Hmm… it is."

I'm so pleased she likes it in here, I can't stop smiling as I open the fridge, pulling out the ham and some tomatoes and mayonnaise. "Do you want to fill the kettle?" I say and she nods her head, doing as I've suggested.

"You have some lovely paintings," she says, putting the kettle back on its stand and switching it on. "I noticed the one in the hallway, but you've got some more in here, too. They look as though they're all painted by the same person."

"That's because they are. Rachel painted them."

"They're very good." She turns around, admiring the two on the far wall, both of the same seascape, at different times of day. One is a sunset, while the other is at dawn, and although the colourings are similar, there are marked differences in the cloud structure, the way she's captured the light, the overall ambience.

"She's very talented."

Millie nods her head, looking back at me, biting on her bottom lip. "Will you be out for very long this afternoon?" Her voice has dropped to a whisper and I take a step forward, so I'm standing right in front of her.

"About half an hour, I should think. But I was going to suggest that you lock the front door while I'm gone. You'll be alone in here, and I think I'll feel a lot happier if I know that anyone who wants to get in has got to knock on the door first."

She lets out a breath, like she's been holding it in for far too long, staring up into my eyes, the moment captivating both of us, until she swallows and nods her head. "O—Okay."

I can still hear a trace of doubt in her voice, and I edge just slightly closer to her. "You'll be safe here, Millie. But if you're scared at all, or if anything happens that worries you, just call me, and I'll come straight back. I can leave you with Tom's number, too, if you like. That way, you can call him as well, if you're really worried."

She shakes her head. "No. I'd rather just call you, if that's okay."

"Of course it is." It's better than okay. "To be honest, I'd probably get here quicker."

"Because you're fitter?" she says, her lips twitching up just slightly.

"No."

"Oh… because Rachel's house is closer than the police station?"

"No. It's further away." Although not by very much.

I say no more, hoping she'll understand that there's nothing on earth that would keep me from getting to her, if she needed me.

The ham and tomato sandwiches were the best I've ever made… or maybe it was the company that made them taste so good. We ate them on the patio, enjoying the shade, along with a very nice cup of tea that Millie had made.

She spent most of the time admiring my garden, which I've never thought of as being much to write home about, and once we were finished, I loaded our cups and plates into the dishwasher and tidied up, before we headed back into the surgery.

My first appointment of the afternoon isn't until two-fifteen, and I'm tempted to spend the intervening forty-five minutes with Millie, except I'm not sure what excuse I could find. There's always the decorating… but that seems a little irrelevant now, and I wait for her to sit at her desk before wandering back into the hall and putting the door on the latch. I've just crossed the threshold into the surgery when the front door opens behind me and I flip around, coming face to face with Tom Hughes.

"Hello." I step back a little further to let him come into my room.

"Good afternoon." He smiles. "I hope you don't mind me just dropping in like this."

"No. It's fine. I'm not seeing anyone until quarter past two."

He looks at his watch and says, "Good. That's plenty of time." He glances over his shoulder. "I've got some news for Millie, but I think it might be best if you were present when I talk to her."

I'm not sure whether that's good or bad, and it's pointless wasting time asking him, so I just nod my head and step around him, going back into the reception, where Millie is typing on her computer.

"Can you come into my office?" She looks up, a frown crossing her face. "Tom's just arrived, and he'd like to speak to you. He's asked if I'll sit in. Is that okay?"

Her face pales, and she gets to her feet. "Yes… of course."

I wait, letting her walk ahead of me into my office, noting that her hair is tied in a more straightforward plait than usual. I don't know why I haven't noticed it before, but I can't blame her for keeping it simple. She probably has too much on her mind to think about how she styles her hair… and in any case, it still looks lovely.

As she gets into my room, she stops, although I'm not sure whether that's because she's uncertain what to do, or whether she's just intimidated by the presence of a six foot five policeman, in full uniform. Fortunately, she's gone far enough that I can get around her without having to touch her, or make a big deal out of her reaction to Tom, and I walk across to the chair at the end of my desk.

"Why don't you sit here, Millie?"

She comes over, like she's on automatic pilot, and sits down, her hands shaking, as she folds them in her lap. I glance up at Tom, and although it takes a moment for me to catch his eye, he quickly understands the nod I give him towards the other chair, which is against the wall, and he pulls it forward, sitting down at a reasonable distance from Millie, without making it too obvious.

I walk around my desk, and take a seat in my chair, although I pull it a little closer to Millie's and turn to face Tom, who focuses on Millie, even though she's staring into space.

"I've been to see Fraser Johnson," he says and Millie's head darts up, a frown settling on her brow, before she turns to me.

"I thought I told you…"

I hold up my hand and she stops talking, although two dots of pink have appeared on her pale cheeks, and I can see the anger in her eyes.

"I know. I asked Tom to get involved… but like I explained to you last night, there are levels of involvement."

She stares for a moment longer, the frown slowly dissipating, and then she nods her head, like she's remembering our conversation. "Yes… and I said I'd leave it with you."

"Exactly. I couldn't just sit back and do nothing… not after what he'd done to you."

Her face softens completely, and she sucks in a breath, letting it out slowly. She doesn't say a word, though, and just turns back to Tom, tilting her head and silently giving him permission to continue.

He clears his throat. "Mr Johnson is denying any wrongdoing… which I think we could all have predicted. He claims you suggested going down the alleyway to get some privacy, but you changed your mind when the chef came out."

Millie shakes her head, then lowers it, although she remains silent.

"So, he's saying it was consensual?" I ask, and Tom nods his head. "Were you able to do anything at all?"

"I can't force him to leave the village, unfortunately, but I made it very clear that I didn't believe a word he was saying, and that if he comes anywhere near Millie again, I'll find an excuse to arrest him, even if I have to invent the charges." Millie looks up at him again, and he turns his smile on her. "It's not official involvement, because you didn't want that, so I've not taken any statements from him. I've just let it be known that I'm watching. In the circumstances, it's the best I can do."

"Do you think he'll take you seriously?" I ask, and Tom turns to me, his frown fading.

"I was at my most intimidating… without actually threatening the man."

"Hmm… it's a shame you couldn't have threatened him, given his track record with women."

Tom sits forward, right on the edge of his seat, only just stopping himself from standing. "Track record? What are you talking about?"

"Just that he's had a lot of girlfriends since he's been here… which, as far as I'm aware, is only a matter of weeks."

"And how do you know this?" He narrows his eyes.

"Because Dan Moyle told me yesterday."

"And you didn't think to mention this last night?"

I can feel myself blush, wondering at my own stupidity now it's been laid before me. "No. Sorry. I was distracted."

Tom shakes his head, his anger abating. "Do we know who any of these women are?"

"No. But I think Dan might."

"Okay. I'll speak to him, just in case there's more to this than the assault on Millie."

He stands and I do the same, getting to Millie's side before he's completely upright. I know she feels a little insecure around him, even though she has no need. Or maybe it's just that he reminds her of last night. Either way, I want her to feel safe, and I stay beside her until Tom's let himself out.

Once the door has closed, I move around in front of her, crouching down.

"Are you angry with me?"

She looks up, unclenching her hands at last. "About speaking to Tom, you mean?"

"Yes."

She shakes her head. "No. I am intrigued, though."

"About why I went to see him?"

"No, about why you were discussing Fraser and his former girlfriends with Dan Moyle."

"He works with Fraser. He knows him… at least better than I do."

"I know that, but I don't understand why you were talking to him about it… or when, for that matter."

"It was yesterday, when I was helping him after he fell and hurt his wrist… and as for the why, I suppose I could claim a sixth sense, except I'm not that intuitive."

"So, you just asked out of curiosity?"

"Something like that." Jealousy would be closer to the mark, but it doesn't feel like the right time to admit to that.

"And he's had a lot of girlfriends since he's been here, has he?"

"According to Dan, yes. I—I would have told you about it, but I wasn't sure how serious things were between you and Fraser, and I didn't want to interfere."

She shakes her head. "It's fine," she mumbles and gets up, forcing me to my feet to give her space.

I grab her hand, and although she doesn't pull back, I can feel how stiff she is. "Millie?" She looks up at me, her eyes glistening and filled with sadness. "If I got it wrong, I'm sorry."

"What do you mean, 'got it wrong'?"

"If you'd rather I'd told you what Dan said…"

"No. Like you said, you weren't to know what was going on."

"Even so, I wish I'd warned you… not that I'm sure what I'd have been warning you about."

She turns around, facing me, and puts her other hand on my arm. "If I'm not allowed to blame myself for what happened, or be a victim in all of this, you're certainly not."

She lets me go with a half-hearted smile, and I release her hand, watching as she walks out of my office. I feel empty without her, and even though she says she doesn't blame me, I feel like I've let her down.

By the time it gets to three o'clock, my appointments are running just a little late, although Imelda Duffy doesn't seem to mind and breezes into my office, like she hasn't a care in the world. As usual, she's wearing a long, flowing dress, and her light brown hair is arranged precariously on top of her head. Because I have access to her medical records, I know for a fact that she's just slightly the wrong side of fifty, but she has the air of someone much younger.

"Hello, Doctor," she says, sitting down. "I haven't been to see you since before Cora left."

"Haven't you?"

"No, and I have to say, your new receptionist is a significant improvement." I'm not about to disagree with her, and I smile. "Cora always struck me as the most unsympathetic of women," she says, which makes me smile even more, although I don't comment. It would be undiplomatic.

"How can I help, Miss Duffy?"

"You can call me Imelda. 'Miss Duffy' makes me sound like a schoolmistress."

I chuckle and nod my head. "Okay. How can I help, Imelda?"

She sits forward on the seat. "It's my ankle."

"The one you broke?"

"Yes."

This happened over a year ago now, and although Imelda required little help from me, most of her care having been undertaken by the hospital, I was aware of what was going on.

"What seems to be the problem with it?"

She raises her skirt, which is almost touching the floor, and I notice she's only wearing flimsy slip-on shoes, and that her ankle seems a little puffy. "As you can see, it swells up over the course of the day, and it gets quite stiff, too."

"The stiffness will be because of the swelling, I imagine." I kneel before her, looking up at her face. "May I?"

"Of course."

I slip off her shoe and hold up her foot, manipulating her ankle. It moves freely enough and my actions don't seem to cause her any pain.

Slipping her shoe back on, I sit up again and lean over. "It's difficult to say precisely what's wrong, but I'd like you to try two things before we do anything drastic, like referring you to the hospital."

She nods her head. "Okay."

"First, I want you to wear more supportive shoes… ones with a back and a low heel."

"That sounds very old-fashioned. What else?"

"I appreciate you spend a lot of the day on your feet, but you're stationary for most of the time, and I'd like you to move your ankle around a little more."

"You want me to walk about while I'm arranging flowers, do you?"

"No. But you could make time in your day for some kind of gentle exercise, like swimming, or cycling."

"Cycling?" She sounds incredulous. "At my age?"

"Why not? You're still young."

"Flattery will get you nowhere, young man."

"I'm not flattering you. I'm telling you the truth. A little light exercise on that ankle will do it the world of good. Try it for a month, and come back to me if there's no improvement."

She looks at me, like I've taken leave of my senses. "Cycling indeed," she mutters under her breath, getting to her feet.

"It doesn't have to be cycling," I say as she turns to go. "I just don't want you to take up anything high impact… like jogging."

"That's even more ridiculous than the thought of me cycling."

She looks over her shoulder at me with a twinkle in her eye and I grin back, waving her away.

Once she's gone, I check the time, sighing when I see it's already gone quarter past three. I'm running late, which means I won't have time to speak to Millie before I go. I was hoping to have the chance to apologise to her again for not revealing Fraser's past. She might have said I shouldn't blame myself, but I do, and it's bothering me.

Still… there's nothing I can do about it right at this minute. I've got to get to Rachel's and be back here for my four o'clock appointment.

I grab my bag, checking I've got everything I need, and then go across the hall and into the reception.

"I'll be off, then."

Millie looks up, that worried expression back on her face, and I wish I could take her with me… except I can't. Someone needs to be here in case the phone rings, at the very least.

"Okay," she says, in a quiet whisper.

"I won't be very long. Once I've gone, make sure you lock the front door."

She nods her head and, aware of the time, I turn and open it, waiting for her to join me before I pass through. I let her push it closed and wait until I hear the latch click before heading down the path and through the gate.

I hurry along to Rachel and Jack's keeping my head down to avoid being stopped by anyone I know… which is practically the entire village, and once I'm outside their house, I knock on the door, waiting just a few seconds for Jack to answer it.

"Are you okay?" he says, frowning at me.

"I'm fine."

He stands back, letting me enter, and I pass through into their living room, where I see Rachel lying out on the sofa. She's wearing a floral dress, her hair tied back in a ponytail, and the moment she sees me, she sits up, her feet flat on the floor, her head tilted to one side.

"Rob?" she says, her brow furrowing. "What's wrong?"

"Nothing's wrong."

"You can't pull the wool over my eyes. Something's happened."

I hate the fact that she can see through me so easily... and that Jack can, too... or so it seems.

"It's nothing I can tell you about."

She sits forward a little, the bump getting in the way. "Is everything okay?"

"No. Something happened to Millie." Rachel pats the seat beside her and I walk across, sitting and putting my bag down next to me. "I can't tell you about it, Rachel, so don't ask."

"I wasn't going to. Just tell me, is she all right?"

"No."

She takes a breath and puts her hand out, resting it on my knee. "Are you, Rob?"

"No."

"Is there anything we can do?"

I shake my head, swallowing down the lump that's suddenly formed in my throat. "No, thanks. I—I can't leave her alone for too long, though."

"You shouldn't have come at all."

"I'm going to pretend I didn't hear that."

"Do you need me to repeat it, then?"

"No. I need you to reassure me you're getting plenty of rest."

"Didn't I look like I was resting when you came in?"

"Yes, but you knew what time I was coming down here. For all I know, you could have been decorating the nursery until ten minutes ago."

"She wasn't," Jack says. "I've been keeping a close eye on her, and the nursery was finished ages ago."

I look up at him, nodding my head. "Did Sue make it in yesterday?"

"Yes." He smiles. "Thanks for arranging that. She couldn't get over here until about half-past six, but at least we could hear the baby's heartbeat, which put our minds at rest."

"That's good."

"It was lovely," Rachel says. "Now, take my blood pressure and get out of here."

"There's gratitude for you."

I nudge my shoulder against hers and she nudges me right back before I lean over and get the blood pressure monitor from my bag, wrapping the cuff around her upper arm. The wait seems to take even longer than usual, but the result is exactly the same as yesterday's.

"More rest?" she says, rolling her eyes.

"Yes." I pack away the monitor, standing up as I close my bag. "Go on then, put your feet up."

Rachel glares at me. "Has anyone ever told you what a bossy-boots you are?"

"Frequently. The problem is, I don't care."

"Well, I do," Jack says, and comes over, lifting her feet and putting them on the sofa, which forces her to fall backwards into its cushions.

"I guess I know what I'll be doing for the rest of the afternoon." Rachel sounds resigned, looking up at me and Jack, both of us nodding our heads, which makes her laugh. She gets herself comfortable, with a little help from Jack, who then steps back to let me pass, on my way to the front door.

He follows, and I turn to him as I'm about to step outside.

"If anything changes, or you're worried, just call me."

"It sounds like you have enough on your plate already."

I shake my head. "I still want you to call if you need me."

I step outside, but feel his hand on my shoulder. "Are you sure there's nothing we can do?"

"No… but thanks for the offer."

He nods his head, and I smile, setting off down the road. I wish I could have told them. I hate keeping things from Rachel. But Millie's story isn't mine to tell, and although I'm grateful for their offers of help, I think this is something we're going to have to work out by ourselves. I'm just grateful she's letting me help her… because the idea of her trying to deal with this by herself isn't something I'm willing to contemplate.

The harbour seems busier than it was earlier, and I dodge between the holidaymakers, taking a few minutes to get back to the surgery, where I let myself in, finding Millie sitting at her desk.

"Are you okay?" I ask, putting the door on the latch again, and closing it.

She nods her head, smiling. "I am now."

God, that sounded good, and I don't think even I can have misunderstood what she meant.

By the end of the day, I still haven't heard from Tom about his visit to Dan, but to be fair, I can't be sure he was going straight there after he left us earlier this afternoon. This isn't even official police business, so something else could easily have taken priority.

When the last patient has gone, I power down my computer and quickly tidy my desk, closing my window and checking I've left everything ready for the morning, before going across the hall to the reception.

Millie's just picking up her handbag, and I stand in the doorway and clear my throat to let her know I'm here, rather than scaring her by speaking.

She looks up, giving me a smile.

"Are you ready?"

Her smile fades. "What for?"

"For me to walk you home."

"You don't have to do that."

"Yes, I do." I tilt my head towards the front door. "Come on."

Her smile returns and she rounds the desk, joining me by the door, which I open, letting her leave before me. I pat my pocket to check I've got my keys and then take the door off the latch and pull it closed.

The heat seems slightly less oppressive, mainly thanks to a stiff breeze coming in off the sea. It catches the loose strands of Millie's hair, blowing them across her face, and I have to put my hands in my pockets to resist the temptation to brush them away… and maybe to let my fingers linger over her soft cheeks.

"What made you decide to become a doctor?" she asks as we get to the bottom of Bell Road. It feels like a slightly forced question, but I realise it would have been here that Fraser jumped out on her last night, and she's probably trying to distract herself. There's a part of me that would rather help her confront that, but now probably isn't the best time.

"I wanted to help people… pure and simple."

"There are other ways of doing that."

"I know. I could have followed in my father's footsteps and become a police officer."

She looks up at me, brushing some of those hairs away from her face herself. "Why didn't you?"

"Because medicine has always fascinated me."

"You never find it awkward, having to treat people you know so well?"

I take a breath before I answer. "I don't treat anyone who really matters to me." Will she pick up on that, bearing in mind I told her last night that she shouldn't register with me? I keep watching her as we walk slowly on, but she doesn't seem to have seen anything significant in what I've said.

"Why is that?" she asks, and I feel a little disappointed that she missed the point.

"Aside from the fact that it's frowned upon, I can't imagine how terrible it would be if I had to deliver terrible news to someone like my mum or dad."

"Would it be any easier with someone like Rachel? She seems to matter to you."

"She does. She's a friend… a very good friend. But she's nothing more than that." I want to reassure her, in case she's wondering. Part of me hopes she is, but again, I'm wary of misreading things.

"Have you known her for very long?"

"Yes. We were at school together."

"But you've never felt the need to ask her to register anywhere else?"

She's fishing now. I know she is. "No. Never."

She nods her head, and I clench my fists in my pockets, just so I don't give in to temptation and take one out so I can hold her hand.

A lot of the shops are already closed, but when we get to the florist's, I'm surprised to find the door is wide open. There's a car parked outside, with a bicycle mounted on the back, and as we pass, Imelda comes out of the shop, accompanied by a man who I recognise as Laura Quick's father. Having only seen him at events such as weddings, when he's been wearing a suit, it makes a change to see him less formally attired in a pair of casual cotton shorts and a polo shirt. He's tall, but not as tall as me, and has the athletic build of someone who's taken care of himself over the years.

He goes to the car, but Imelda stops and looks up at me.

"Not a word, young man."

I turn, as does Millie. "About what?"

"This." She nods towards the bicycle that Laura's father is currently removing from the rear of his car.

"You mean, this is yours?"

"Yes."

I have to smile. "But you only came to see me this afternoon, Imelda, and I seem to recall you said cycling was a ridiculous idea."

"Yes… well… that was before I remembered Grayson likes to cycle. I called him on my way back here, and he said he'd help me choose a bicycle, and that we could go riding together."

Grayson puts the bike down on the pavement and Imelda holds it upright while he looks up at me. "It seemed best to strike while the iron was hot, before she changed her mind again."

"Honestly, to listen to you two, anyone would think I was fickle." Imelda glares at him and then me.

I take my hands from my pockets, holding them up in surrender. "I'm not getting involved in this. But I'm glad you're going to be exercising that ankle."

"I'll make sure she does," Grayson says. "I can easily strap my bike to the back of the car and drive over here, and then we can go out together." He looks down at her. "We can even take a picnic, if you like."

"That sounds lovely." She looks up at him, with a dreamy expression on her face, and I can't help grinning as Millie and I continue on our way.

We've gone a few paces when she glances up at me. "Are they a couple?"

"Not that I'm aware of, but it wouldn't surprise me. They certainly seem quite attached, don't they?"

She nods her head, smiling, and we move along the harbour, turning right into Church Lane. Millie's smile fades almost instantly and I feel her tense beside me. She reacted in the same way this morning, when we were about to cross the road by the Italian restaurant, and I walked her further down, crossing nearer to the police station instead. I know I could do the same thing again, and cross over here, but she needs to face this, or the fear is just going to build inside her.

She holds back, but I take her hand.

"Come on. You'll be fine." I feel her tug against me, and I turn slightly, holding her hand a little tighter. "You'll be safe, Millie. I promise. I won't let anything happen to you."

She gazes up at me and then nods her head, letting me lead her further up the road until we're right outside the restaurant. I can feel the tension pouring off of her, but I don't let her dwell and instead, I check for traffic and quickly guide her across the road to the other side.

Once we're firmly on the pavement again, she visibly relaxes, and she looks up at me. There are tears in her eyes and I stop walking.

"Are you okay?"

She nods. "Yes. Thank you."

"What are you thanking me for?"

"For making me do that. I couldn't face it this morning, and to be honest, if you hadn't been with me, I don't think I could have faced it now."

I start walking again, and she falls into step beside me. She hasn't pulled her hand from mine and there's no way I'm letting go of her, so we walk further up the road, hand-in-hand, turning into Chapel Mews.

We get to her front door far too quickly, and unfortunately, she lets go of my hand to retrieve her keys from her handbag, putting them into the lock and turning them.

"I'll see you up," I say, before she can get a word out.

"You don't have to."

"This is a door-to-door service."

She giggles and lets us both inside. It feels a little airless, although I'm not sure that's entirely because of the weather, and I follow her up the stairs, all the way to the top of the house, where she pauses outside her door. I wait, letting her open it, and then as she looks up at me, I know I have to say something. I can't go home feeling like this.

"I'm sorry, Millie."

She frowns. "What for?"

"For not telling you about Fraser's background. I feel that if I'd spoken out sooner, none of this would have happened."

She shakes her head, stepping a little closer to me and looking up into my eyes. "I thought we covered this already. You're not allowed to blame yourself."

"Maybe not. But I still do. I feel like I let you down."

"You didn't. It's not your fault." She lowers her head as she's speaking, her voice fading.

"It's not your fault either, Millie."

She looks up again. "You don't believe him, then?"

"Believe him? You think I'd believe someone like that, over you? Of course I don't believe him. I know you've told me the truth, and I trust you completely... in everything you say and do."

Could I make it more plain than that?

She blinks a couple of times. "Thank you."

"Has that been worrying you? That I'd believe Fraser's version of events?"

"Yes." She nods her head, and it takes every ounce of willpower I possess not to pull her into my arms.

"Then don't let it bother you any more. I know you didn't ask him to take you down that alleyway, just like I know you didn't lead Damian into doing what he did."

"Even though I admitted to wanting him?"

"Yes. Wanting someone doesn't give them the right to take something that isn't on offer." She sighs and I step closer, so we're almost touching… almost, but not quite. "You're not to blame for anything that's happened. Okay?"

"Neither are you. You did nothing wrong by not telling me about Fraser's past." She steps back slightly and holds out her hand, offering it to me. I take it and she shakes mine. "Deal?"

"Deal."

"Thank you for walking me home, Robson."

"You can call me Rob, you know? Quite a lot of people do."

She smiles, taking her hand from mine. "Okay."

I step away, letting her go into her flat. "And remember to phone if you can't sleep."

"You too."

I smile at her and wait until she's closed the door before floating down the stairs.

Chapter Fifteen

Millie

I think I slept even better last night.

In a way, though, I wish I hadn't. I wish I'd had an excuse to call Robson... or Rob, as he told me to call him. It would have been nice to hear his voice.

I guess I slept so soundly because of him, though... or at least because of the conversation we had at my door last night. That did a lot to allay my fears about what he might think of me after Tom's revelations at the surgery. Of course, Tom's reassurances probably helped too, in a way. While I hated the thought that Fraser was trying to claim that what he did was consensual, at least Tom had warned him off. There was something vaguely satisfying about that.

I get up, wandering straight into the shower, and as I turn on the water, I think back over that conversation with Rob, and how keen he was to reassure me he believed in me. That was comforting, although I still didn't understand why he'd been asking about Fraser's background in the first place. 'Curiosity' is hardly a reason for prying into the private life of someone you don't even know, although I accepted his explanation at the time because he'd almost immediately started apologising for not telling me. He said he hadn't wanted to interfere, which suggested he believed me to be serious about my supposed relationship with Fraser… and that's my fault. I should have been honest with Rob when he asked me about Fraser in the first place.

If anyone's to blame for what happened and for all the misunderstandings, it's me.

I should have just told him how I feel about him.

Of course, at the time, I believed him to be disinterested… to put it mildly. I think it would be fairer to say, I didn't think he realised I existed.

That's all changed now, though.

Now, he couldn't be any more attentive.

Not that it helps.

I still don't know how to tell him I'm in love with him.

Although I came close to blurting it out several times yesterday, most notably when he came back from visiting Rachel. Being on my own at the surgery was so much harder than I'd expected. I've done it before, several times, but yesterday was different. I watched the seconds tick by on the clock, wishing Rob would come back. Every sound made me jump, although the silence was so deafening, and by the time I heard his key in the lock, I was a nervous wreck.

The first thing he did was to ask if I was okay, and I was so relieved to see him, and to feel safe again, I just said, "I am now," because it was the truth. I wanted to ask him to stay with me, so I could tell him how much I'd missed him, and why, but he was running late and had to get ready for his next patient.

That was the story of the rest of his afternoon, but when he offered to walk me home, I was so relieved. I might have said he didn't have to, but I was only being polite. I didn't just want his company, or his protection, I wanted to spend some more time with him… just the two of us.

What I hadn't expected – although I ought to have done – was that when we got to Church Lane, I'd be overwhelmed with fear. It was so much worse than this morning; I suppose because the journey was the same as it had been last night… even though the company was so different. I half expected Rob to cross the road further down, like we did on the way to work, but he took my hand and led me up the hill, making me cross at the place where I usually would… at the place where I'd been going to cross last night, when Fraser dragged me into that alley.

I was terrified. My legs were like jelly, and my heart was beating so hard and so fast, I was struggling to put one foot in front of the other. Rob was a tower of strength though, and he made me go through with it… made me face my fears, so they couldn't fester and grow out of proportion. I'm not unrealistic enough to think 'that's it' now… that I'm cured of my fear of that place. But I've done it once. Hopefully, doing it the next time won't be quite so hard.

Thanks to Robson.

I get out of the shower, drying off, and try to think of something other than yesterday, my fears, and my unanswered question. My brain lands on the day ahead, and the new patient Robson has coming to see him first thing this morning.

He came to register yesterday afternoon, while Rob was busy with other patients, and after he'd filled in all the necessary paperwork, he asked if he could make an appointment straight away. I told him it would take a while to get his records from his previous GP, but he seemed insistent, so I made the appointment anyway, hoping for the best. The problem is, with everything else that was going on yesterday, I forgot to check with Robson whether I'd done the right thing, and now the man is due in at nine, and it's too late to change his appointment.

I could kick myself for being so pre-occupied, but I'll have to mention it to Robson as soon as I get to work, and hope he's not too angry with me.

I wander back into the living area, and over to the bed, finding a yellow dress, which I pull on over my underwear, and then I assess myself in the mirror. I feel like I could try styling my hair a little more thoroughly today and I take my accessories bag from the hook on the side of the chest of drawers, delving into it to find some ribbons. There's a nice bright yellow one, and a white one, which will go well with my dress, and setting them down, I brush through my hair. Then I comb it out, parting it on the left, and I take a large section from the front, pulling it over, while I separate off two smaller pieces, tying a ribbon on to each, as close to the root as I can get it. Once they're secure, I take the larger section and braid it. As I work my way down, I incorporate the strands that have the ribbons tied on, including the ribbons with them. It's a little fiddly, because there are so many strands to control, and it's important to ensure that the ribbons are always on top, and not buried beneath the plait. Sometimes, when I'm doing this, I feel like an extra pair of hands would be useful, but eventually, I reach the end, grateful that I'm doing it at the side of my head and not the back, so at least I can see what I'm doing, and correct the occasional twist in the ribbon. I use an elastic to tie it off, and then cover that with another ribbon, in a slightly paler yellow.

That just leaves breakfast, but as I go over to the kitchen, my stomach churns. The thought of food makes me feel sick, and rather than pouring out cereal that I'll only waste, I just make myself a coffee, sitting down on the sofa to drink it. I know I ought to eat something. After all, I may have got all the ingredients out of my fridge to make a salad last night, but I didn't actually do anything with them, and after staring at everything for about ten minutes, I put it all away and went to bed. I guess that makes it a good thing that Robson fed me yesterday lunchtime… otherwise, I'd be wasting away.

Once I've finished my coffee, I put the cup into the sink, unplug my phone from its charger, and put it in my bag, then head out of the door. After I've locked it, I double check, and then put the keys away, rushing down the stairs before I can be tempted to check the door for a third time. At the bottom, I take a deep breath, and open the front door, squinting against the sunshine, and then smiling when I see Robson exactly where he was yesterday morning, leaning against the wall opposite.

He comes over, his eyes fixed on mine, my body heating with every step he takes.

"You're here again," I say, and he grins.

"Yes. Although I decided against hiding behind your door this morning, just in case I scared you."

"Thank you."

"And, just so you know, I'll be here every day for as long as you need me."

So, that'll be forever, then.

I can't tell him that, but I look up at him and smile, hoping he might get the message, regardless of my silence.

He turns and I pull the door closed, taking my place beside him as we start our walk to work.

"Can I take you slept okay?" I ask. "Only I didn't hear from you, so…"

He smiles, looking down at me. "I slept very well, thank you."

"Good. Me too."

"I guessed as much, because I didn't hear from you, either."

I suddenly remember my thoughts from earlier… not the ones about yesterday and how kind he was, but about his first patient of the day, and I know I have to tell him… sooner rather than later.

"I've got a confession."

"What's that? You're not going to tell me you've been lying awake all night, and you didn't call?"

"No. I honestly slept really well. But I remembered this morning that I made an appointment for you this morning with a new patient. He's coming in at nine, but he only registered yesterday afternoon."

"So, I won't have his records," he says, understanding the problem straight away.

"No. I'm sorry."

"Don't worry about it. This kind of thing happens all the time."

He seems very relaxed, although I'm sure I've made his life more complicated than it needs to be, and I'm about to make sure he's okay with what I've done when we turn the corner into Church Lane and I feel myself panicking. I can see the Italian restaurant from here, and despite my earlier bravado, the thought of going anywhere near the place is still terrifying.

I feel Robson's hand slide into mine and when I look up, he's gazing down at me.

"Remember? I won't let anything happen to you. You're safe, Millie. Just trust me."

"I do."

He nods his head and, checking for cars, he leads me across the road and straight down the hill. He makes it seem so simple, even though it's anything but, and although I know I should probably pull my hand from his, I don't want to. It's not as though I actually need his physical support any more… and yet I do. I think I always will.

He makes no move to let me go, and we carry on, getting around the corner and onto the harbour before he slows the pace and looks down at me. "Okay?" I nod my head, and he smiles. "Shall I make my confession now?"

"What confession?"

"I decided last night that I won't visit Rachel during the day today. I'll go after surgery finishes, instead."

"Okay."

He shakes his head. "You don't understand, do you?"

"Understand what?"

"Going to Rachel's after surgery means I'll be taking you with me."

"Why?"

"Because I'll be walking you home."

I feel pleased and grateful about that, but I don't know if I want to be part of his house call, especially not when the patient is one of his closest friends.

"I'm sure I'll be fine…"

He stops, pulling me back with him and looks down at me, a serious expression on his face. "If you're about to say you're sure you'll be fine walking home on your own, I think we both know that's not true. And as for staying at the office by yourself, I could see how worried you were yesterday, so I'm not leaving you like that again. I only have to take Rachel's blood pressure, and she won't mind you being there."

"You don't think she'll find it a little odd?"

"No."

It occurs to me that he might have told her about what Fraser did to me, and I pull my hand from his, which seems to surprise him.

"What's wrong, Millie?"

"Did you tell her about me? About what happened to me?"

"Of course not." He shakes his head. "I had to tell her something had happened to you." I take a half step backwards, but he moves forward, keeping the gap between us the same.

"Why? Why did you have to do that?"

"Because she'd guessed something was wrong. I didn't say what, though. I'd never reveal that to anyone. Not even Tom knows all of it. I told you, everything you said to me was in confidence, which means I won't repeat it to a living soul."

I look up into his perfect face, wishing I'd never doubted him now. For a moment, I wonder why Rachel might have guessed something was wrong, but then I remember, he changed the time of their appointment, which makes sense…

"Won't Rachel want to know more?"

"No. I've already explained that I can't tell her, and you don't have to. She's very understanding. When we get to work, I'll send Jack a message, letting him know our plans."

Our plans?

That sounds good, and I can't argue with him anymore.

Instead, I put my hand in his and we start walking again, neither of us saying another word, all the way to work.

Unfortunately, he has to release me to get his keys out of his pocket, and once he's opened the door, he stands back, letting me go in ahead of him.

"I'll open the windows, shall I?"

He nods his head. "And I'll make the coffee. I get the feeling it might be the last time I see the coffee machine all morning."

He's not wrong. The morning's schedule is very full, and he's only just finished making us both a cup of coffee when Sebastian Baxter arrives. He's a few minutes early, for which he apologises, looking nervous, although he barely even glances at me. A tall man, he's casually dressed in jeans and a turquoise polo shirt, probably in his mid-forties, with greying hair, which he wears in a wind-swept, slightly messy style. He also has a much greyer beard, which ought to make him look older, but doesn't. Robson greets him, still carrying his coffee, although he's put mine on my desk, and the two of them disappear into Robson's office.

By the time Mr Baxter leaves, there are already two other patients waiting, with a third one due any minute, and I know this means the morning is going to be spent catching up and apologising. Most people are very understanding, although a couple of them make a point of checking their watches at regular intervals. They're the ones who, when it's their turn, take longer than everyone else... which always makes me smile. They don't like to be kept waiting themselves, but don't have a problem with making others wait in turn.

At lunchtime, as the final patient of the morning leaves, Robson comes out into the reception, looking weary.

"Do you feel like having lunch with me? I'm only offering ham sandwiches again, and a shortened lunch break, thanks to my appalling time-keeping this morning, but..." He lets his sentence hang, and I smile up at him.

"I'd love to have lunch with you. I'm starving, actually."

He comes around my desk, perching on the edge. "You are eating properly, aren't you?"

Am I that transparent? I guess I must be, and I lower my head. "I'm doing my best."

He holds out his hand, putting it in my line of sight, and I look up at him. "Come on... let's feed you."

I take his hand and let him pull me from my seat towards the back of the house, through the door and down the hall into his kitchen... which is so much more than just a kitchen.

It's the perfect living space, the walls being the palest of pale greens, and the floor a light wood. To the left is the kitchen, which has cream coloured units and a granite work surface, separated from the living room by a rectangular oak table that has six chairs surrounding it. The living area itself features an open stone fireplace with a heavy wooden mantel above it, and a long, wide sofa and two matching chairs, all covered in cream fabric. There are cushions scattered all over the furniture in shades of green, and a soft throw over the back of one of the chairs. The room is so relaxing, I could happily stay here forever, but Robson heads straight for the kitchen, opening the fridge door and reminding me we're on a tight schedule today.

"Shall I put the kettle on?" I say.

"Yes, please."

I set about making the tea, fetching the pale blue mugs from the cupboard. He showed me where to find them yesterday, along with the tea bags and spoons, which are in a drawer beneath the draining board. He cuts some bread on a thick wooden board, and while I watch him, waiting for the kettle to boil, I wonder if now might be the right time to ask him about his curiosity over Fraser's past.

I open my mouth, but before anything can come out, Robson turns his head, looking at me.

"That was an interesting morning," he says.

"It was?"

"Yes. At least, it was to start with. Did you realise we have a minor celebrity living in our midst?"

"No. Who's the celebrity?"

"Sebastian Baxter."

"I'm sorry… what's he famous for?"

He smiles. "Around here, he's famous for renting his house from Sean Clayton."

"You mean the novelist?"

"Yes."

"He owns a house here?"

"Yes. It's the one on top of the cliff and Sean used to live here until earlier this year."

"Really?"

He nods his head. "He's moved away now, but he's rented his house out to Sebastian Baxter."

"Who I've still never heard of."

"Neither had I until he told me what he does."

"Which is?"

"He illustrates children's books. To be honest, I still wasn't any the wiser, until he revealed the names of a few of them." He cuts up the tomato, laying it out on the buttered bread. "There's a series of books, the name of which I can't remember, but we've got a couple of them in the children's box in the waiting room. There's one about a hiccuping hippo, and another which has got something to do with an ant called Atticus."

"Oh, yes. I've picked them up countless times. I can't say I've ever looked inside either of them, but the illustrations on the covers are superb."

"They are, aren't they? And now we know who's responsible."

I find it interesting that, even though he's happy to share this snippet of information about his patient, he doesn't explain what was wrong with him, or why their consultation overran by nearly half an hour this morning. That's one of the things I love most about Robson. He's so trustworthy. I know he'd never reveal a patient's secrets to me, any more than he'd reveal my secrets to anyone else. I should never have doubted that.

Today's ham sandwiches are just as good as yesterday's, and afterwards, he hands me an apple from the fruit bowl on his kitchen work surface.

"Eat this."

"But I'm already quite full."

"Then take it back to your desk with you and eat it later this afternoon. We can't have you fading away through malnutrition."

"After a lunch like that?"

He chuckles and checks his watch. "I'm afraid there's no peace for the wicked. My next patient is due in five minutes."

We quickly clear away and go back through to the front of the house, leaving the peace of his living room behind for another day.

I look up from my computer as the front door swings open. There's no-one expected for at least another fifteen minutes, and I feel myself tense, until Tom appears around the door, and rather than being intimidated, like I was yesterday, I relax, and even smile at him.

He smiles back and nods towards Robson's closed door.

"Is Rob free?"

"He will be in a minute."

Tom nods his head. "I've got some news, but I think I'd rather tell you both together."

"Oh…. okay."

"He hasn't got another patient due, has he?"

"Not for a little while. Someone cancelled, so he's got a break coming up."

He nods his head, just as Robson's door opens and his patient comes out, clearly surprised to see Tom standing there, blocking the doorway. He moves aside and the middle-aged lady steps outside, Robson coming into the hallway.

"Did you want to see me?" he says, looking up at Tom.

"I wanted to see both of you." He finally steps into my room, and it occurs to me he's been waiting in the hall because he didn't want to crowd me without Robson being here.

Robson follows and, while Tom goes and sits on one of the chairs, Rob perches on the end of my desk. "Has something happened?" he asks.

"That's one way of putting it." Tom leans forward. "I went to see Dan Moyle over at the surf school straight after I left here yesterday. I didn't give him very much detail, but told him I needed to know what he could tell me about the women Fraser Johnson might have dated since he's been here."

"Was he able to help?" Robson asks.

"He went through their client lists and worked out two of them for sure, and three other possibles."

"Five in total?" I'm surprised, and can't hold it in.

"Yes. Fortunately, Dan had contact details for the two he was sure about, and I spoke to them both on the phone yesterday afternoon. They told similar tales, and although I couldn't lead them into any specific answers, there's a definite pattern to Fraser's behaviour."

"He's done this before?" Rob says.

"Not exactly. You didn't give me very much detail the other night, but as you know, what you told me was enough for me to classify what he did to Millie as a sexual assault. What the other two women described was different."

He's holding something back. That much is obvious. But that may be because he's not allowed to give us the details, any more than he was probably allowed to tell these other women about what Fraser had done to me.

"Does any of that help?" I ask.

"Yes," he says, nodding his head. "I went back to the surf club this morning and spoke to Sam."

"Who's Sam?"

Robson turns around so he's facing me. "He owns the surf club and has done for years."

Tom nods. "I didn't tell him who was involved, so he knows nothing about what happened to you, but I gave him enough information to worry him, and he decided he couldn't have someone like Fraser working for him."

"You mean he fired him?" Robsons says.

"Yes. There and then, right in front of me. He needs to trust the people who work for him, and he obviously didn't feel Fraser fell into that category anymore."

"How did he take it?"

"Not well. I think Sam was glad of my presence in the end, because Fraser lost it."

"He got violent?"

"I think he might have done if I hadn't been there. As it was, he just threw a half-empty mug across the room. Unfortunately, it didn't hit anyone, because if it had, I could have arrested him for assault. As it was, he followed up the poorly directed cup throwing by yelling at Sam that he didn't want to stay in a dump like Porthgarrion anymore. Then he packed up his locker and left."

"Just like that?"

"Yes."

I sit forward. "You mean, he's gone?"

"Yes. Obviously Sam's not happy about it, because Dan's injured and even though Fraser was only doing really basic work, he's now two men down."

I feel a shiver of fear creep up my spine. "Hang on a second. Are we sure we're all talking about the same man?"

Tom frowns at me and Robson stands, coming to crouch in front of me, taking my hands in his. "Why do you ask," he says.

"Because the Fraser I knew wasn't doing basic work. One of the many boring things he told me was that he was having to take over doing all the surf training because his colleague – which I presume is Dan Moyle – had injured his wrist."

"That was a lie," Rob says. "When I was treating Dan's sprained wrist, he was worried about how Sam was going to react to him being out of action for a while, and I suggested he could get Fraser to take over. Dan explained that Fraser's limits were handing out boards and going through safety checks. His precise words were that Sam would rather close the surf school than let Fraser do anything more than that."

"Did he lie to me about everything?" I look into Rob's eyes and he lets out a sigh.

"I don't know. According to Dan, Fraser was a fraud. He may or may not have been a lifeguard at some time, but Dan reckons he's got very little experience on a surfboard."

"But he was telling me about a competition. I can't remember much about it now, but he said he'd been invited to take part in it."

"It wasn't called The Eddie, was it?"

"Yes, I think it might have been."

"I'm sorry. That was a lie, too."

"But he said he'd come close to winning it last year."

"He can't have done. Dan told me they didn't even run it last year, because the waves weren't high enough."

"I feel so stupid for believing him… for even pretending to listen to him."

"Hey… we've been through this several times now, but I'll repeat it as often as I have to. This isn't your fault, Millie."

"It's not," Tom says from the other side of the room, getting to his feet. "But it's over now. He's gone."

"What if he does it again, though? Or something far worse?" For the first time, I regret not reporting him… not making this an official complaint.

Rob grips my hands more tightly. "Before you blame yourself for things that haven't even happened yet, you had a good reason for not wanting to take this any further, and no-one's going to hold that against you."

Tom steps closer, standing on the other side of my desk. "Rob's right. You can't take responsibility for Fraser's behaviour. I checked him out, and he's got no police record… so I think we have to assume this is the first time he's done anything this serious. Hopefully, he's learned his lesson, and he won't be making the same mistake again."

I do my best to feel reassured, but before I can say anything, the front door opens and Robson's next patient comes in. He gets to his feet, letting go of me, and Tom makes his excuses, saying he's got to get back on patrol.

Within moments, I'm alone, unsure whether to feel relieved that Fraser has gone, or sad that Rob isn't holding my hands anymore.

Although Robson doesn't fall behind for the rest of the day, his patients are back-to-back, so there's not even the chance of exchanging a nod, let alone a few words. By the time six o'clock comes around, I'm more than ready to head for home, although in a way, I'm not sorry now that we're due to stop off at Rachel's. Aside from the opportunity to spend more time with Robson, I might get the chance to talk to him, because now I know he and Dan Moyle had such a detailed conversation about Fraser's past, I'm feeling even more intrigued about why Robson felt compelled to raise the subject in the first place.

He comes out, just as I'm powering down my computer, his bag in his hand.

"Are you ready?"

"Almost."

He closes the window at the front of the reception, while I pick up my handbag, walking around my desk to join him.

"I'm sorry about this. We won't be long at Rachel's."

"It's fine. Don't worry."

He opens his mouth to say something else, just as his phone rings, and he pulls it from his pocket, frowning slightly. "It's Jack. I'd better…" He connects the call, holding the phone to his ear, but doesn't get the chance to speak, before I hear Jack's voice, as an incoherent, tinny whisper. "Calm down, will you?" Robson says eventually. "I'll be there in five minutes."

He ends the call without another word, and turns, rushing back into his room. I follow, marvelling, as he opens drawers, grabbing various things and throwing them into his bag.

"Can I help?"

He turns, just briefly. "No. But can you drive?"

"To Rachel's house?"

"No, in general. Do you drive? Do you have a car?"

"Yes. It's parked outside my flat."

He nods his head, looking inside his bag, which he closes, coming over, and grabbing my hand. "Come on, let's go."

It's obvious where we're going, but I hadn't expected to be taking it at quite this pace, and we rush headlong from the house, only pausing to slam the door shut behind us, before we run down the path and out onto the street. Robson keeps a hold of my hand, even as we pelt down Bell Road and onto the harbour.

"Wouldn't it have been quicker to drive?" I say, panting for breath.

"No. It takes about five minutes to get my car out of the garage."

We're already turning into Church Lane, and he glances over my head to check for traffic as we run across the street and into St. Mary's Road. Within seconds, we're standing outside a pretty house, which is painted white, with blue window frames and roses growing around the door, both of us dragging air into our lungs.

Robson knocks and a couple of moments later, the door opens, and we're faced with a tall man, wearing shorts and a t-shirt, with nothing on his feet. His dark blond hair is a mess, and his blue eyes are filled with fear.

"Thank God you're here," he says, stepping aside.

Robson practically pushes me in through the door ahead of him, and the man stares down at me for a second or two, confusion etched on his face.

"Jack, meet Millie. Millie, this is Rachel's fiancé, Jack." We nod at each other, and Robson turns to Jack. "Where is she? Upstairs?"

"Yes." We edge further into the living room, although I'm left behind as the two of them climb the stairs, listening to Jack as they go. "It all started about an hour ago, so we called the maternity unit, only to be told they had no beds."

"So you phoned for an ambulance?" Rob says.

"Yes, but it broke down."

"And, of course, Margaret's away, so…" Robson's voice is fading and I guess they're going into a bedroom. I can't hear anything else, and I turn around, taking in the room before me. Rachel's tastes differ greatly from Robson's. Where his colour palette is muted, hers is much bolder. Her sofa is bright blue, although it's covered with throws in various shades of the same colour, and beyond that is a dining table, with mis-matched chairs surrounding it. There isn't a single internal door in sight, and I can see into the kitchen, to the pale yellow cabinets and light wood work surface. I'm not sure what to do, and am just about to sit down on the sofa when I hear footsteps coming down the stairs, and turn to see Robson, who stops when he gets to the third step from the bottom.

"I'm sorry," he says. "I didn't mean to abandon you. Are you okay?"

"I'm fine. Is there anything you want me to do?"

"No. I don't think this is going to take very long."

"Okay. Go and be a doctor."

He smiles and turns, taking the stairs two at a time as he goes back up. I hear a female cry of anguish, which gets louder, and then Jack's voice saying, "Is that better? Is there more air with the door open?"

I can't hear the reply, but whatever it is, I can hear them all much more clearly now, so I guess having the door open is an improvement.

To distract myself, I spend a little while looking at the paintings on the walls, trying to ignore the intermittent cries from upstairs. The paintings are clearly by Rachel. I recognise the style from the ones in Robson's house. They're very good, and I have to agree with him, she's very talented.

I can't think what else to do with myself, but then I realise, if it's hot upstairs, they might appreciate a drink… and I wander into the kitchen, and put the kettle on to boil. The tea bags are in a fairly obvious canister, but I take a while to find the cups.

"I'm never letting you near me again!" I hear Rachel's scream, even from here, and I have to smile, wandering to the bottom of the stairs.

"I'm not responsible for this. Jack is." That's Robson, and his reply makes me giggle.

"He's never coming in the same room as me… not after this."

"I believe you," Jack says.

"I mean it, Jack." I can hear a threat in her voice, although her words are followed by a hearty male laugh.

"No you don't."

"I hate you. I really hate you… both of you."

"That's fine," Robson says, with the most soothing of voices. "We don't mind."

"Stop being so bloody patronising, Doctor Carew."

I giggle, returning to the kitchen. The kettle has boiled, but I'm not sure about making the tea yet. If they're as busy as they sound, I'd only be interrupting… and besides, how would I get it up to them? I don't feel as though I can go up there, and I can hardly ask either Jack or Robson to come down, just for the sake of a cup of tea.

I decide to leave it for now, and as the back door is open, I wander out into the courtyard garden, a smile forming on my lips. This is lovely. I'm surrounded by pots of herbs and shrubs, and there's a table and chairs, painted in the boldest of colours, which ought not to fit in this haven of greenery… and yet it does.

Pulling out a bright yellow chair, I sit down and take a deep breath, letting myself relax. The evening sunshine is gentle on my face, and I tip my head back, relaxing for the first time in days.

"There you are." I sit up, jolting awake, and stare up at Robson. He's standing in front of me, looking worried. "I thought you'd left without telling me."

"Why would I do that?"

He shrugs. "I don't know, but I came down and couldn't find you."

"Sorry. I just stepped out here for some fresh air. I must have fallen asleep."

He crouches, taking my hands in his. "Don't apologise. I was just scared for a moment, that's all."

That's the second time he's admitted to being scared about me, and although there was no need, the fact that he cares enough to be so worried makes me feel warm and safe... both of which are very welcome.

"Shouldn't you be looking after your patient?"

He smiles. "I'm giving her and Jack some time to get to know their daughter."

"You mean, the baby's here?"

"Yes. I told you it wouldn't take long."

"Are they both okay?"

He nods his head. "Rachel's stopped calling Jack names, and has fallen in love with him all over again."

"I heard some of the things she was saying."

"I think most of the village did." I giggle and he sighs.

"What happens now?"

"I'm afraid we'll have to hang on for just a little while. You don't mind, do you?"

"No."

He nods his head. "I can manage with births, and making sure mother and baby are okay, but there are a few things that need to be done… not the least of which is weighing little Beatrice. I don't have all the equipment necessary for that, but the community midwives do."

"They're calling her Beatrice?"

"Yes. It's a lovely name, isn't it?"

"It is. What are you going to do about the midwife, though? Margaret's on holiday, isn't she?"

"Yes. But I've called Sue already, and she says she should be able to get here within an hour."

"Okay. I was going to make some tea before I fell asleep."

"That's a marvellous idea. Jack could probably do with something stronger, but I think we'd all appreciate a cup of tea."

"Shall I bring it up?"

"Would you mind? I should probably check on Rachel and Beatrice. The bedroom is on the left at the top of the stairs."

"I'll find it."

He stands, and because he's still holding my hands, I copy him, and for a second or two, we gaze into each other's eyes.

"Thank you for being here," he says.

"I wouldn't have wanted to be anywhere else."

It's true. I've realised over the last couple of days, I need to be wherever he is.

Chapter Sixteen

Robson

By the time Millie brings up the tea, Rachel's looking a lot more presentable. She's re-fastened her ponytail and put on one of Jack's shirts. She wore a t-shirt during the birth – mainly because she had it on when I arrived, and there wasn't time to worry about taking it off – but it's a little the worse for wear now.

I make the introductions, and although Rachel and Jack are both aware of something having happened to Millie, neither of them shows any sign of wanting further details. That's probably because they're so enamoured with their little girl, but I like to think it's also because they're good friends, not willing to pry into something they've obviously realised is difficult… just from my reactions.

Millie comes over, bringing a cup with her, and hands it to me.

"Are you okay?" I look down into her eyes, and she smiles, nodding her head. "Where's your tea?"

"I left it downstairs. I wondered if Rachel and Jack would like me to make something for their supper, to save them the trouble."

We both glance over at the bed, where the happy parents are cradling their daughter, and I smile when I realise that neither of them has registered a word Millie just said.

"I'm sorry to interrupt, but Millie was wondering if you'd like her to make something for your supper?"

Jack looks up, although it takes Rachel a moment longer to drag her eyes away from Beatrice.

"We couldn't ask that…" he says, his voice fading as he turns to Rachel, like he wants to leave the decision to her.

"That's very kind." Rachel smiles at Millie. "I couldn't possibly expect you to—"

"I honestly don't mind," Millie says. "Although I can't guarantee anything exciting."

"We've had more than enough excitement for one day." Jack chuckles and Rachel joins in, stopping abruptly and wincing.

"Don't make me laugh. It hurts."

"It won't for long," I tell her, and she narrows her eyes at me.

"You're a man. How would you know?"

Millie stifles a laugh and steps away from me, much to my regret. "I'll see what I can put together."

She's gone in the blink of an eye, and I stare after her, even though I can hear her footsteps on the stairs.

"She's lovely," Rachel says in a quiet whisper.

I turn to her, to find she's smiling at me now. "I know."

Rachel hands Beatrice to Jack, who nestles her in the crook of his arm, and then she sits up, with some difficulty, and pats the edge of her bed. "Come and sit down." I do as I'm told, perching on the mattress by her knees, my body twisted so I can see her. "I know you won't tell me what's happened to her, but are you sure she's okay? She looks nervous… and haunted."

I hate to hear Millie being described like that, especially by someone who barely knows her. "She is… nervous and haunted, that is. As for being okay, she's getting there."

"With your help?"

"I'd like to think so."

She reaches out, resting her hand on mine. "I'm sure you're doing an excellent job, but if you ever think she'd benefit from talking to another woman, as opposed to a man, or a doctor, let her know I'm a reasonably good listener, and I'm happy to help."

I smile, placing my other hand over hers. "You're an excellent listener, and if the need ever arises, I'll suggest it to Millie and see what she says."

I glance across at Jack, but he's so busy gazing at his daughter, he hasn't even noticed me holding hands with his fiancée. Rachel gives me a smile and then pulls her hand from mine, leaning in to Jack.

"She's perfect, isn't she?"

He nods his head, turning to her. "Hmm… just like her mum."

Rachel blinks a couple of times. "It's so strange to think of myself as a mother."

"Why?" I say, getting to my feet and moving to the end of the bed. "You've had nine months to prepare for it."

"I know, but it still comes as a surprise when it happens."

"Do you feel the same way, Jack?" I ask and he looks up at me, tilting his head, like he's considering my question.

"Yes. I think so. You're right. We've had a long time to get ready for this, but now Beatrice is here, it's all so much more than I expected. I feel a weight of responsibility I'd never expected."

"A bad weight? The responsibility doesn't scare you?" It's odd, but I suddenly want to know.

He smiles. "No. There's nothing bad or scary about this at all. Fatherhood is the most fabulous feeling in the world."

He turns to Rachel, and she kisses him, and then brushes her fingertips across their baby's forehead, a lump rising in my throat.

I hadn't expected that and I turn away, pretending to be busy with my bag, so they don't notice how jealous I am.

By the time Millie and I leave, it's dark. Sue arrived a while ago, but she wanted me to stay while she carried out her checks, being as Rachel and Beatrice aren't her patients, and because there had been complications with Rachel's blood pressure. It made sense, in case there were any issues that required a follow-up. Not that I thought there would be, but I could see the logic behind her suggestion.

Everything was fine, though, and once Jack had shown Sue out, Millie and I followed. She'd left a mild vegetable curry cooking in the oven for them, and Jack made a point of thanking her without getting too close. Her shyness is obvious for anyone to see, even if I haven't been able to explain it.

"I'll call tomorrow to check up on Rachel and the baby," I say as he opens the door. "But I won't come by unless you need me."

"We're being thrown in at the deep end, are we?"

"Like all new parents… yes. And why is it you assume I know anything about being a parent? Just because I'm a doctor doesn't mean I can help with night feeds and nappy changing."

"Damn. I was assuming you'd be here at four in the morning to take the strain."

"Not a chance."

He holds out his hand and I take it, letting him give me the firmest of handshakes. "I know I've thanked you already, but I owe you."

"No, you don't. Just take care of them."

"I will."

Releasing myself from Jack's grip, I take Millie's hand and lead her from the house. I've got no intention of letting her go, or walking very quickly, and we saunter down St. Mary's Road at a snail's pace.

"Can I ask a question?" Millie says, breaking our comfortable silence.

"Of course." I look down to see she's smiling up at me.

"Why did you ask if I could drive, and whether I have a car?"

I smile back at her. "Because if things had gone wrong, I'd have needed someone to drive us to the hospital. My job would have been looking after Rachel, and I doubt Jack would have been capable of driving anywhere. So, it would have fallen to you."

She nods her head. "You took that very much in your stride."

"Probably because that's not the first baby I've delivered."

"It's not?"

"No. I shouldn't think it'll be the last, either. Situations like that can arise from time to time, and in small villages like this, you have to be prepared to step in when required."

"Don't you worry things might go wrong?"

"Yes. That's why I was so relieved you were there." She frowns, like she doesn't understand. "If I'd been by myself, without you, or even Jack, and I'd needed to get Rachel to the hospital, I don't know what I'd have done."

Her face clears, and she nods her head. "Has it ever gone wrong like that?"

"No. Thanks goodness. Not badly. Although there was a delivery I was involved with a few years ago, that got a little fraught."

"Why? What happened?"

"It was only my second winter as the village GP, and the weather was atrocious. We had a terrible storm, with gale force winds and torrential rain. The mum went into labour right in the middle of all that, and she called the dad to tell him to come home from work to take her to the hospital… except his car broke down, so she phoned for an ambulance instead, and that got held up when a tree was felled in the winds. That was when she phoned me. I got concerned when the labour wasn't progressing as I'd have expected, and I wanted to take her to hospital..."

"But you were by yourself?"

"Yes. In the middle of one of the worst storms in living memory."

"What did you do?"

"I called the police station. My dad answered, and I explained what was wrong. The next thing I knew, Rory Quick was at the house with a police car, telling me he'd left one of the PCSOs in charge of the station and sent my dad to find the baby's father."

"Did he get you to the hospital in time?"

"Yes. It was an interesting car journey, and not one I'd care to repeat, but I was relieved to hand the mother over to the maternity unit, and the baby was born by emergency Caesarian section not long afterwards."

"And the dad?"

"He arrived just in time to see his son enter the world." I shake my head. "God knows why, but the experience didn't put the parents off, and they've had another little boy since, although they timed it better, and he was born in the summer, by elective Caesarian."

"Did it make a difference today that it was Rachel who was giving birth?"

I wonder for a moment if she's going to overreact to me having been so intimate with Rachel in the course of my work.

"Why would it?"

"Because she's your friend. It must have put more pressure on you."

I smile, leaning in a little closer to her. "I suppose, but when you're in the middle of something like that, you're more preoccupied with doing your job than anything else. To be honest, I didn't even pay too much attention to the fact that it was Rachel until afterwards, when she was apologising for calling me all the names under the sun."

Millie chuckles. "Why did she aim that at you, and not Jack?"

"Oh, Jack didn't escape. The problem was, I was at the end of the bed. It put me directly in her line of sight… and therefore, in the line of fire. Besides, by the end, I think she just had a general hatred of men. Still, it's all forgotten now."

"And she's fallen in love with Jack all over again?"

"God… yes."

I look up, surprised to find we're already approaching the house where Millie's flat is, even though we've dawdled all the way here, and I know we're about to have to say goodnight.

The problem is, I don't want to… and not only that, I'm not sure where I stand anymore. With Fraser gone, she won't need me to walk her to work, or to walk her home, and while I'd love to keep coming down here in the mornings, I don't want her to feel crowded by me. Should I ask her what she wants me to do? Or should I come down in the morning anyway and see how she reacts? I can't decide, but time is running out. We're almost at her front door, and I need to decide.

"Can I ask another question?" she says, distracting me.

"Yes." *Especially if you're going to ask me to continue walking you to work. That would be wonderful.*

She hesitates for a moment, and then says, "I know this might not seem very relevant, considering everything else that's happened this evening, but it's been driving me mad, and I need to know…"

"Know what?"

"Why did you ask Dan Moyle about Fraser's past? I know you said it was just curiosity, but was it?"

"No." My answer is instinctive, even if her question has just taken me by surprise, and she looks up at me, her face lit up by the moon, and the glimmer of lights from the flats and houses beside us.

"Then why?"

"I didn't specifically ask about his past. I just asked Dan if he knew anything about Fraser, because I didn't like him."

"But you never met him."

"I know." I take a breath and step a little closer to her. "My dislike was based on the fact that he was going out with you, and I didn't want him to." I hear her suck in a breath and hope I haven't gone too far… revealed too much. Her eyes widen and she stares at me for a moment before releasing that breath.

"You didn't want him to?"

"No."

She lets out a sigh. "I was so stupid to say yes to him."

I shake my head. "You weren't to know what he'd be like."

"That's not what I mean."

Okay… I'm confused now, although that's probably not helped by the fact that we're standing so close together, or by the way she's looking up into my face, studying me, like she's seeing me for the first time.

"What do you mean, then?"

"That I was stupid to say yes to him, when it was you I wanted to go out with all along."

The air around us stills, and I gaze down into her eyes, wondering how silly I must look with my mouth open. More than anything, I want to pull her into my arms and kiss her, but I can't. Partly that's because of what's happened to her, but it's also because I feel guilty.

"I didn't know, Millie," I whisper, shaking my head. "I feel awful now… like I caused the problem."

"Why?"

"Because if I'd asked you out when I wanted to, none of it would have happened."

She blinks, her lips parting, although nothing comes out of them for a moment, and then she chokes, like she'd been holding her breath, and had suddenly remembered to breathe again.

"Y—You wanted to ask me out?"

"Yes. I've wanted to for ages, but I didn't think you were interested in me. I'd convinced myself I didn't stand a chance, but had decided to throw caution to the wind and ask you anyway on the day I saw you outside with Fraser for the first time."

"You mean the day he and I met?"

"Yes, I suppose it must have been. I asked you if he was your boyfriend when you came in, and…"

"And I made a complete hash of things." She closes her eyes for a second or two, shaking her head. "I didn't know what to say when you asked that, so I just said the first thing that came into my head." I sigh, realising the extent of the misunderstanding at last. "Please forgive me," she whispers.

"There's nothing to forgive. You're not to blame, Millie." She stares up at me, attempting a smile, and I smile back, edging even closer to her, so we're almost touching. She doesn't flinch or pull back, and I gaze at her lips for a moment. "Would… Would it be okay if I kissed you?" I hear her slight gasp and although I know I can't touch her, I reach out instinctively, my fingers poised about an inch from her face. "If it's too soon…"

"I don't know if it's too soon, but I'd like to try, if that's okay with you." I smile and nod my head, but before I can move, she says, "I apologise in advance if I freak out at you."

"You don't need to apologise."

"Maybe not. But if anything goes wrong, please don't take it personally."

"I won't."

I bend my head as she tips hers back, my nose touching hers as we both tilt our heads, then our foreheads meet for a second before I change the angle slightly and my lips dust over hers. I keep it gentle, aware of her reactions. Her breathing hitches, but in a good way, I think, and I bring up my hands, cradling her face and just let my lips caress hers, over and over. I'm surprised to find I'm trembling… but so is she, although she shows no sign of wanting to stop, and I let my kisses linger, moaning gently into her mouth every so often. I'm reluctant to pull back, but I know I have to, and when I do, I hold her gaze.

"Okay?" I whisper.

She nods her head. "Yes, thank you."

"Why are you thanking me?"

"Because the way you did that was so different to anything I've ever felt before. There was no way I could freak out about something that felt so lovely."

I smile, unable to help myself. "That's good." I move closer, my hands still clasped around her face. "Would you like to do it again?" She nods and I tilt her head, covering her lips with mine. This time, I take a chance and brush my tongue along the seam of her mouth. She jumps, stiffening in my arms, and I pull back.

"Sorry. Was it too soon for that?"

She looks up at me. "Not necessarily. I—I just wasn't expecting it."

I bend my head again, resuming our kiss, and give her a moment to adjust before I flick my tongue across her lips. This time, she opens her mouth and as her tongue meets mine, I feel her arms come around my waist, her breasts crushing against my chest. Her sighs meet my moans, and after a while, I pull back, separating us while I can still remember how.

"We should get you up to your flat, and then I ought to go home." Not that I want to, but I think it's for the best.

The look of disappointment in her eyes makes me smile, but I know leaving is the right thing to do. We have to take this in small steps, or risk the consequences of getting it wrong... and that's not something I wish to contemplate.

I drop my hands from her face, and she delves into her handbag, finding her keys before she turns and opens the front door. Tonight, she doesn't query whether I'll see her upstairs. Instead, she waits for me to follow her inside and then I close the door behind us and she leads me up the stairs to the top of the house.

Once we're outside her flat, she looks up at me and, unable to resist, I lean back against the wall beside her door, and I pull her into my arms, our lips meeting at the same time as our bodies. She rests against me, and I keep one arm around her waist, while the other roams up her back, my hand coming to a halt on her neck, which makes her shudder. My fingers caress her soft skin, and she brings her hands up, resting them on my shoulders, clinging to me... which feels so good, I have to focus really hard not to flex my hips, because I want her so much, I ache.

This time, it's Millie who pulls back, and I wonder if it's too much for her, although the look in her eyes tells me it's not, and she smiles up at me, biting on her bottom lip in the sexiest move I've ever seen... made more so because I don't think she's even aware of it.

"You'd better go in."

"Hmm... it's getting late."

She steps back, moving away, and I push myself off the wall. "Before I go, will you promise me one thing?"

"Of course." She gazes up at me, her eyes alight.

"Will you promise me you'll eat something? I know it's late, but you haven't been eating properly and I need to know you'll at least have something before you go to bed."

She nods her head. "I've still got all the ingredients for the salad I didn't bother to make last night."

"Okay. Then promise me you'll have it tonight?"

"I promise."

She puts her key in the lock, turning it, and opens the door.

"I'll see you tomorrow."

"Yes."

She's about to step inside when I take her hand, and she stops. "One last kiss?"

She smiles and I pull her into my arms again, claiming her mouth with mine. She gasps and sighs, her body relaxing into mine, and I hold her close to me, being careful where I put my hands, letting her know she's safe… and mine.

"Sleep well," she whispers, when we both pull back.

"You too. And call me if you need me."

She nods and steps inside the flat. I wait until she's closed the door, and then I turn away, drifting along the hall and back down the stairs.

Once I'm outside, I close the door, making sure it's locked behind me, and then I set off for home, my feet still barely making contact with the ground.

How did that happen?

The day has been so chaotic, full of so many highs and lows, but how on earth did we end up here?

Not that it matters… the point is, we're together, and that means, even though I didn't get to ask the question, I'll definitely be coming to meet her in the morning. Wild horses couldn't keep me away.

I'm in such a daze, I can barely think straight. My lips are still tingling from Millie's kisses and my mind is a maelstrom of emotions… all of them good.

I've never felt anything like this before, and although I'm vaguely aware of putting one foot in front of the other, I'm not conscious of anything around me.

That's probably why I almost walk into the man who's standing at the corner of Church Lane, and I step aside, towards the kerb.

"I'm sorry."

I need to pay more attention.

As I go to walk forward again, I find the man is still in my way, and I glance up, taking in his muscular frame, just as the blow hits me in the stomach, winding me. I bend, but instinctively raise my arms, protecting my head.

"Thought you could have her, did you?" he hisses in my ear, a second punch striking me in the ribs, pain shooting through me. "I know it was you that reported me to the police. I know why, too. It's because you want her for yourself, don't you? But it's time you learned when to back off, you pathetic piece of shit. She's mine… got it?" A third blow follows the second, in exactly the same place, and I let out a cry. "Ha!" He chuckles. "Still think she'll want you when she knows what a loser you are?" He punches me again, and although I do my best not to show it, that one really hurt. I've had enough now, not just of being hit, but of his words, and I brace my feet, steadying myself, before I stand up straight, looking into the blazing eyes of Fraser Johnson…

Chapter Seventeen

Millie

Robson said he'd see me this morning, but I'm not sure whether he meant at work or outside my flat. I know which I'd rather, after last night, and I have to smile when I open the front door and see him standing opposite, leaning against the wall.

He smiles back, and I pull the door closed behind me, strolling over to him, his eyes locked on mine. I can't help recalling his kisses, the memory of which kept me awake for some time last night. I wasn't about to phone him and tell him that, though. He might have suggested coming over… and I'm not sure what would have happened if he'd done that.

I think I might have been tempted to do a lot more than kiss… but I know, deep down, it's too soon. I'm not ready yet, and I think he knows that, too. That's why he left last night, rather than waiting for me to ask him in.

Because he understands… and I'm grateful for that.

As I get to him, he pushes himself off the wall and I walk straight into his open arms, putting mine around his waist. I hug him, just like I did last night, only this time he winces, flinching when I apply even the slightest of pressure, and I pull back, looking up into his eyes.

"What's wrong?"

"Nothing."

"It's not nothing. All I did was put my arms around you, and it hurt… so, what's wrong?"

He takes my hands in his, holding them between us. "I had an altercation on my way home last night."

"An altercation?"

"Yes. With Fraser Johnson." I try to pull my hands away, but he won't let me, keeping them clasped in his, and moving closer, so our bodies are almost touching, his eyes gazing deeply into mine. "It's okay, Millie. He's firmly behind bars now."

"I—I don't understand. What did he do? How did it happen?"

"He was waiting for me at the end of your road," Robson says, nodding in that direction. "I didn't even realise it was him to start with… not until he punched me."

"Where?" I examine his face, but can't see any signs of bruising.

"In the stomach. That winded me… as well as taking me by surprise."

"Oh, God… what did he do to you?" I pull one hand free, caressing his firm stomach over the top of his shirt, and he glances down, smiling. I should probably feel self-conscious about touching him, but I don't, and I wait for him to reply, which he does eventually, raising his eyes and looking right at me.

"He didn't *do* anything very much. Fortunately, as with most things, Fraser probably talks a better fight than he could ever manage in reality, and after the third or fourth blow to my ribs, I'd had enough of listening to him whining on."

"What about?"

"All sorts of things. He said he knew it was me who'd reported him to the police."

"How?"

He shrugs. "I don't know. Maybe he guessed. He didn't bother explaining himself. He just said he knew I did it, because I wanted you for myself, but that you were his…"

I gasp, torn between anger and fear. "No, I'm not. I never was."

"Hey." Robson pulls me into a hug, which has to hurt, although he doesn't seem to notice. "Hey, don't be scared. You're safe. I promise."

"What happened? I mean, you said you'd had enough, but what did you do?"

"I took advantage of the fact that he forgot the first rule of fighting."

"Which is?"

"Always protect your head. He didn't. So I knocked him out."

I smile… my smile becoming a grin, which in turn becomes a giggle. "You knocked him out?"

"Yes." He shrugs his shoulders. "When I was younger, I used to go to martial arts classes in Padstow. It's not something you forget." He brings his right hand around from behind me, examining his knuckles. "That said, it's been over ten years since I've actually used it, and even then, I never hit anyone in anger. I wasn't sure I'd knocked him out with any degree of success, so I rolled him onto his front and basically sat on him while I called Tom."

I giggle again, imagining the sight. "Did he come down here?"

"Yes, and he brought Rory Quick with him. Rory must have called my dad, because the next thing I knew, he arrived as well. Fraser was waking up by then, so Tom and Rory took him to the police station, and Dad walked me back to his place."

"Was your mum at home?"

"Yes, and she immediately panicked." He rolls his eyes. "Dad and I sat her down on the sofa, and while Dad made her a cup of sweet tea, I reassured her everything was fine."

"How can you be so blasé about it all?"

"Because nothing much happened... not really. And the main thing is, you're okay."

He leans in and kisses me, and although I'm tempted to kiss him back, out of gratitude if nothing else, I've got too many questions.

"Does this mean your parents know about what happened to me?"

"Mum definitely doesn't. Even if Dad was aware of it, he wouldn't discuss it with her. But I'm not sure how much Dad knows. He didn't mention it, and as it wasn't an official police matter, Tom might not have said anything about it to him."

I nod my head. "And us? Do they know about us?"

He smiles. "Not from me."

"Didn't they wonder what you were doing at the end of my road at that time of night?"

"Dad might have done, but Mum was making so much fuss about my ribs, he didn't get the chance to ask me about it."

I manage a half-laugh and he copies me, although he winces against the pain in his ribs. "Are you sure you're just bruised? You haven't broken anything?"

"Fraser didn't hit me hard enough for that." He pulls me closer, holding on to me. "Now, before I walk you to work, can you answer me a question?"

"Yes, but are you well enough to work?"

"Of course I am... and stop changing the subject."

"Sorry. What's the question?"

"Did you eat last night?"

"Yes. I had a bowl of salad with some chicken. I even had breakfast, too."

"Well done."

"What about you? Did you eat anything yesterday evening?"

"I was at my mother's. Of course I ate."

I laugh, and he kisses the tip of my nose, releasing me from his embrace before he takes my hand in his and we start walking.

"I wasn't sure you were going to be here this morning," I say, looking up at him. "But I suppose, after what happened last night, it makes sense that you'd…"

"I was going to come down anyway, even before Fraser decided to use me as a punchbag."

"I'm glad you're here."

He smiles. "So am I."

We turn out onto Church Lane and I feel myself tense already, the sight of the Italian restaurant getting to me once more.

"I'm still so scared, Rob."

He holds my hand a little tighter. "I know. But do you realise, you ran across this road with me last night, and you didn't give it a second thought?"

I look up at him, remembering our sprint to Rachel's house. "Yes, I did, didn't I? How on earth did I do that?"

"Because you weren't thinking about Fraser and what he'd done to you. You were thinking about Rachel, and the fact that I needed to get to her. Something else took priority over your fear."

"Maybe. But that's not going to happen every day, is it?"

"No, but you don't need it to. What last night proves is that you can conquer this."

"Then why am I still so scared today?"

He smiles. "Because these things take time. You just need to keep reminding yourself that you've done it once, so you can do it again… and one day, you will."

As he finishes speaking, he leads me across the road, down the hill and out onto the harbour.

"Do you think I might have felt more scared today because of what Fraser did last night? Do you think it was knowing that he'd been following me?"

"Maybe. But he's not following you now."

I smile up at him, loving his simple logic. "What's going to happen to him?"

"I don't know. Rory didn't say too much about it last night, and I haven't had the chance to speak to him yet this morning."

"Why was Rory handling it all and not Tom?"

"Because he's the senior police officer here. He takes a very dim view of people being assaulted in the middle of the night… especially when they're the son of one of his colleagues. I'm sure he'll let us know what's happening later on, though."

"Do you think he'll expect me to press charges, now Fraser's been arrested?"

Robson stops walking, and I turn, looking up at him. "Let's deal with one thing at a time, shall we? We'll wait and see what Rory says, and then you can decide what you want to do. It'll still be your decision, Millie, whatever happens."

I nod my head, and he leans in, kissing my forehead.

Desperate for a change of subject as we continue on our way, I ask after Rachel. "Have you heard anything from her or Jack this morning?"

"No. I'll give Jack a call later to see how they're getting along. My schedule's fairly busy today, though, so unless I get a panicking phone call in between, I'll probably have to do it at lunchtime." His face falls. "Except…"

"Except what?"

"If I phone Jack, I might not have enough time to have lunch with you."

"It can't be helped, Rob. And in any case, if Fraser's locked up, it's safe for me to go out now, isn't it? I could pop to the baker's and get us something."

"You could… but I enjoy having lunch with you."

"I enjoy having lunch with you, too."

"In which case, will you let me make it up to you by taking you out for dinner instead?" I nod my head and he smiles. "Okay… assuming no-one else gives birth this evening, shall we go to the pub after work?"

My heart races, almost to the point of becoming painful, and I struggle to swallow, let alone speak.

Robson must sense my fear, because he stops walking and turns to me, looking down into my eyes.

"Millie?" I stare up at him, my stomach churning. "Millie? What's wrong?"

I pull my hand from his, and although he goes to grab it back, I don't let him. Instead, I put my hands on his shoulders and lean in to him. "Please, Rob… not the pub."

"Oh… shit," he whispers, and, taking hold of my arms, he leans back, looking into my eyes. "I'm sorry. I should have thought. It was a stupid, insensitive suggestion."

I reach up, caressing his cheek. "No. It's okay."

He shakes his head. "It's not okay. I should have remembered he took you there." He pulls me in to him, holding me tight, even though it must hurt. "I'll drive us somewhere. We'll find another pub, away from here."

I lean back, gazing up into his eyes. "Are you sure you can drive, with your ribs and everything?"

"I'm positive."

He bends his head, kissing me gently, and then takes my hand in his, as we continue on our way.

When we get to the surgery, he lets us in, and I open the window in the reception, before going around my desk and switching on my computer. It's only then that I turn to find Rob's standing in the doorway, watching me.

"I meant to say earlier, your hair looks lovely."

"Thank you."

The style I chose today is called a topsy-turvy ponytail, which is really simple, but looks effective. I've tied it with a red ribbon that matches the flowers on my dress. Robson walks over slowly, coming around to my side of the desk.

"It's going to be very difficult not to keep coming out here all day, to steal kisses. You know that, don't you?"

I smile, resting my hands against his chest, noticing how his eyes widen when I do. "It might be an idea to try… unless you want everyone in the village to gossip about us."

He shakes his head. "Given the fact that we walked here hand-in-hand, that I held you several times, and that we've kissed in public more than once already this morning, I think it's a little late for that. I imagine the news is already half-way round the village."

"Oh."

He frowns. "Is that a problem?"

"No. It's just… I don't like being the centre of attention."

"Don't worry. It'll be me they're talking about."

He steps away, going back towards the door.

"That didn't sound at all arrogant, Robson."

He turns, grinning. "It wasn't supposed to. What I meant was, everyone is going to be asking the same question."

"They are?"

He reaches the door, pausing on the threshold, his hands buried in his pockets. "Yes. They're all going to be asking, how on earth did the doctor get so lucky?"

Before I can say a word, he disappears, and I'm left staring at the space he just vacated, knowing that, in this relationship, I'm the lucky one.

It's almost lunchtime, and I'll admit that, even though I had breakfast, I'm starving. I'm just trying to decide whether Robson will think me greedy if I buy a cake to go with our lunch when the door opens, and a policeman walks in. This isn't Tom. This man is a little shorter for one thing, and he's older, too.

He steps into the room, coming up to my desk.

"You must be Miss Adams."

"Yes."

He smiles. "Is the doctor available?"

I check the clock on my computer screen. "He should be very soon. The patient who's with him now has been in there for quite some time. He's got someone else waiting, though."

I glance to my right, to where Miss Woodward, Robson's twelve-fifteen patient, is sitting, thumbing through a magazine.

The policeman turns, a smile forming on his lips. "Hello, Nicki. What are you doing here?" He stops talking, shaking his head. "Forget I said that. It's none of my business."

She smiles and gets up, putting the magazine down on the table before she walks over. "Don't worry about it, Rory. I'm not ill, or anything like that. It's just a check-up."

She's not lying. I know from having made the appointment that she's on HRT, and has come in for her yearly follow-up. I've never met her before, but she seems very nice, and judging from the fact that she and the policeman are kissing each other on the cheek, she clearly knows him... and at least I know his name now. This must be Rory Quick.

Once they've finished greeting one another, he steps back slightly, looking down at her. She's tiny by comparison, and I'm almost tempted to smile at the difference in their heights.

"Would you think me really rude if I asked to push in ahead of you?"

"Is everything all right?" She looks concerned, and he smiles.

"With me? Absolutely. It's just that I need a word with Doctor Carew, that's all."

"Is this about the man who attacked him last night?"

He rolls his eyes. "Honestly, is nothing sacred around here?"

"I don't know about sacred, but as for secret… not a chance. This is Porthgarrion, Rory. You know what it's like better than anyone."

I feel myself blush, hoping I'm not the subject of gossip, and notice Sergeant Quick turning towards me just briefly, although it's only a glimpse, before he looks back at Miss Woodward.

"I'll need to borrow Miss Adams here, as well."

Miss Woodward nods her head and glances over at me. "I can hold the fort, if it helps."

"Y—You can?"

"Of course. I haven't got anywhere else to be."

"You haven't? The schools haven't broken up just yet, have they?" he says, and she shakes her head.

"No, but now the exams are over, I only have to go in for the first two lessons on a Friday morning. The rest of my day used to be spent teaching year eleven students, and they've all gone now, which means I'm home by just after half-past eleven."

"I'm sure Ed's not complaining."

She grins. "He wouldn't be, if I wasn't using the time to prepare for next term."

Rory laughs, just as the door to Robson's surgery opens and his patient comes out, going straight through the front door without looking into the reception.

"You two go on in," Miss Woodward says, looking at me. "If the phone rings, I'll take a message."

"Thank you."

The sergeant waits for me to walk across the hall ahead of him, and I knock on Robson's door, noting the surprised look on his face when he sees me.

"Millie? Is…" He looks over my head, seeing Sergeant Quick behind me and gets to his feet. "Rory?"

"Robson." The sergeant comes into the room behind me and closes the door. "I hope you don't mind me interrupting your appointments. I've spoken to Nicki, and she's happy to wait while I speak to you and Miss Adams."

"Have you got news for us, then?"

Rob comes around the desk, standing right beside me, and we both stare at the policeman before us. He doesn't wear quite the same uniform as Tom, having less equipment, by the looks of things.

"Yes, I have. Tom and I interviewed Fraser Johnson this morning, and not only has he admitted to assaulting you, but he's also confessed to the sexual assault on Miss Adams here."

"He's what?" I can't believe I'm hearing this. "He's confessed?"

"Yes. While he was at it, he admitted to two further assaults in another village further down the coast. I've liaised with my opposite number there and, although he was unaware of any such crime being committed, he's now pursuing his own enquiries. Mr Johnson will be handed over to officers in St. Austell this afternoon, and they'll take over from there. I just wanted to let you know."

Robson shakes his head. "I—I don't understand. How did you get him to admit to it all?"

The sergeant smiles. "You can thank Tom for that. He might be my son-in-law, but I wouldn't want to get on the wrong side of him."

"Why? What did he do?"

"Nothing illegal, I can assure you, but he ran so many rings around Mr Johnson, he didn't know which way was up. In the end, I think he'd have confessed to kidnapping Shergar, if Tom had felt like adding it to the list of misdemeanours."

"Even though he wasn't born at the time?" Robson says, and Rory chuckles.

"I don't think he cared by the end."

"Will he go to prison?" I ask, and he turns to me.

"I can't guarantee what will happen to him. That's for the courts to decide, but he's facing three charges of sexual assault, and one of actual bodily harm."

"I won't have to testify, will I?"

"No. Not now he's confessed... not unless he changes his plea when the case comes to court. But I doubt that, not given the confession he's just signed. It was very detailed, and he'd have a hard time backing out of it."

"Does this mean it's over?" Robson asks, and the sergeant nods his head.

"For both of you, yes. I'll notify you when the case comes to court, but like I say, unless he changes his plea, you won't need to attend... not unless you want to."

I'm suddenly overwhelmed with relief and I burst into tears, unable to help myself. Robson pulls me into his arms, stroking my hair as I rest my head against his chest.

"It's okay," he says. "You're safe, Millie. I'll keep you safe."

I glance up, to see he's looking down at me, and then he averts his gaze, raising his eyebrows at the police sergeant. I twist around so I can see him, and I notice the smile touching the corners of his lips.

"I'll let myself out, shall I?" he says, turning away.

"Thank you," I murmur before he goes, and he looks back. "And thank Tom for me as well, will you?"

He nods his head. "Of course I will, Miss Adams."

"Call me Millie... please?"

He smiles, and without another word, he opens the door and steps outside, closing it behind him.

"I'd better let Miss Woodward in, but before I do, are you okay?" Robson asks, and I look back up at him.

"I think so. It's all such a shock to think it's over… just like that." I lean in to him, only now realising that I've been crushing his ribs all this time. "God… I'm sorry. I must be hurting you."

He leans down, kissing me, his lips brushing over mine, so gently. "I can't feel a thing."

Miss Woodward comes out of Robson's office, pausing to give me a smile before she leaves.

"Thank you for holding the fort earlier."

Her smile widens. "Oh, that's okay. Nothing happened."

I nod my head, getting up from my seat as she goes out through the front door, and I wander across the hall, letting it off the latch and knocking on Robson's door.

There's no call to 'come in', so I wait, assuming he must be busy with something, and then jump when the door opens and he grabs hold of me, pulling me into his arms.

"I've missed you," he whispers.

"You only saw me fifteen minutes ago."

"I know. And that's fifteen minutes too long."

I lean against his chest, my hands on his shoulders, taking care not to crush his ribs. "Shall I get us some lunch?"

"I suppose so. I'd rather just keep you here, but we've got to eat, and I don't really have time to make sandwiches today."

"No." I tip my head back, looking up at him. "You've still got to phone Rachel, haven't you?"

"Yes. Although I'll probably call Jack, in case Rachel's busy." I nod my head, pulling back from him, and he smiles. "I'd never normally advocate this, but why don't you pick us up a cake while you're out? It feels like we have cause to celebrate."

I can't help smiling. "Are you psychic?"

"Not that I'm aware of," he says, which makes me laugh. "Why do you ask?"

"Because I was thinking about getting a cake earlier, just because I'm hungry. Celebrating sounds like a much better excuse."

He chuckles and kisses the tip of my nose, and then stares into my eyes for a second, all thoughts of cake forgotten as he dips his head and kisses my lips. I like it when he does this. It makes me feel warm and safe, and comfortable... like we belong together... which it seems we do.

I break the kiss eventually, feeling a little breathless, and he smiles down at me.

"You'd better go before I get carried away."

I nod my head, knowing how easy it would be to get carried away with him... and that I'm not ready for that yet. I'd like to be, but I'm not... especially not after Sergeant Quick's visit. Despite his news, I still feel vulnerable, and what I need from Rob is someone to lean on, more than anything else.

It feels like he understands that, though... just like he understands everything else.

The hot topic in the bakery appears to be Rachel's baby, which I suppose isn't that surprising when you consider she owns this place.

Everyone seems to like the name they've chosen. The lady in front of me asks the lady behind the counter if Beatrice is a name from either Jack's or Rachel's families.

"I don't think so," she says, shaking her head as she puts a loaf of bread into a paper bag, handing it over to the woman. She takes the five-pound note the customer offers, retrieving her change and giving it back, and at that moment, she looks up at me. "You were there last night, weren't you?"

"Yes." I feel myself blush as everyone turns to gawp at me.

The woman in front of me puts her change in her purse, but shows no sign of leaving the shop and I step forward, ordering a tuna and sweetcorn sandwich for myself and a chicken and salad one for Robson.

"How is Rachel?" the woman behind the counter asks, and I look up at her, dragging my eyes away from the display of cakes.

"As far as I'm aware, she's fine."

"Was it a straightforward birth?" The customer with the loaf of bread steps a little closer, lowering her voice.

"I don't know. I wasn't in the room."

"But surely the doctor must have told you."

I shake my head. I remember this woman now. She's been to the surgery twice, and although I don't know what for, I doubt she'd like to have her medical problems bandied around the harbour. "Doctor Carew doesn't discuss his patients with me unless I need to know something specific. I'm sure you can appreciate that."

She blushes and makes a fuss about putting her bread into a carrier bag.

I turn, looking back at the woman behind the counter. "Can I have two chocolate muffins, please?"

She reaches for them, but pauses. "Is one of them for Doctor Carew?"

"Yes." I'm not so greedy that I'd eat two chocolate muffins all to myself.

"In that case, you'd be better off getting him a lemon one. He doesn't like chocolate very much."

I nod my head, hating that she knows him better than I do, and once she's handed everything over to me, I give her the exact money and leave.

I hurry back, almost letting out a scream when a man comes out of the Harbour Store and bumps into me. He apologises and moves on, but I'm reminded of the day I met Fraser, and of everything that happened afterwards. Was that really only the beginning of this week? It feels like a lifetime ago.

I pick up my pace, almost running back to the surgery, and let myself in with my key, leaning on the door once I've closed it, to catch my breath.

Luckily, I can hear Robson's voice coming from his office, so he must still be on the phone and, once I'm sure my legs will support me, I push myself off the door and go through to my office, dumping the sandwiches and cakes on my desk and sitting on my chair.

It was silly of me to get so scared, especially when I know there's nothing Fraser can do to me anymore… but I couldn't help it, and I wish now that Robson had been with me.

"Are you all right?"

I look up, surprised to see Robson standing in the doorway, his arms folded across his chest, staring down at me. He must have finished his call without me realising.

"I'm fine." I smile up at him, but he frowns, less than convinced, I think. "We'd better have lunch, or we'll run out of time."

He nods, coming further into the room, and I gather up our sandwiches and cakes, although he takes them from me and leads the way into the back of the house.

"I don't think we've got time to make tea today," he says, setting everything down on the table. "We could have a glass of water with lunch and save our cakes for later, and have them with a cup of coffee sometime this afternoon."

"Sounds good to me."

He fetches some glasses from the cupboard next to the fridge, filling them with iced water, and brings them back to the table. Then he sits opposite me, and I hand him his sandwich.

"Was it busy out?" he asks, unwrapping it.

"Very. Rachel was the hot topic of conversation in the baker's."

He shrugs his shoulders, taking a bite of his sandwich. "I suppose that's understandable. Her baby's arrival has been much anticipated."

"The people in the shop wanted details about what had happened and how the birth had gone, but I didn't say anything."

He nods his head. "Well done. If they want to know more, they'll have to ask Rachel, and it'll be up to her to decide what she wants to tell them."

"I thought you'd probably say something like that, and to be honest, I was so relieved they weren't talking about us, or what Fraser did to you last night, I just bought the sandwiches and got out of there."

"I'm sure they'll get around to gossiping about us in due course," he says, and I shudder, just thinking about it.

Robson puts down his sandwich and reaches across the table, taking my hand in his. "Are you okay?" he says. "You haven't seemed quite right since you got back."

"That's because I'm not."

He stands, letting go of my hand, and comes around the table, crouching beside me and looking into my eyes. "What's wrong, Millie? Has something happened?"

"Nothing specific, no. It's just that I didn't feel as confident as I'd thought I would."

"When you were out, you mean?"

I nod my head. "Even knowing that Fraser can't do anything to me now doesn't seem to help."

He puts his arm around me, resting it across my lap so he can grasp my waist with his hand. "Give it time. Things will get better. And just remember, I'm here." He strokes his thumb against my ribs. "I'm not going anywhere, Millie."

I smile at him and bend over slightly so I'm resting against him... leaning on him. He takes my weight, supporting me... just like I knew he would.

*

By the time the last patient leaves at ten to six, I have to admit to feeling ravenous. We may have found ten minutes to stop for a cup of coffee and our muffins earlier on this afternoon, but I think my eating habits have been so erratic over the last few days, my body doesn't know what's going on.

So, when Robson asks if I want to go home and change before we go to dinner, I'm not in any hurry to say 'yes'.

"Would it be okay if we just went straight to the pub, rather than changing?"

"Of course." He smiles, coming into my room and closing the window for me. "I've got one in mind," he says, turning to face me.

"Is it far?"

He chuckles. "No, but what's the rush?"

"I'm hungry."

"Again?"

"Yes." I can feel myself blush and he comes around my desk, putting his hands on my waist and looking into my eyes. "I think I must be making up for not eating earlier in the week."

He shakes his head. "It could be that, or maybe the relief of it all being over and done with has affected your appetite."

"Is that a medical opinion?"

"No." He kisses me just briefly. "I'd love to linger, but I think we'd better get you fed."

I chuckle and grab my bag as he takes my hand and leads me to the back of the house.

"Where are we going?"

"If we're driving to the pub, we'll need my car."

I feel like such an idiot for not realising, but I stay silent, waiting while he unlocks the patio doors. He lets me go out ahead of him, and then closes and locks the doors again, taking my hand in his once more and leading me down to the end of his short garden. There's a wall with a gate in it, and we pass through, finding a garage with a small hard-standing, leading out onto a narrow track.

"I didn't even realise this was here."

"I can't imagine it was when the house was originally built," he says, unlocking the wooden garage doors and pulling them open. "I think it was added in the nineteen-fifties."

"Making the garden much smaller?"

"Yes. But I don't mind. I'm not much of a gardener, and it's useful to have somewhere secure to park the car." He smiles down at me. "Unfortunately, when the garage was built, cars were significantly smaller, so you'll have to wait here while I get it out."

I stand aside and watch him go into the garage, turning sideways to fit down the narrow gap between his car and the wall, noticing the four joining circles on the front, just above the number plate. It's an Audi... I know that much, but other than that, and the fact that it's dark grey, I'm lost.

He starts the engine, driving the car out, and pulls it to a stop right in front of me. Before I can move, he jumps out and comes around, taking my hand and helping me into the passenger seat. Then he goes back and closes the garage doors again.

Once he rejoins me, sitting in the driver's seat and pulling on his safety belt, I look across at him.

"You could have bought a smaller car, you know?"

He chuckles. "Would you think me very odd if I told you I went around the car dealerships with a tape measure?"

I tilt my head to my right and then my left. "Not very... but a little."

"I wanted the most comfortable car I could fit into my garage... and this was it. Believe me, I looked at dozens before reaching that conclusion."

"I'm sure you did."

He smiles and selects first gear, driving slowly down the track, which appears to lead behind his neighbours' houses, bending sharply after a while.

"I've never noticed this before," I say, as he turns left out of the track and onto Bell Road.

"You'd have no reason to."

He's right. Unless you needed to come down here, it would just appear to be a track leading to nowhere.

At the top of Bell Road, he turns right, driving with confidence.

"What do you drive?" he asks.

"A Ford Fiesta. It's what I learned to drive in, and it seemed like the most obvious choice."

"I did that when I bought my first car."

"I think a lot of people do, don't they?"

"Probably."

We get to a roundabout and stop talking long enough for him to negotiate it, and then he speeds up again. I like the way he drives, and for a while, I sit and watch him. He doesn't seem to mind, and occasionally just smiles over at me, like he doesn't understand what I'm looking at.

"Am I doing something wrong?" he asks, after his third glance in my direction.

"No. I just like looking at you." I can't believe I said that, but the words are out there now, and he slows the car, taking more time to turn his gaze on me.

"I like looking at you too, Millie."

I feel myself blush and bite on my bottom lip, nerves getting the better of me. "Why don't you get us to this pub? Then we can look at each other."

He chuckles. "What you mean is, why don't I get us to this pub, so you can eat?"

"Yes… while looking at you."

His chuckle becomes a fully fledged laugh, and he accelerates again, taking the next right and turning left almost immediately afterwards. The pub is about five hundred yards down on the left, and he parks the car outside in one of several available bays, getting out without a word and coming around to help me to my feet.

"I'd hate to keep a lady from her food," he says, locking the car and leading me towards the front entrance. He pauses on the threshold to let me go in ahead of him, but I hang back.

"No… you go first."

He smiles, and walks in ahead of me, waiting on the other side of the door and taking my hand again, guiding me to the bar.

There are brass plaques attached to the many dark beams, and a flagstone floor on which my heels click loudly, despite it being quite busy. A fire at the far end of the room remains unlit, and the deep window sills appear to make a suitable home for various nautical nicknacks.

"What would you like to drink?" Robson asks, and I survey the array of bottles on display.

"Can I have a dry white wine?"

"Of course."

He turns to the barman, who's waiting for our order. I'd guess he's around the same age as Rob, with lighter hair and very pale blue eyes, which seem to keep darting towards me. I move slightly, so I'm shielded by Rob and when the man goes to get his mineral water, Rob looks down at me.

"Are you okay?"

"Yes. I just don't like him looking at me."

"Neither do I."

"You noticed, then?"

"It was hard to miss."

I heave out a sigh of relief. "I thought I was being paranoid."

"No. You're being beautiful." I shake my head, but he smiles at me and reaches out, cupping my face with his hand. "You're beautiful, Millie." He leans down and kisses me, just as the man comes back, announcing himself with a slight cough.

He pushes our drinks across the bar, and Robson asks him to set up a tab for us.

"Do you want some menus?" the man asks, looking anywhere but at me now, which makes me wonder if that was the purpose of Robson's kiss… to stake a claim. I don't mind if it was. I feel much safer now.

"Yes, please."

The man disappears, returning moments later with two menus, encapsulated in plastic, which he hands to Robson, who passes them to me, while he picks up our drinks.

"Let's sit, shall we?" he says, nodding to a table by the window.

I lead the way, taking a seat that means I have my back to the bar, and he sits opposite, with his back to the window, putting the drinks down between us. I hand him one of the menus, holding on to it until he's pulled his phone from his pocket, placing it on the table.

"Sorry." He glances down at it. "Occupational hazard, I'm afraid. I'm never really off duty."

"That's okay."

He takes the menu and we both look down, although rather than deciding what I want, I can't help wondering what he's going to choose, and in the end, curiosity gets the better of me, and I lay my menu flat on the table and lean forward.

"What kind of foods do you like?"

He puts down his own menu, taking a sip of his water, and says, "Pretty much everything."

"That's not true though, is it?"

"Isn't it?" He frowns, looking confused.

"No. When I was in the baker's today, I was going to buy you a chocolate muffin, but the lady in the shop said you don't like chocolate, and suggested I get you a lemon one instead."

He reaches over the table, taking my hand in his. "I'll admit, chocolate isn't my favourite thing, and of the two, I'd prefer lemon, but I'd have eaten the chocolate muffin if you'd bought it." I nod my head and he stares at me for a moment. "What's wrong, Millie?"

"I know this is going to sound silly, but I didn't like the fact that the lady in the baker's knew more about you than I do."

"She doesn't. She just knows I don't like chocolate as much as I like lemon." He pushes his menu aside, leaning a little closer, and glances down at mine. "Why don't you choose my dinner for me?"

"How can I? I don't know what you'd like."

"Then guess. You know me fairly well."

I gaze at him, and he smiles. I have to smile back, unable to stop myself and he nods to my menu, raising his eyebrows, although he doesn't say another word, and I lower my gaze, studying the options. There are a few things I can dismiss straight away, simply because I've already established that Robson is quite a healthy eater... and I doubt he'd want a burger with all the trimmings, even if it sounds delicious. He's definitely not a vegetarian, having served me ham sandwiches, and eaten a chicken one today, and somehow I can't imagine he brought me to a pub to eat pizza. My eyes alight on two fish dishes, and I read through the accompaniments, trying to decide.

"You look confused," he says.

"I am. I can't decide between the grilled sea bass and the whole trout."

He nods his head, his lips twitching upwards. "I'd love either of them. What do they come with?"

I look down, reading from the menu. "They both come with new potatoes, and the sea bass also has green beans and a caper and lemon sauce."

"Sounds incredible. What about the trout?"

"That comes with spinach and a tomato and mushroom butter."

"Well… now I'm as confused as you are. I want them both."

I shake my head. "That really would be greedy."

He chuckles. "I know. The good thing is, I'm leaving the choice to you."

"In that case, it's not so hard, because I don't like spinach very much, so I'd probably choose the sea bass."

"Fine. Sea bass it is. I can always have the trout the next time we come here."

I smile, thinking about 'the next time', and put the menu down. "Okay… it's your turn now."

"My turn to what?"

"Choose what I'm going to eat." He nods his head and picks up his menu, studying it for a few moments before he puts it down again. "That was quick."

"Hmm…" He doesn't say a word, but just sits, smiling at me.

"Stop teasing, Robson. What am I eating?"

"The burger," he says, frowning when I shake my head. "Did I get it wrong?"

"No. That's the whole point. I hate that you got it right so easily… and that compared to your dinner, it's so unhealthy."

He chuckles. "You don't eat unhealthy food as a rule, but you've had a truly terrible week, and I figured as it's Friday, you'd probably want to treat yourself."

"I do. But how do you know I'm not generally an unhealthy eater?"

"Because I've seen the contents of your fridge."

"Oh, yes… of course." I narrow my eyes at him. "That gave you an unfair advantage. You had prior knowledge of my eating habits."

"I know… but I never said I'd play fair."

He gets up, taking my menu, and grabbing his own, and walks over to the bar.

He returns within minutes, and sits down again, taking my hands in his and leaning closer. "So… tell me about your brother."

"My brother?"

"Yes. I know you said he went to university down here, but does he work here, too?"

I know he's doing this to stop me from thinking about my terrible week, as he called it, and I'm grateful. Talking about Ellis has got to be better than thinking about Fraser.

"No, he works in Scotland."

"Oh?" I can tell that's surprised him.

"I know. He couldn't be much further away if he tried."

"Does it bother you? That he's so far away, I mean?"

"It used to." I gaze into his eyes, hoping he'll understand that I don't feel the need to rely on Ellis anymore.

He smiles, his eyes shining, like he got the message, and he says, "Have you always been close?"

I laugh. "No. Not at all. Until I was about thirteen, he regarded me as nothing more than a minor annoyance."

"What changed when you were thirteen?"

"I don't know, but that was when he suddenly became super protective of me."

Robson nods his head. "Probably because he thought you'd start seeing boys around then." I shake my head and he leans a little closer. "I know you didn't…. you were too busy being studious."

"What about you?"

"What about me?"

"Were you busy being studious too, when you were a teenager?"

I'm fishing, but I want to know the answer, and Robson smiles at me. I think he realises I'm fishing, too, and he squeezes my hands a little tighter.

"I was fairly studious. You don't get to be a doctor by ignoring your studies."

"But you had fun, too?"

"Sometimes." I raise my eyebrows and he smiles. "You want details?"

"Not graphic ones, but…"

He nods his head. "Okay… without going into graphic detail, I had my first kiss when I was fourteen."

"With anyone I know, or am likely to bump into in the baker's?"

He smiles. "If you're thinking it might have been Rachel, then the answer is no."

"What about the other woman? The one who knew you prefer lemon to chocolate."

"That was probably Vicky. She's about ten years older than me. I think she was already married by the time I turned fourteen. She's divorced now, and she likes to flirt… not just with me, with everyone. Don't worry, she's harmless enough."

"I see. In that case, your first kiss…?"

"Was with a girl called Clare. We only went out with each other for a couple of months, and kissing was our limit. She left the village when she was in her early twenties and hasn't come back."

I nod my head. "Okay, so that covers your first kiss."

"Hmm… moving forward, I had a few more girlfriends after Clare, but nothing serious – or at least nothing that involved any nudity – until I was eighteen."

"Four years later?"

"Yes. I waited until I left for university. In villages like this, people tend to gossip… in case you haven't noticed."

"And you didn't want to be a subject of tittle-tattle?"

"Not particularly." He pulls one hand away from mine, but only while he takes a sip of his drink, and then he puts it back again. "After that first introduction to nudity, I had a few more girlfriends, while I worked my way through med school… but work was the optimum word. That was my priority."

"And did all your relationships involve nudity?"

"No."

I smile, and he smiles back. "What about after med school?"

"Since I've been living back here, you mean?"

"Yes."

"I've been out with a few women – again, not all involving nudity – but they've all been from outside the village."

"Because of the gossips?"

He shakes his head. "No. Because if they'd lived in Porthgarrion, I'd have been their doctor, and that's not just frowned upon, it could lose me my job." He smiles, leaning even closer. "I'm happy to tell you more, if that's what you want… if that's what you need. But it's all in the past, Millie. None of it matters now."

"Like I said, I don't want details. I just have one question."

"What's that?"

"Have you ever been in love?" I don't know why, but it feels important to know the answer to that.

He stares at me for an uncomfortably long time, and then takes a breath and says, "I've never loved any of the women I've been with in the past."

That feels like a very long-winded way of saying 'no', but I still can't help myself from smiling. I like his answer.

I pull my left hand free, taking a sip of my wine, but the moment my glass is back on the table, Robson grabs my hand again.

"Can I ask you a question now?"

"Yes."

"If your brother is so protective of you, does that mean I've got to pass some kind of test?"

I shake my head. "No. Why would you?" He lets go of my hands, sitting back in his seat, his face a picture of hurt and disappointment, and although I lean forward, he makes no move to take my hands again. Instead, he just sits, staring. "What's wrong, Rob?"

"Nothing. I just thought…"

"You thought what?"

"I thought you said there was an 'us'. This morning, when we were talking about my parents, you said there was an 'us'. After that, and our kisses last night, and during today, I assumed that meant we were together… that we were seeing each other, and that your brother would want to… you know… vet me."

I reach right over and take his hand… the only one he's left on the table. "We are together. We are seeing each other, and there is an 'us'." He smiles again and captures my hand in both of his. "But you don't have to worry about Ellis. He'll be fine with you. He's always fine, as long as I'm happy."

He sits right forward. "Does that mean you're happy with me?"

"Yes."

"That's a relief… because I'm absolutely delirious with you."

I can't help laughing and he joins in, that moment of insecurity forgotten.

Our dinner was lovely. That burger was exactly what I needed, and according to Robson, I made the right choice for him, too. He said the sea bass was cooked perfectly. I'd thought I'd be hungry enough to have a dessert, but the burger was so filling, I couldn't have squeezed in another bite, and once we'd finished, Robson paid and then drove us home, parking outside my flat.

As he turns off the engine, I expect him to get out, but he doesn't and instead he turns to me, and even in the dim light, I can see the smile on his face.

"I've had a lovely evening," he says.

"Me too."

"Can I see you tomorrow?"

I've been hoping he would ask, and I nod my head. "I've got to get some washing done in the morning, and maybe some tidying up too…"

"So have I, but why don't I come down around twelve and take you to lunch at the café? Then we can decide what we want to do afterwards… unless you don't want to spend the rest of the day with me?"

"I'd love to spend the rest of the day with you. I like being with you."

His smile widens. "I like being with you, too."

Part of me wishes he'd lean over and kiss me, but he doesn't. He gets out of the car, coming around to my side to help me out, and keeping a hold of my hand, he leads me to my front door. I retrieve my keys, letting us in, and he follows me up the stairs, both of us stopping outside the door to my flat. I've still got my keys in my hand, but rather than putting them into the lock, I turn and look up at him, and as I do, he clasps my cheeks between his hands, bending his head to kiss me.

There's something different about this kiss. It's more intense, his tongue delving more deeply into my mouth, his lips crushing harder against mine. His groans are a little louder than before, and I struggle to breathe, clinging to his shoulders for support.

When he pulls back, although he moves his left hand down, putting it around my waist, there's a look of uncertainty in his eyes.

"Was that okay?"

"It was lovely."

"I'm sorry to keep asking, but…"

I move my right hand down, resting it on his chest, and he stops talking. "Don't apologise. I like that you care enough to bother."

He moves closer, holding me tight against him. "I care, Millie. Believe me, I care."

I reach up with my left hand, caressing his cheek. "I know you probably want more, but I——"

"Hey… it's okay. I'm happy with where we are. Just seeing your beautiful face, holding you in my arms like this, kissing you whenever I get the chance… this is good. Everything else can wait."

I suck in a breath and cup his face with my hand. "Just so you know, there's no-one else I'd want to do everything else with. It's just that I need a little longer."

"That's okay. It's been a traumatic few days. However long it takes for you to feel comfortable, is just fine with me."

Chapter Eighteen

Robson

Millie and I have spent every spare moment of the last week together, starting with last Saturday. After lunch at the café, we went for a long walk up on the cliffs above the village, only getting back in the early evening. I wanted to take Millie out to dinner again, but she said she'd rather cook, and we went back to her place, where she demonstrated her ability to make healthy meals, by preparing us a prawn and courgette tagliatelle. It was loaded with garlic and lemon, and tasted delicious, and after we'd eaten, we sat on the sofa and watched a film. I didn't do anything other than hold her in my arms and occasionally kiss her, because I'd meant everything I'd said to her the previous evening. Yes, I want more. But I'm happy to wait until she's ready, and in the meantime, I love absolutely everything we're doing together... almost as much as I love her.

Since then, we've spent a lot of time at her flat. I think she feels more comfortable there, and I guess that's fair enough, considering everything that's happened to her.

To make things even better, my ribs are now completely healed, and I'm relieved about that. It means she can hug me without it hurting, and I'm definitely not going to complain about that.

One thing I might start to complain about soon is this weather. It's been sweltering today, and although I'm fairly sure Millie intended for us to go back to her place after work, I think I'd rather stay here and sit in the garden.

I don't know how she'll feel about that, though, and once my last patient of the day has gone, I lock the front door and wander into her office. She's typing something into her computer and I stand in the doorway and watch her for a moment. She really is beautiful, and although I'd never have believed it possible, I think she's become even more so over the last week. The worry has gone from her face, and she seems more alive than before.

She looks up, smiling at me, and without taking her eyes from mine, she finishes what she's typing and then sits back.

"Are you ready to go?"

I move further into the room. "I was just coming to talk to you about that."

"Oh?"

"Yes. I was going to ask how you'd feel about staying here for this evening. It's boiling, and I was thinking we could barbecue something, and make some salad, and eat outside."

She sighs. "That's sounds idyllic. The more I think about going home and cooking in my flat, the more I keep dreading it."

"Then we'll stay here, shall we?"

She nods her head, but then stops, doubt creeping across her face. "Do you have anything for us to eat?"

"No."

She giggles. "That's not surprising, I suppose. We've eaten at my place all week, so your fridge must be practically empty."

"Almost."

We've been buying the things we need each night on the way back to Millie's flat, and I've kept my fridge stocked up with the things we need for lunch, but there's nothing here we could hope to make into a satisfying evening meal.

She smiles. "I could use a shower and a change of clothes, so why don't I go back to my place and shower there, while you do the shopping?"

"Or… we could both go back to your place, you could pick up some clothes, and then we could stop off at the store on the way back, and you can shower in the guest room upstairs, while I get the barbecue started." She frowns, like she thinks my plan is nowhere near as sensible as hers… which it probably isn't, until you take one important factor into consideration. "That way, we can be together."

Her lips twist up at the corners, and she nods her head. "I like that idea."

"Hmm… so do I."

She powers down her computer while I close the window, wishing I didn't have to, and then I take her hand, leading her out through the front door.

I think most of the village knows about us now. They seem to have become used to seeing us walking around hand-in-hand, and no-one bats an eyelid anymore. A few people raised an eyebrow, or smiled at us to start with, but we're much less exciting than we feared we'd be… and I think we're both relieved about that.

Millie's flat is just as stuffy as we'd thought it might be, and I'm pleased she fell in with my plans to stay at my place. Fortunately, it doesn't take her long to put a few things into a bag, and once she's done so, I take it from her and she opens the door, waiting for me to pass through before she locks it behind her. She puts the keys into her handbag and I smile.

"What's wrong?" she says, looking up at me.

"That's the first time since we've been together that you haven't double checked your door."

She blushes, her cheeks pinking in the most adorable way. "I didn't realise you'd noticed."

"I notice everything about you. I know it was anxiety that made you do it, but when did it start?"

"After Damian."

"And has it got worse since Fraser?"

Neither of us has mentioned his name all week, but rather than flinching against the sound of it, she tilts her head, like she's thinking about my question.

"I don't think so. It just became an instinct."

"One you've broken, by the looks of things."

"Hopefully."

She puts her hand in mine, and we go down the stairs.

Outside, Millie closes the front door without a second thought, and we make our way back. She may be getting out of the habit of checking her door, but she still tenses whenever we go near the Italian restaurant. I guess that's going to take a while longer to get over, and I don't make a fuss about it anymore. I just hold her hand and lead her across the road and out onto the harbour, stopping at the store to pick up some salad ingredients and chicken breasts. For the recipe I've got in mind, I need a lime, but they only have lemons, which should do just as well, and I grab some sesame seeds.

"What exactly are we having?" Millie asks, as I pay Bryn behind the counter.

"It's a kind of Korean spiced chicken, but I'll tone it down."

"You remembered I don't like things too spicy?"

"Of course."

She smiles up at me, and I take the bag from Bryn, as we depart the shop.

Fortunately, it's only a short walk back to the surgery, and when we get there, I let us in through the side door.

"I've never come in this way before," Millie says.

"Well… get used to it."

She grins, and I let her go ahead of me, down the hall and into the living room. I follow behind, putting the bags on the kitchen table, and emptying our shopping into the fridge.

"Did you want something to drink? Or would you rather shower first?"

"Shower, I think."

"Okay."

I grab her bag, and lead her to the stairs, which are in the corner of the room behind a door. Millie follows and I make my way up them, to the landing, off of which there are four doors.

"It's so much bigger up here than you think it's going to be," she says, looking around.

"It's deceptive because downstairs, I only live in the back of the house, whereas up here, I have the whole of it."

She smiles and I lead her into the guest bedroom, which has its own ensuite bathroom. "This is lovely."

"Do you remember me saying I had some work done up here?"

"Yes." She turns and looks at me.

"Well… basically, I took what was a four bedroomed house, and turned it into a three bedroomed one, and then I added the ensuite to this room."

"What happened to the extra bedroom?"

"I incorporated it into my room, so I've got an enormous bathroom, and a bedroom that's big enough to fit not only the bed but also a couch as well."

"It sounds really nice."

Hopefully, you'll see it one day soon.

"It is. Can you just give me a minute?" She nods, and I put her bag down on the bed and pop out of the room, going to mine to grab a couple of towels from the cupboard in my bathroom, and returning to Millie within moments. "The shower is pretty self-explanatory," I say, handing them to her. "Did you need a hairdryer?"

"You possess one?" She looks up at my hair, which I know is a mess.

"Surprisingly, yes."

She shakes her head, smiling. "I'll manage without one."

"Okay. I'll be downstairs when you're finished, but if you need anything, just shout."

I walk backwards as I'm talking, heading towards the door, feeling unsure what more to say, or if I need to say anything at all. She watches me go, and I wink at her when I get to the threshold, which makes her giggle.

I don't recall ever feeling this happy, and it only takes me a few minutes to change out of my work clothes and into a pair of navy shorts and a grey t-shirt, after which I go back downstairs again. I can hear the shower running in the guest room, but I do my best to ignore all thoughts of Millie, and what she might be doing, and instead I get on with mixing up a marinade for the chicken, and letting it rest in the fridge while I get the barbecue ready.

I'm not sure how much time has passed, but it hasn't been very long, when Millie appears at the french windows, leaning against the frame and looking down the garden at me. She's tied her hair back, although from here, I can't see how, but what catches my breath, is the sight of her wearing a pair of cut-off denim shorts and a sleeveless blouse, which is white, with tiny flowers on it. She looks incredible, and even though I know I'm staring, I can't help myself.

"Is everything okay?" she asks, eventually.

"Um… yes." I come to my senses, checking the barbecue is okay, and wander back towards the house, trying not to focus too much on how good her legs look. "Was the shower all right?"

"It was great, thanks. Would you like me to chop things up for the salad?"

"You could do. I don't think it'll be long now before I can start cooking the chicken."

We head inside, and between us, take everything out of the fridge. It's impossible not to touch her every so often, and although most of the time it's accidental, I'll admit that there are few occasions when I deliberately get in her way. She doesn't seem to mind, though, and by the time I take the chicken outside to cook it, I've already decided I really like having her here… and I don't want her to leave.

I'm not sure how I can make that happen, though… not if she's not ready, so rather than beating myself up over things that can't be, I concentrate on cooking, and before long, Millie comes out of the house, carrying a bowl of salad.

"Is it nearly ready?" she calls and I nod my head.

"There's some wine in the fridge, if you want to bring it out."

She goes back inside, returning with the wine and some glasses, and I put the cooked chicken onto a plate and carry it back towards the patio.

"I hope I haven't made it too spicy for you," I say as she helps herself, adding salad to her plate.

"I'm sure it'll be fine."

We both start eating, and she makes all the right noises, which is good, because even though the chicken is less spicy than I'd usually make it, I added more lemon and ginger, just to keep it interesting… and it seems to have worked.

We've almost finished eating, and I'm just pouring us both a second glass of wine, when without warning, the heavens open.

"Oh, my God."

Millie scrambles to her feet, and I do the same, both of us trying to gather up the plates and glasses, as the rain pelts down on us. To be honest, we needed a storm, and it's not unpleasant being out in it… it's just that we're both now drenched, and as we go back into the kitchen, loaded with crockery and cutlery, dumping it onto the work surface, I can't help laughing.

"You look soaked," Millie says, giggling at me as we both kick off our shoes.

"I feel soaked."

Her blouse is stuck to her, and I do my best not to lower my eyes, despite the obvious temptation.

"Thank goodness I've got a change of clothes," she says, running her hand down her wet arm. "I can put my dress back on to go home."

Or you could just stay here.

I nod my head. "Maybe we should both get changed."

"I think we should."

She leads the way to the stairs, which makes me smile… just because she knows her way around now, and once we get to the top, she heads into the guest room, while I go in the opposite direction, and open my bedroom door.

I close it gently and pull my t-shirt off over my head, wandering into the bathroom for a towel, which I rub over my chest, just as there's an enormous bolt of lightning, which coincides with a huge clap of thunder. I hear Millie scream at the same time and, without thinking of the consequences, I drop the towel and run from my room, across the landing and straight into hers.

She's standing with her back to the door, naked from the waist up, her hair now unbraided and hanging in loose waves around her shoulders.

"Millie?" She spins around at the sound of my voice, and I see she's clutching a towel to her chest. "Are you okay?"

She shakes her head, and I step forward slightly. "No. I'm sorry. I've always been terrified of thunder. Don't ask me why, but…"

At that moment, there's another tremendous clap, the lightning flashing across the sky, and she jumps, rushing straight into my arms.

"It's okay."

I hold her as she looks up at me… and I can't resist any longer. I lower my head and touch my lips to hers, deepening the kiss as she tilts her head back, welcoming me. She brings her arms up around my neck – both of them – and then she deliberately shifts her body away from mine, allowing the towel to fall. Her naked breasts are pressed against my chest and I put a hand on her back, pulling her closer. Every other time we've kissed, I've made an effort to prevent her from feeling my arousal… but not this time. This time, I flex my hips, and she surprises me by mirroring my action, rolling hers into mine. I know I didn't mistake that move, or the moan that accompanied it, but I need to know if it means anything, and I break the kiss, looking down into her eyes.

"What do you want, Millie? Do you want to stop, or…?"

She shakes her head. "No," she breathes. "Please don't stop."

"You want to carry on? You want everything?"

She gazes up at me. "I want you, if that's what you mean."

"It is. But are you sure?"

"I'm positive. I'm sick of being scared, of crying all the time… of not being myself."

"Then come with me."

I step back, trying not to groan out loud at the sight of her perfect breasts, and take her hand, leading her back into my bedroom. She gasps as we cross the threshold, and I turn, looking down at her.

"This is so beautiful, Rob."

She glances around, but I clasp her chin in my hand, raising her face to mine. "We'll admire the scenery later." She smiles and I bend, kissing her just briefly, bringing my free hand up to cup her breast. I half expect her to pull back, but she doesn't. She deepens the kiss, moaning into my mouth. I take heart from that, and let my other hand drop from her chin, bringing it between us, and undoing the button of her shorts. She doesn't object, so I lower the zip, my fingers sliding between her velvety skin and the soft lace of her knickers, finding swollen lips, the touch of which makes her jump.

"Shh… it's okay," I whisper, breaking our kiss, and she nods her head.

"I know… don't stop." I circle my finger over her tight bud, and she shudders against me. "Oh… oh, yes, Rob." She clutches my shoulders, staring up into my eyes. "That feels so good."

She's rolling her hips, her body trembling, as I alternate between the slightest of touches, and a harder circling, pinching her nipple between my finger and thumb at the same time.

Suddenly, without any warning, she starts to shake, a squeal emitting from her lips. I move my hand from her breast, putting my arm around her waist and hold her up, as she struggles to ride through her orgasm, her legs on the verge of giving way beneath her.

"I—I need to sit," she says, finally calming.

I walk her backwards to the bed, lowering her to the mattress, and I kneel before her.

"Are you okay?"

"God, yes." She smiles at me. I smile back.

"We can stop, if you want?"

"No. I said I want everything."

"You're sure?"

"Yes. Please, Rob."

I stand again, putting my fingers in the top of her shorts. "Lift up," I say and she raises her backside off the bed, letting me pull them down, along with her underwear. She gazes up at me, and I undo my own shorts, my eyes never leaving hers as I lower them, along with my trunks. She doesn't look down, and I'm not sure I want her to, just in case the reality frightens her. Instead, I lift her, moving her further onto the bed, and she lies down, averting her gaze to the ceiling while I grab a condom from the bedside table and roll it over my erection. She must know what I'm doing, but the fact that she doesn't want to watch makes me even more certain she's not ready to see me naked yet.

I climb up over her body, taking in her toned thighs, that triangle of trimmed dark hair at their apex… her slim waist and rounded, firm breasts… and the moment my face comes level with hers, she lowers her gaze to mine again.

"I know you say you don't me want to stop, but if you change your mind…"

"I'll tell you, don't worry."

"Good."

I part her legs with mine, and she takes them a little further still, like she knows where they need to be, and I raise myself above her, balancing on one arm, while I position myself at her entrance.

She sucks in a breath and I stare down into her beautiful face, realising my mistake.

I pull back and lower myself down over her again, resting on my elbows so I'm not crushing her, and she frowns at me.

"What's wrong, Rob?"

"Nothing's wrong. It's just that I need to say something before we do this."

"It can't wait?"

I sense she's psyched herself up for this moment, and my timing isn't helping, but this needs to be said. I shake my head. "No. Sorry. It can't."

"Why? What's so important?"

"I need to tell you I'm in love with you." She blinks twice, and then very slowly, her lips curl up into the most beautiful smile. "I've been in love with you for so long, Millie, and it doesn't feel right to do this without telling you that first." She's still staring at me, and although that smile is firmly etched on her lips, I'm getting a little worried by her lack of response. "If you want to change your mind about…"

She startles, like she's waking from a dream, and puts her hands on my shoulders, holding me still. "No. That's the last thing I want. Sorry, I zoned out then. It's just that I feel as though I've been living in a nightmare for the last couple of years. This past week with you has been magical. Better than I would have thought possible. But hearing you say that… it's like being taken into a parallel universe, where the past is a distant blur, and everything is just… perfect."

"Can I take it you're okay with me loving you, then? It's not too much?"

She chuckles. "No. It's not too much. Why would it be? I've been in love with you for such a long time, it's like second nature now… like breathing."

"Oh, God…"

I cover her lips with mine, reaching between us to re-position my erection, and edging inside her as we kiss. She sucks in a breath, parting her legs a little wider, and I whisper the word, "Sorry," into her mouth as I push all the way in. She lets out just a very slight cry, which I swallow down, and then I still, waiting while she gets used to where we are. After a minute or two, it's Millie who flexes her hips first, letting me know it's okay to move again… so I do.

I break our kiss, leaning up slightly, although I'm still resting on my elbows, my fingers caressing her cheeks, cradling her face. I want to ask if she's okay, but now doesn't feel like the time for words, and she's making soft mewling sounds, which suggest she's more than okay with what we're doing. She matches me stroke for stroke, regardless of whether I increase or decrease the pace, taking her a little faster, or a little slower. It's like we're in tune with each other, rising and falling at the same time… together.

It feels like we were made for this… which, of course, we were.

I could stay here forever, gazing into her eyes, our bodies joined, but I can feel my climax building, and I'm about to ask if she's close, when suddenly I feel her tighten around me. The question is superfluous. I plunge a little deeper with my next stroke and her expression changes. She looks bewildered, like she's struggling against what's about to happen.

"It's okay… just go with it," I whisper.

"I—I can't."

"Yes, you can. I've got you."

My words seem to calm her, and instead of tensing against her orgasm, she releases her body into it. I hold on long enough to see the rapture on her face, to watch her writhe and thrash, her body curling up in ecstasy, before my climax claims me and I throw my head back, calling out her name as I explode deep inside her.

Nothing feels the same, and I wonder if it ever will again. It's like my entire world has been altered, which is probably why it takes me a moment to realise that the continued shuddering of Millie's body isn't the dying embers of her orgasm…

She's crying.

"Oh, God… what's wrong?" I cradle her in my arms. Has she been reminded of her nightmares? Was it too soon? "Did I hurt you?" That's the only other option I can think of, and although that wouldn't be great, I think I'd rather it was that than our love and our future being forever haunted by her past. "Please, Millie… talk to me?" *I'm dying here.*

She swallows hard, struggling against her tears, and blinks, looking up at me. "Don't look so scared."

"How can I not be scared when you're crying like this?"

"I'm sorry. I—I just didn't realise…"

"Didn't realise what?"

"That it could be so good."

I sigh out my relief. "You're crying because what we just did was good?"

"Yes."

"In that case, you cry as much as you like." I lean down and kiss her, relieved when she kisses me back. "If you're not careful, I might even join you." She frowns up at me, and I let my forehead rest against hers. "It's never been that good for me, either."

"But you've done it all before... lots of times, I imagine."

"Maybe, but never like this."

"What was different?" she asks and I raise myself up above her, smiling down at her inquisitive face.

"Love," I say simply, and I kiss her. Hard.

"I didn't mean to scare you," she whispers, when I break the kiss, leaning up and looking down at her flushed cheeks, her sparkling eyes.

"That's okay. Did you... did you like it?"

"Oh, God... yes." She smiles, nodding her head, and then she bites her lip, which is very distracting. So much so, I have to lean in and free it with another kiss.

"Stay the night?" I whisper into her mouth.

"Can I?" She leans back, pushing her head into the mattress, and gazes up at me.

"Of course you can."

I turn us onto our sides, still joined for now, and wrapped up in each other, her head on my chest. "This feels nice," she murmurs against my skin.

"Hmm... it does." It feels perfect. I hold her tight to me. "You realise I might never let you go, don't you?"

She twists her head and looks up at me. "You realise I might not want you to..."

Chapter Nineteen

Millie

It's been over a month since I first stayed the night with Robson... and he was quite right. He didn't let me go.

I've spent every night with him since, because I wasn't joking when I said I didn't want him to.

Initially, just for those first few nights, we alternated between my place and his, depending on where we ended up after eating out or dining in. But now, I'm living at Robson's house and have officially moved out of my flat. I sent my parents' friend an email, thanking him for helping me out when I needed it, and letting him know I'd found somewhere more permanent. I didn't give him any more information than that, but I still expected to hear from my parents shortly afterwards, wanting more information... that was until I remembered they were on holiday, which made the timing even more perfect.

I wasn't in the mood for having my decisions questioned.

Why would I be, when I know I've done the right thing? I love living at Robson's place. It's more practical for one thing. Not only do we both work here, but he's got so much more space. The rooms are really light and airy, with lovely soft furnishings, in neutral colours.

I especially like his bedroom… not just because it's where we spend most time together, but also because of how it looks, and how it makes me feel. It's just as big as he described, decorated in an off-white colour, which is not quite yellow, but getting there. The furniture is light wood, and the only splash of colour is the mustard sofa which lies at the end of the bed. It's a room full of romance, just like our relationship. I feel so safe and happy here, and I love falling asleep on him, and waking up beside him… and everything else we do in here, as well.

It's not just his house I like, though. He has a lovely garden, too.

That's where we entertained Rachel, Jack and Beatrice on the first weekend after I moved in. We probably should have been unpacking my things, but I got the feeling Rachel wanted to meet me in an official capacity, at a time when she hadn't just given birth, and I knew it was important to Robson that I should get along with his best friend. I couldn't see any reason I wouldn't, although he was incredibly nervous as we awaited their arrival. I wasn't sure why, but everything became clear when, with about thirty minutes to go, he sat me down on the sofa in the living room and knelt before me.

"I have a confession to make."

"You do?"

He nodded his head. "I know you've met Rachel before, when Beatrice was born, and at the surgery, but this is the first time you're going to meet properly, for any length of time, and while I know I told you she wasn't my first kiss, I need to own up that she and I nearly slept together once."

I leant back, moving away from him, because whatever I'd expected him to say, that wasn't it.

He frowned at my response and bent over, resting his arms on my legs.

"Don't shy away from me. Please, Millie… I'm trying to be honest here."

"Does Jack know?" I needed to understand if I was being expected to keep secrets from Rachel's fiancée… if that was the point of his confession.

"Yes, Jack knows." That was a relief. I didn't think I could lie… not about something like that.

"And he's okay with it?"

"Yes. Because he knows what happened."

"Okay. In that case, I'd like you to tell me, too."

He sighed and sat up beside me, turning in his seat so we were facing each other. "There's not very much to tell, really. We were having a drink at her place one evening. Rachel was bemoaning her love life, and I was going through a dry patch and feeling sorry for myself. One drink led to another, and another… and the way the conversation took us, we ended up hugging. But because we were drunk, the hugging became something more."

"How much more?"

"To be honest, I can't remember. Everything became a blur. All I know is we backed out before we went too far."

"You both backed out? It was a mutual thing?"

"Rachel's always said so, and I don't recall it being any different."

"What about your rule? The one you have about not sleeping with patients?"

"I was excessively drunk. Rules weren't foremost in my mind. It occurred to me the following day that the consequences could have been dire… at least for me, although I'm not sure that's ever dawned on Rachel."

I sucked in a breath, feeling a little bruised. "Do you regret it? Do you wish you'd been able to take things further with her?"

"God, no." His response was immediate and unmistakable, and he reached over, taking my hands in his and staring down at them for a moment before he looked back at me. "Neither of us regretted it. In fact, we both felt the complete opposite. The next day, we met up, nursing twin hangovers from hell, and we agreed we make great friends, but that we would have made lousy lovers."

"How can you know that if you didn't try?"

"You don't have to sleep with everyone you meet to know they wouldn't be right for you," he said, staring into my eyes. "I love Rachel, in a purely platonic way… probably in the same way that you love your brother. But if you asked me to live with her for any length of time, I think I'd rather have my appendix removed without an anaesthetic."

I giggled, unable to help myself. "That's not very kind, Robson."

"Maybe not. But could you live with your brother, day in, day out, as an adult?"

I thought about the prospect and shook my head. "No. I don't think I could."

"Exactly. And I imagine Rachel feels the same way about me. We can be friends because we can tolerate each other's foibles in a way that we couldn't if we lived together. Friendship enables you to escape each other's idiosyncrasies, by hiding in your own. But you can't do that with a lover… not if you want the relationship to work. There can't be anywhere to hide, because you have to be open about who and what you are. You can't keep secrets. Which is why I'm telling you about this."

"In case Rachel or Jack bring it up?"

"No. I doubt they would. But in any case, I'm telling you because I don't want to keep anything from you. I want you to know everything there is to know about me." He shifted closer. "Do you understand?"

"I think so." I stared up at him. "Can you just explain why you haven't told me about this before?"

He nodded his head. "It's nothing sinister. It's just that you only moved in here a few days ago, and we've been… a little preoccupied." His eyes sparkled as he spoke and I couldn't deny we'd been busy… most of our spare time having been spent in bed. "Do you know how much I love you?" he whispered.

"Yes."

"Do you know you have nothing to fear from me or my past?"

"Yes. I've never felt safer than I do when I'm with you."

He smiled. "Good. That's how it's meant to be."

He kissed me then, only stopping when Rachel and Jack arrived.

We spent a lovely afternoon together, and even if I'd had any doubts about Rob and Rachel's friendship – which I didn't – they'd have been dispelled by witnessing how much love she has for Jack and their newborn baby. They make such a lovely family, and although I know it's early days for me and Robson, I couldn't help feeling a little jealous of what they've got.

Most of the afternoon was spent talking and laughing, a great deal of which seemed to be at Jack and Robson's expense, and I got the feeling Rachel and I could become friends. I held Beatrice a few times, while she found things in her changing bag, or went to the bathroom, as Jack was busy talking to Robson, or helping to make the tea, and at one stage, I caught sight of Robson staring at me, while I cradled the baby in my arms. He had the strangest look on his face, but I didn't get the chance to ask him about it… not until much later, when we were lying in bed.

He turned to me, pulling me closer in his arms. "You looked good like that," he said, offering his explanation.

"With a baby in my arms?"

"Yes." He smiled and traced a line of kisses from my lips down to my jawline and then up to my ear. "How would you feel about holding our baby, instead of someone else's? Not straight away, but one day… soon?"

My body tingled, and I leant back, looking into his twinkling eyes. He was clearly waiting for an answer, so I nodded my head, because it was what I wanted, too, and he smiled, kissing me… very thoroughly.

I might have escaped the scrutiny of my parents, but the same didn't apply to my brother. He called, out of the blue, on the Monday after Rachel and Jack's visit, and being as I was sitting on the sofa with Rob, having just eaten dinner, I could hardly lie to Ellis about what was going on. I made a point of not mentioning Fraser, though. I'd already decided that the fewer people who knew about what had happened with him, the better.

My brother seemed surprised that I'd moved in with Robson so quickly, and didn't hang back in saying so.

"If you're that bothered, why don't you come down and meet him?"

"Okay. I've got some time off next week, so I can come down at the weekend."

"This weekend?" I hadn't expected that.

"Yes. I was planning on going to Mum and Dad's, but I can come via you."

"We're hardly on the way, Ellis."

"It's fine. I don't mind the detour." He asked for Robson's address, and I couldn't think of a single reason not to give it to him.

When we ended our call, I turned to Robson, feeling a blush creep up my cheeks.

"Can I take it your brother's coming at the weekend?"

"Yes."

He laughed, pulling me into his arms. "I told you he'd want to check me out."

As it turned out, I was worrying about nothing. Robson and Ellis got along really well.

My brother arrived on the Saturday lunchtime, having flown down from Aberdeen to Newquay, where he hired a car and drove to Porthgarrion. He greeted me warmly, and although he seemed a little suspicious of Robson to start with, he soon mellowed over lunch at the pub. I'd overcome my fear of the place by then, and we spent the rest of the afternoon in the village, having a barbecue in the garden that evening. Ellis stayed in the guest bedroom and joined us for brunch at the café on the Sunday morning before starting the drive to our parents' house. When he left, he shook Robson's hand and gave me a hug, whispering in my ear that he'd never seen me looking so happy.

Whatever his doubts about Robson, they were unfounded, and he knew it.

I have to admit, I've never felt so good in my life, and now, as I gaze out of the french doors, staring at Robson as he sits in the garden, listening to the cricket, I can't help almost bursting with happiness.

Life is so perfect now, I can barely remember the pain of before. I can't remember the last time I cried, either.

And that's all because of Robson.

Chapter Twenty

Robson

What a month it's been…

When Ellis left, he must have gone straight to his and Millie's parents' place and told them all about us living together, because the next thing we knew, they were on the phone, and a visit had been arranged for the following weekend.

Given the choice, I'd have delayed them. Not because I was worried about meeting them, but because I felt like Millie and I needed some time on our own. We'd barely had a moment to unpack her things, let alone get used to living together. But I knew her parents were bound to want to meet me.

They drove down from Hampshire, arriving in time for a late lunch at the pub, and before we'd even chosen what to eat, they'd already mentioned Damian's name. As she sipped on her orange juice and lemonade, her mother enquired of Millie whether she'd informed me of what Damian had done to her. I answered for her, making it clear that Millie and I had no secrets. They referred to him again during the afternoon, although that time it was her father who brought him up, and only as 'Millie's ex-boyfriend'. It was all very awkward and by the time we climbed into bed that evening, I could tell how stressed Millie was by the whole thing.

It was easy to see that her parents were struggling to let go of their anger at what had happened, but they weren't helping. So, the next day, over lunch at a pub in Padstow, where I'd driven us to get away from the village, and the chance of any prying ears, I decided to say my piece.

I didn't bring it up in conversation. I'm not that insensitive. But the opportunity arose quite naturally, when Millie's mum asked if she'd thought any more about going back to university, after 'what that man did to you'.

Millie opened her mouth to answer, but I took her hand, giving it a squeeze, and sat forward slightly.

"Millie's happy working with me right now," I said and her mum looked at me, her surprise quite obvious.

"I'm sure she is, but what you're probably not aware of is that she wanted to be a lawyer. She was on the verge of…"

I held up my hand, stopping her mid-sentence, and she frowned at me. "I know all about Millie's past. As I explained last night, we don't have any secrets. She's told me everything, including her ambitions, and how they were thwarted. I'm sure she hasn't dismissed the idea of returning to formal education at some stage, but as I say, right now, she's happy working with me."

"I am," Millie said. "I'm very happy with Rob."

She smiled at me, and I could see the gratitude in her eyes.

"But you wanted it so much," her father reasoned. "And Damian stole that from you."

I felt Millie tense against me. "I don't think it's very helpful to look at it like that," I said firmly. "This is Millie's decision, not Damian's. She's in control now. She has to be, otherwise he's won, and nobody wants that for her. If she chooses to go back and take her degree, she can… and she will. On her terms." Her father was glaring at me, but I knew I had to finish what I was saying. "The thing is, Millie wants to leave the past behind her, and I think it would be best for her if you could do the same."

They both stared at me, their mouths open, and then I heard her father mutter the word 'fool', and mumble something about me not understanding.

The rest of our meal was fairly silent, and we were both relieved when they left later that afternoon.

Millie apologised to me, but I told her there was no need.

"They'll come round," I said, trying to reassure her. "I think they're frustrated because they weren't there when it happened. By the time they came home, it was all over and done with, as far as the authorities were concerned, even if the outcome was so unsatisfactory. I imagine they wonder if things might have been different if they'd been at home, and they probably feel helpless because there was nothing they could do to make it better."

"What on earth would they be like if they knew about Fraser?" She rolled her eyes, and I held her tight, and listened when she sat beside me and phoned her brother, asking him to intervene. He said he'd talk to them and see what he could do, but told her she'd probably just have to wait for them to accept that she'd moved on… even if they hadn't.

Over the course of the next few days, she was a little quiet, but then she started asking about my parents, wondering why I hadn't introduced her to them yet. I could see her point. I'd met her family, and they all lived miles away. My parents were only around the corner, and she'd never met either of them.

Dad was thrilled when I suggested Sunday lunch last weekend, and although it meant our fourth weekend together would be spent with other people, Millie didn't seem to mind… and neither did I, really. I knew it would be easier than entertaining her parents. My mum and dad are very easygoing.

They clearly loved Millie, right from the first moment they met her. Mum went out of her way to embarrass me at every opportunity, which had Millie in stitches over lunch, as Mum regaled her with stories of that time when I'd cooked for them before going to university.

Dad, on the other hand, was much quieter.

I wasn't sure why until later in the afternoon, when Mum and Millie were out in the garden and, rather than joining them, he pulled me back into the kitchen, and looked up into my face.

"Is she all right?" he asked.

"Who? Millie?"

He nodded his head. "Of course. Who else?"

"Why wouldn't she be all right?"

"Oh, come on, son. I know about the assault on you, and I know what Fraser Johnson did to Millie, too."

"You do?"

"Of course I do. The man confessed. How could I not know?"

I shrugged my shoulders, realising how stupid I'd been. "I suppose I'd just assumed, because you hadn't said anything…"

"I kept quiet, because it's nothing to do with me… not really. But that doesn't mean I don't care. These things take time to get over. It might be months before she's even ready to come to terms with it, and…"

I put my hand on his arm. "She's fine, Dad. Honestly." I couldn't tell him about Damian, but I needed to say something. "We've talked everything through and she knows it's best left in the past… she doesn't want to be a victim."

"She got that from you, did she?" he asked, smiling.

"Maybe. But you shouldn't complain. I got it from you." He chuckled, shaking his head. "You don't need to worry, Dad. I'm keeping an eye on her."

He nodded and stepped out into the garden. I watched him go, joining Mum and Millie, and I knew, as he looked down at my girlfriend, that he and the rest of Porthgarrion's police force would be keeping an eye on her, too.

The last month hasn't just been about meeting new people and watching over Millie, though.

I've had half an eye on Rachel and her baby daughter. Margaret might be back now, doing all the routine work, but this is Rachel we're talking about, so I have to check up on her every so often, just to make sure.

She's brought the baby into the surgery several times, just for a visit, and she and Millie get along really well. On a couple of occasions, I've come out of my office to find Millie holding Beatrice, and I have to admit, that sight always makes me smile… just like it did that weekend, when they came over for tea.

I've never thought about becoming a father before, but seeing Jack with Beatrice, and then watching Millie like that, cradling an infant, the thought has been making a home in my head, and in my heart. I asked Millie how she felt about it, later that night, and she seemed as keen as me, although we agreed there's no rush. Naturally, I'll always be guided by Millie, but I don't think I want to wait too long…

As well as Millie, Rachel and Beatrice, I've had a couple of other people on my mind over the last few weeks.

First, there was Joan Evans, who came back to see me, looking a lot better. She had a smile on her face and a spring in her step, and before she'd said a word, I knew the new regime was working. She told me Bryn was joining in and seeing the benefits, too.

I haven't seen Imelda Duffy at the surgery, although I've caught a glimpse of her on her bicycle, riding around the village with Laura's father. I can only assume her ankle is better, and she's too busy enjoying herself to come and tell me… which is fine by me.

And then there's Sebastian Baxter.

When he came to see me that first time, it was because he'd found a suspicious-looking mole on his back. He was clearly concerned and had every right to be. I referred him to the hospital in Truro, and although he only had to wait ten days to be seen, I knew how anxious he must have been.

As it transpires, it was nothing to worry about. He popped in on Tuesday to tell me he'd finally had all the tests done and had been back to see the consultant, to be told that everything was fine. He couldn't remember the name of what the doctor told him was wrong, but it wasn't cancer, and that was all he cared about. I received written confirmation on Friday that it was a pyogenic granuloma, which the consultant said they're going to leave for now, asking me to monitor it, and refer the patient back if it becomes troublesome, so they can surgically remove it.

I'll admit, I was almost as relieved as Sebastian, and I filed the letter with a significantly lighter heart.

That's one of things about being a doctor in somewhere like Porthgarrion… you can't not care.

I have to keep my cares and my worries to myself for the best part, but that doesn't mean they're not important to me… like my patients.

None of them are as important as Millie, though, and as today is the first Sunday we've had to ourselves since she moved in, I've got every intention of enjoying it.

The day started well, with a shower, which we took together, with breathlessly spectacular results, after which we enjoyed brunch on the patio.

Now, I'm sitting in the garden, while Millie makes us some tea, and I've got the radio beside me, so I can listen to the latest test match.

It's been a struggle to keep up with the cricket over the last few weeks, but I've managed, in between patients, and as I lie back in my deckchair, I close my eyes, hoping Millie will bring her tea out and join me, even though the cricket is on. She might bring a book, I suppose…

She loves to read, just as much as I do, and my bookshelves are now heaving. We'll have to buy some more, but that can wait… because England are batting with an achievable score to chase. Providing they don't suffer an embarrassing collapse, it should be a good day's cricket.

"Where do you want your tea?"

I open my eyes and look up to see Millie standing beside me, with a cup of tea in each hand. "I'll take it."

I sit up, as she hands me the cup, putting hers down on the low wall beside her deckchair, making it clear she's planning on sitting out here with me, which is nice, although I don't want her to get bored… or ask me to turn the cricket off.

"Are you going to get a book?" I ask, and she looks over at me as she sits down.

"What on earth for?"

"Because the cricket's on."

"I know it is. What's the score?"

I sit up even further, almost falling off of my deckchair. "Don't tell me you like cricket?"

Her eyes light up as she smiles. "I do."

"How did I not know this?"

She shrugs her shoulders. "I guess because we've been so busy over the last few weeks, we've barely had time to talk… not about ourselves, anyway."

I turn, facing her, the cricket forgotten for a moment. "Okay… so what other sports do you like? Or is it limited to cricket?"

"It's not limited at all. I enjoy watching football and rugby in the winter, and I'm not averse to tennis, either."

I jump to my feet, pulling her up from her chair and into my arms. "That's it… we're getting married." She giggles and I lean back, looking down at her. "What's funny?"

"You are?"

"Why? I wasn't joking."

She falls silent, her mouth falling open. "Y—You mean…?"

I drop to one knee, just as England score a six, and the crowd cheer, which is distracting, so I reach over and turn off the radio, looking back up at her.

"I love you, Millie. I want to spend the rest of my life loving you, and keeping you safe, and listening to the cricket with you… while our grandchildren run around the garden. So, will you marry me and make all my dreams come true?" She nods her head, smiling again, her eyes glistening, and I stand. "Say it out loud."

"Yes." I lean in, kissing her deeply, holding her body tight against mine. After a while, she pulls back, looking up at me. "Can I ask you something?"

"Anything. I'll do anything for you. Just name it, and it's yours, no matter what it is."

She smiles. "In that case, can you turn the cricket back on?"

The End

Thank you for reading *It Started with Tears*. I hope you enjoyed it, and if you did, I hope you'll take the time to leave a short review.

The characters of Porthgarrion will return soon in
It Started with Ice Cream. This story is all about Ember Penrose, who owns the ice cream parlour, and what happens when she finally succumbs to the charms of local farmer, Adrian Roskelly. Will he melt her heart? Or will her troublesome sister ensure it stays frozen forever?